Buckled

PAM GODWIN

Copyright © 2018 by Pam Godwin
All rights reserved.
Proofreader: Lesa Godwin
Cover Designer: Hang Le
Interior Designer: Pam Godwin

This is a work of fiction. Names, characters, places, and incidents are the product of the author's imagination or are used fictitiously, and any resemblance to actual persons, living or dead, events, or locales is entirely coincidental.
No part of this book may be reproduced in any form, except for the inclusion of brief quotations in a review or article, without written permission from the author.

Visit my website at pamgodwin.com

Disclaimer

Each book in the TRAILS OF SIN series
is a different couple,
but they should be read in order.

KNOTTED (#1)
BUCKLED (#2)
BOOTED (#3)

Prologue

Jarret

SIX MONTHS AGO…

Some might say I'm unethical. Maybe even depraved. But the things I've witnessed and the crimes committed against those I love tainted me. Provoked me. Gave birth to the anger and strength blazing through my veins.

I make no apology for it.

Leaning against the wall in the hallway outside my father's office, I glare at the closed door. Dad is in there right now, completely oblivious to his fate.

Most men look at their fathers and feel protective. Loyal. When I look at mine, I see an unworthy creature made of frail bones and greed. An abomination I want to destroy.

I don't just want to hurt John Holsten. I want to throw him into the ravine and dump truckloads of earth atop his broken body until his lying goddamn mouth overflows with dirt. I want to hear his pained cries while boulders rain down and crush his organs. I want to see the life drain from his deceitful eyes as the gorge swallows him whole.

This is the exact method my brother and I used last week to murder Rogan Schroeder.

The vest-pocket loan shark was the biggest threat against Conor Cassidy's life. His network of black-market creditors loaned money to our fathers and demanded repayment with impossible interest rates.

Rogan Schroeder didn't just want to be repaid. He wanted a piece of Julep Ranch. Specifically, the oil-rich land. My father bowed to his demands, working with him to keep the land owners, Conor and Lorne Cassidy, out of the picture while oil rigs chewed up the property.

The Cassidys will return eventually. Conor, to honor our blood oath. Lorne, when he's released from prison. Rogan intended to have them murdered the moment they stepped foot on the ranch.

So Jake and I eliminated him.

In doing so, there will be no more contract killers. No more debts. No more threats against the girl I love like a sister.

After Jake and I deal with Dad, Conor will finally be able to live safely at the ranch. Lorne still has a few years to serve in prison, but when he's free, we'll be able to welcome him home with open arms.

I drum my fingers against my thigh, listening for my brother's footsteps, so fucking ready to put this shit behind us.

A few minutes later, he rounds the corner of the hall and strides toward me with a laptop tucked under an arm.

Despite how close we are to getting Conor back, his mood hasn't improved from the surly, miserable funk he's been immersed in for the past five years.

Because Conor has a boyfriend. A man she now lives with on her college campus. That revelation is ripping Jake apart, day after day.

"Ready?" His whisper snags, his jaw so tight it

doesn't give.

With a nod, I step toward the office door.

We were raised under a strict code of conduct, to honor our father, his rules, and his privacy. That includes knocking before we enter his quarters.

He lost all honor the moment he put Conor and Lorne in harm's way. Still, it goes against the grain to open that door without permission.

Jake casts me an irritated glare and swings open the door himself.

"What the—?" Behind the desk, Dad shoves his chair back and causes something to fall at his feet. His hands fly to his lap, his eyes murderous. "Get out!"

I follow Jake in, and we skid to a stop at the sight of the woman rising from the floor behind the desk.

Long black hair and beautiful Native American features, Dad's girlfriend, Raina, hugs her nude chest.

Fucking great. I share a disgusted look with Jake.

"I said, *Get out!"* Dad zips his pants, his face crimson with rage and utter disbelief.

Interrupting a blow job is one thing, but we're blatantly ignoring his booming order. He has no idea how much leverage we hold over him.

"Raina." Jake approaches the desk without looking at the woman. "Leave us."

I spot her shirt on the floor and toss it at her.

She catches it, keeping her tits covered with the cloak of her hair. She slips it on without a bra and looks to Dad for permission to leave.

I don't know what her interest is in him. She's a stunning woman. At age twenty-two, she's a year younger than Jake and me. Way too young for a sixty-year-old man.

If she thinks he's loaded, she's sorely mistaken. He's penniless, and after this meeting, he'll be homeless. Or *dead.*

"Wait in my bedroom while I deal with this." Dad waves her away.

She turns and heads out of the office, shoulders square and expression unreadable. She's been staying at the ranch for the past month and hasn't so much as met my eyes, let alone spoken to me. Even now, as Jake and I glare holes through her, she doesn't look at us.

Something feels off about her. Nothing indicates she's here against her will, but she's not exactly warm around my father, either. Whatever it is pings at my protective instinct.

"You boys might be grown." Dad nudges the white Stetson up his angry brow. "But I'm fixing to whoop your asses. You better have a damn good reason for barging in and disobeying me."

"We do." Jake sets the laptop on the desk.

While it powers on, I follow Raina into the hall.

"Hold up." Out of view of the office, I grab her elbow. "Are you in trouble?"

She yanks free and steps back, folding her arms across her chest. "Trouble with whom?"

"You tell me." I cock my head. "You know the old man is broke, right?"

"You're sticking your nose where it doesn't belong." She pivots in the direction of Dad's bedroom and strides away. "Stay away from me."

Well, I tried. Maybe she just has a thing for older men.

With a shudder, I return to the office and close the door behind me.

"What the fuck is this?" Dad glares at the laptop screen, his face paling from furious red to ghost white as realization dawns.

The screen angles away from me, but I hear the video snippets. Captured with hidden cameras over the past couple of years, the recordings serve as evidence against Dad's criminal activities. His discussions about the hits on Conor and Lorne, meetings with Rogan Schroeder and other dangerous moneylenders, illegal negotiations with Sheriff Fletcher—all of it would put him away for a very long time.

"How did you get this?" Dad's dark eyes jump between mine and Jake's.

"You underestimate us." Jake removes a small camera from the nearby bookcase and rips the wires free.

I'm not a tech guy. Neither is my brother. But Jake found what we needed online and wired an amateur setup. It was easy enough, seeing how Dad still looks at us like we're kids. Like we're naive and simple-minded with aspirations that don't stray from herding cattle.

At least, he *did.* He's not looking at us like that now.

His bulging eyes are overly bright, his hands white-knuckling the armrests. "You have no idea what you've done."

"We know Conor and Lorne own the land." I lower into the chair across the desk from him. "We know if they lived here, they could revoke the Power of Attorney that allows you to drill on land that isn't yours." I lean forward. "We know your creditors are dead, your enemies gone."

"What the hell are you talking about?"

"We know it was *you!*" Jake slams a fist onto the desk, making Dad jump. *"You* hired the men who raped and brutalized Conor. *You* put the hit on her and Lorne." His face twists with five years of deep-seeded pain. "How could you, Dad? They're family! And Conor..." His hoarse voice scorches the air. "She's my entire fucking world, and you took her from me!"

"Calm down, son." Dad's breathing accelerates as he discreetly reaches for the desk drawer that holds his pistol. "Just listen for a—"

"Are you going to shoot us?" I direct my eyes toward his wandering hand. "Have you fallen that far?"

"You're my sons." A muscle flutters across his jaw, and he abandons the drawer to stare at me like I've lost my mind. "I'd put a bullet in my own head before turning a gun on you."

Maybe so, but just in case, I removed the guns from this room this morning.

"What happened to Conor…" Dad steals a glance at Jake and frowns. "It was supposed to be quick. A quick, painless death–"

Jake launches over the desk, roaring and reaching for Dad's neck.

I catch my brother around the waist, hauling him back and manhandling him into the chair. "Keep it together."

Bloodthirst spikes through me, too, but killing our father is a last resort. Jake and I discussed this endlessly. As much as we want him dead and as many men as we already buried, murdering the man who raised us would alter us irreparably. It would make us as fucked-up as he is.

"Look, I'm sorry about Conor and Lorne." Dad straightens, his deep voice soothing, seemingly trying to temper the confrontation. "I made some bad decisions that put everyone in jeopardy, and in the end, it came down to your lives or the Cassidys. I didn't have a choice. I would do anything to protect you."

Eliminating Conor and Lorne may have appeased his enemies and kept them from hurting Jake and me, but it was never a solution. If the old man doesn't see that now, he never will.

"They're our closest friends." I meet his eyes. "Closer than blood. You had no right."

"Do you know that Dalton beat her in Chicago?" Jake stares at his lap, his hands clenching. "He took out his anger on her for two years."

Dad's lips thin, and his head makes a slight shake. "I'm sorry, son."

"I don't give a fuck if you're sorry. I don't want to hear it." Jake rises from the chair and paces beside me. "You should've told us about the trouble you were in. We could've worked through it together." His voice explodes. "*Before* you tried to kill my girl!"

"We could've helped." I touch Jake's arm as he passes, a reminder to keep himself in check, and return my gaze to Dad. "We respected you back then. Loved you. We would've worked harder on the ranch, figured out a way to make more money. But instead of coming to us, you took away the two people who mean the most to this family. In one night, you twisted us into the vengeful, bitter men we are today, and we won't stop until this is finished. I hope you're proud."

"What do you mean you won't stop?" Dad looks at the laptop, at Jake, and back at me, his eyes widening with understanding. "You're behind the disappearances?" His throat bobs. "You're the reason my business partners are missing?" He drags a hand down his pallid face, his voice a whisper. "What have you done?"

"We took care of your debts." I return to the chair and rest a loose fist beneath my chin, watching him. "Rogan Schroeder won't threaten this family again."

Dad removes his white Stetson and carefully places it on the desk. "That's why he didn't show for our meeting last week."

Oh, he showed. Jake and I intercepted him a few miles away. The arrogant fuck was alone when we shot out his tires and forced him off the dirt road. His body and pickup truck lay at the bottom of the ravine, buried beneath the very earth he drilled out of the south pasture.

Dad doesn't need the details. He comprehends

enough. It burns in his red-rimmed eyes. "You don't know who Rogan Schroeder is, do you?"

"A criminal loan shark intent on taking this land."

A hollow laugh bursts from his chest. "I suppose I owe you a thank you?"

"You owe us more than that." Jake glances at the clock on the wall. "Our lawyer will be here any minute."

"A lawyer for what?" Dad peeks at the desk drawer again, eyes wild. "You boys think you're going to turn me in?"

"No, you worthless piece of shit." I angle forward and let my expression convey the lethal conviction of my words. "You're going to sign over ownership of the cattle operation and all assets on the property to us. Then you're going to take your whore and disappear. Quietly. *Permanently.*"

"Or what?"

"Or you stop breathing." I shrug.

"You're threatening me?" He rises with a wide stance and swipes a hand across the desk, crashing computer equipment to the floor. "I'm your father!"

"That's the only reason we're giving you the option to live." I remain seated, unmoved by his posturing.

A knock sounds at the front door, and Jake steps out of the office to greet the lawyer.

"I won't agree to this." Dad snarls at me. "The cattle business is all I have left."

A business he acquired from my mother and ran into the ground after her death. He never deserved Julep Ranch.

"If you don't sign the papers and leave town, I will kill you." My tone doesn't waver, my eye contact steady and brutally honest. "I'll disembowel you just to see how long you live without your toxic insides. The truth is, *Dad,* I would enjoy it. And why is that? Did I inherit that sickness from you?"

"No." A clammy sheen shines on his brow, and he

slumps into the chair, studying my expression as horror strains his own. "I've never killed anyone."

"That's right. You hire out the dirty work. Because you don't have the stomach for it. Because you're a weak, pathetic old man."

His jaw tightens, and his eyes grow cold.

I'm baiting him. Mostly, I want to see if he has what it takes to reach for the gun that no longer sits in that drawer. But I already know he won't. He didn't have the balls to kill Conor and Lorne himself, and he certainly doesn't have it in him to kill his own sons.

Jake returns with the business attorney, and the room coils with silent tension. As papers are laid out with signature boxes marked with tabs, Dad stares at the documents, his eyes swirling with resentment and conflict.

I slide a pen across the desk. "What we're offering is more than you deserve. Sign the fucking papers."

"The business is steeped in debt. It won't make you rich, boy."

"This isn't about money. It's about taking what rightfully belongs to us and making sure you lose everything our mother built. As far as revenge goes, this is trivial."

"If I sign," he says, his voice lowering with waning resistance, "you'll let this go?"

"Yes. We'll let *you* go. Gladly."

He snatches the pen and angrily scrawls his signature, one page after another without reading the terms. "I don't want to lose you boys."

"You already have." Jake gathers the signed paperwork and hands it off to the quiet, middle-aged lawyer. "I'll walk you out."

He leaves me alone with Dad again, putting a helluva lot of trust in me that I won't kill him. Or maybe he's hoping I'll do exactly that.

"I want you and Raina gone by nightfall." I glance at the position of the sun beyond the office window. "You have three hours to gather your shit."

It feels weird standing on this side of a confrontation with him. Giving orders rather than receiving them. It's empowering.

"It doesn't have to be like this." Dad scans the office, his usual dominant demeanor weakening by the second. "Let me stay. I'll pull my weight on the ranch and make it up to you."

He looks tired, a defeated old man who long ago exhausted his sixty years. He still has his hair—thick and dark, peppered with silver. He's still physically fit, strong limbs and a sturdy build. Except for his gut, which extends past his belt buckle from years of laziness and self-indulgence. Maybe his appearance hasn't changed much, but I see him differently now. He no longer holds power over me, and he knows it.

"We're five years past amnesty." I stand and head toward the door, lingering on the threshold. "If you turn us in for crimes you believe we committed, we'll kill you. If you harm a hair on Conor's head, we'll kill you. If you kill us, the evidence we hold against you will be delivered to people we trust. People on the right side of the law who would love to put you and Sheriff Fletcher behind bars for the rest of your miserable lives."

Lorne has access to every piece of evidence we hold and can do a hellacious amount of damage with it from prison.

"I pity you." Dad rises from the chair and circles the desk, his posture relaxed and nonthreatening. "You think you're smarter than me? A better man? Yet you're willing to kill your own flesh and blood. That makes you truly evil."

The fact that I'm letting him live proves him wrong. But there's an iota of truth in his statement. A man cannot be good unless he possesses the capacity to be evil. Decency is a choice. It's being tempted by hatred and following a different path no matter how difficult. It's looking inward with a magnifying glass and acknowledging the flaws and weaknesses in one's character.

It's the terrible ache for revenge and choosing to let it go.

"We're showing you mercy." I grip the door frame, giving him my back. "Don't squander it. You have three hours to disappear."

I leave him there to regret his consequences. Or to make more mistakes. Whatever happens next is up to him.

Walking from one end of our eight-thousand-square-foot estate to the other, I enter the Cassidy wing. Jake completely renovated this space with his bare hands. He rebuilt it for him and Conor, knowing full well he may have lost her for good.

I find him in the master suite, staring at the mural that represents the horse impressionist paintings Conor collected as a child.

"Will he give us trouble?" Jake asks, without moving his eyes from the wall.

"Not sure." I lower onto the bed behind him. "He knows we did him a favor by erasing his debts, and he gains nothing by going after us."

"Except revenge."

"Maybe. But I think he's too tired to take us on. He's not the same man who raised us."

"We're not the same, either." He reaches out and traces a brush stroke along one of the painted stallions. "I used to be worthy of Conor. I was a proud, dependable man with a lot to offer her. But not anymore. Even if she returns—"

"You're still that man, Jake. And she *will* return."

"For the blood oath. She won't come back for *me*.

Not that I blame her. I chased her away, as effectively as possible. And now… If she's happy with that fucking professor…" His shoulders tense, and he grips his brow as if in pain. "If she's truly happy, I won't interfere. I've caused her enough heartbreak."

"Will you tell her about that night in the barn?"

"I'll tell her everything. She deserves to know."

My lovesick brother waited years to have sex, just so he could give her his virginity. Since it was anonymous, in the darkness of an abandoned barn, Conor doesn't know it was him. He gave himself to her, and she thinks she had sex with a stranger. He won't admit it, but I know that hurts him more than anything.

He lowers his arms, flexing his hands at his sides. Then he slides down the wall and pulls his knees to his brow.

Every tense inch of him radiates misery and loneliness. He's been watching Conor from afar for the past few years. The moment she began dating Miles York, Jake lost parts of himself he'll never get back.

He started fucking a lot of women, night after night, treating them in ways I didn't think he was capable. He used them to channel his rage. His grief. But it only heightened his guilt over the wrongs that were done to Conor.

Over the past month, he's returned to celibacy, and frankly, it makes him unbearable to be around.

"You need to go out and get laid." I rise from the bed and approach him slowly.

"I can't." He removes his hat and tilts his head back against the wall, revealing the dampness in his eyes. "I miss her so fucking much she's all I see."

"I miss her, too." I sit beside him and stare at the leather cuff on his wrist. He hasn't removed it since Conor left it for him on her eighteenth birthday.

I don't have a sister, but she fills that space. The ranch is dull and meaningless without her.

Now that Dad and Rogan Schroeder are dealt with, Jake could bring her home. He could drive to OSU this very minute and force her back to the ranch. Screaming and kicking, if necessary. But he won't. He would never disrupt the life she's built for herself. Not if she's happy.

"I asked the private investigator to tail her boyfriend." Jake rubs a thumb over the leather cuff. "If he finds anything that Conor wouldn't approve of..."

"All bets are off."

"Damn straight."

We ebb into a span of silent minutes, lost in our thoughts. I wonder if Dad is packing. I wonder if he was a better man when our mother married him. I wonder what she would think about the choices Jake and I have made.

Jake cuts his eyes at me. "When are you going to scoop out your heart for a woman? You're missing out on a lifetime of pain."

"Well, when you put it like that..."

"The happiness that comes before the hurt is the best feeling in the world." He closes his eyes, his whisper riding on a shredded breath. "It's worth it."

"I'm all for self-destruction. I just haven't found my own Conor to lay it all on the line for."

"She's one of a kind." His lips pull into a sad smile. "I was a lucky son of a bitch. I still am. I had her for sixteen years."

During those years, I had a front row seat to the evolving relationship between him and Conor. I watched in awe and envy as their love forged into something legendary. Something so bright and powerful it eclipsed everything around them.

Jake's a good guy, but Conor Cassidy sets the bar. I've been with countless women, and no one comes close to the contagious passion and soulful strength that Conor possesses. I suspect no one ever will.

Fuck it all if I find that person. I'll latch on so tightly she won't stand a chance.

I'll move mountains.

Stake my claim.

Piss all over my territory.

Rearrange my entire existence until we buckle together beneath the intensity.

I want what Jake had with Conor. I fucking crave it.

He and I might be different in many ways, but we share one thing in common.

We don't just love.

We love hard, with every bone, sinew, and breath in our bodies.

The Big Sugar is the biggest bar in Sandbank, Oklahoma. Actually, it's the only bar in this godforsaken town. I don't belong here, and every boot-scuffing, flannel-wearing redneck in the joint knows it.

These people have a deafening way of judging and accusing without opening their mouths. They watch me without staring. Avoid me without moving out of the way. Insult me without uttering a sound from the pinched lines of their lips.

To say I'm not welcome here is an understatement.

Do they give all out-of-towners the same treatment? Or just the ones wearing ill-chosen high heels to a bar littered with peanut shells?

I teeter over the mess on the floor, certain I'll break an ankle. When I sink onto the first available stool at the counter, I heave a sigh of relief.

The bartender ignores me. Just as well. I don't drink when I'm working.

I call it *work.* This assignment is officially unofficial.

In Chicago, I write for a few beauty and fashion columns under different pen names. Horribly boring and uneventful, but it pays the bills. Or rather, it *paid.*

I lost those jobs. Over the past six months, I lost everything. Which is why I'm here. Trying to put my life back together.

Jake and Jarret Holsten are going to help me with that. But first, I need to run into them. Make it look like a fluke encounter. They would be more likely to divulge personal information during a casual conversation than if I knocked on their door and demanded answers.

"Excuse me." I tap the shoulder of the thirty-something brunette beside me. When she turns, I plaster on my warmest smile. "Hey, there."

She squints at my silk button-up, starched black trousers, and cute red pumps. "You're not from around here."

"I get the feeling that's a curse in this town, as if I'm bringing in an infectious disease or something. I swear I'm current on all my shots."

I laugh. She doesn't.

Where's the southern hospitality I always heard about? Maybe I need to wander farther south for that.

"I was wondering..." I pat down the unruly curls around my shoulders. "Do you happen to know the Holsten family? There are two sons—"

"The twins?" Mascara clumps in the slits of her eyes. "What of them?"

The only photo I found of them was a grainy black-and-white snapshot in the newspaper. I had to visit the local library to dig up that one, and I still don't have a clear idea what they look like.

"Do you know where they hang out?" What I really want to ask is if they're here in the bar tonight, but I don't want to look stupid.

"I don't know who you are or where you come from, but your interest in those boys is a waste of time. They ain't friendly with outsiders."

"I just need a few minutes—"

"No single gal wants just a few minutes with them." She scowls at my ringless left hand and lifts her chin. "I hear Jake is off the market, but don't go getting your hopes up about Jarret. He'll settle down with one of our own before he marries the likes of you."

"Marriage?"

"He won't take kindly to you asking about them, neither."

I can't even wrap my mind around this conversation.

Her eyes dart to the front entryway, and a hitch cuts her breath.

I follow her line of sight and stifle my own gasp.

Good God Almighty. Cowboys do nothing for me, but the two men who just strolled in redefine my preconceived notions of rugged ranchers.

Maybe I've watched too many old westerns, but I expected sweat-soaked dirt rings around the collar, unwashed and overlong hair, iconic mustaches, and rotten teeth. Most of the guys in this bar fit that description. But not these two.

They're definitely twins, but not identical. One has a narrower face, paler eyes, and a darker hairline beneath the wide brim of his hat. His almost-smile is far more personable than the almost-scowl the other one wears. He exudes charisma, which makes him the most attractive of the two.

And the most dangerous.

Finely-honed brawn bunches and contracts as they move through the bar. Sculpted biceps and pectorals, flat stomachs, and powerful thighs—they're built the same, as if carved from a single hunk of testosterone-infused stone.

Golden complexions. Six-foot-and-several-intimidating-inches tall. Clean-shaved faces. Squared jaw lines. Broad, sloping shoulders. Well-worn denim encases well-endowed packages that draw the eye. There's so much to take in.

Holy hell, I'm staring, and I can't stop.

It isn't just their hotter-than-hot surface area that compels me. There's an air about them, a confidence, an authoritative intensity that grabs a woman by the ovaries and reduces her to her most primitive core. It's the same instinct that drives females of any species to mate with the strongest male, to birth the fittest, most viable offspring.

Jesus. I'm not even interested in that. I'm so fucking done with men, especially the good-looking ones. Yet here I am, slurping back drool as it leaks from my gaping mouth.

I'm here for the Holsten twins, to learn about them, and hopefully, to get answers. If I wasn't already certain I found them, the petite redhead between them would be a dead giveaway.

Conor Cassidy.

One doesn't need to be a journalist to know her story. A simple online search on *Sandbank* brings up dozens of results related to the brutal attack on her six years ago. What the articles don't mention is the Holsten family's involvement that night.

I didn't expect her to be in town. Last time I checked, she was still at OSU. I certainly didn't expect to see her all cozy with the family who caused her so much pain.

The one with the darker eyes and the arm hooked around her shoulders must be Jake. Rumor has it they were the sweethearts of Sandbank, right up until the attack.

Her brother, Lorne Cassidy, went to prison for

killing the wrong man, and her father moved her to Chicago. To *my* hometown. She doesn't have a clue who I am or how we're connected, and I hope to God I never have to be the person to tell her.

I drag my eyes away from the magnetic trio as they sit around a nearby high-top table. That's when I notice that every woman in the bar is caught in their spell.

Conor stands out with her outrageous beauty and colorful sleeves of tattoos, but it's the Holstens who coax the far-away looks beneath the feminine lashes around me. Not to mention, the irritated scowls of their male companions.

Jake and Conor share a few whispered words. Then he makes his way to the bar and orders drinks.

I glance back at the table and find the other brother, Jarret, staring right at me.

Shit. I look away and curse myself for flinching. I won't be unnerved by him, no matter how goddamn sexy he is.

I force my gaze back to his.

He's still staring, and the effect that has on me is bizarre. It feels like victory, like I just won a competition against every female in the bar. There are thirty or forty women he can stare at, but he's looking at me. An unwavering, potent look from the most potent man I've ever seen.

I may not be accustomed to this kind of scrutiny, but if I don't get a grip on my headspace—and other hungrier spaces inside me—he'll eat me alive before I spit out two words.

Conor speaks to him, and he touches her hand on her lap, keeping his eyes on me.

That stare... Fuck me, it's too much. I turn my focus to Jake at the counter. He would be easier to approach. He hasn't glanced at me or any other woman since he walked in here.

I slide a hand over my hair, pressing down the blond disaster. The humidity is a nightmare on natural curls. I hate the frizz when it's this long. I hate it more when it's short. I really hate that I can't stop touching the tangles when I'm anxious.

The bartender turns toward Jake with his beers, and I dare another peek at Jarret.

He's still watching me.

Damn. There's nothing discreet about him, and now that he's caught me looking multiple times, I might as well get on with this.

I rise from the stool, and he drags his tongue along his lip, speaking to Conor. He laughs at something she says and sobers when he realizes I'm heading his way.

That's right, Jarret Holsten. I'm not as shy as I look.

He might be intimidating as all hell, but I'm not leaving town until I get what I came for.

As I cross the room, the damn peanut shells make it difficult to navigate on heels. First thing tomorrow, I'll find a second-hand clothing store and replace my shoes with something practical.

When I reach the table, Jake slips past me and settles next to Conor.

"Um... Hi." Oh God, I sound like an idiot. I hook a thumb under the purse strap on my shoulder and strengthen my voice. "You're the Holsten twins, right?"

"Yup." Jarret drinks from his beer and rudely stares at my chest.

Conor kicks him under the table. "Women don't like to be leered at."

She would know. Her beauty is really something to behold. I bet she gets ogled and catcalled everywhere she goes.

I tip my head at her in thanks. "You must be Conor Cassidy."

Jake gives me direct eye contact for the first time.

"And you are?"

"Maybe."

"Maybe?" Jarret wings up a brow. "That's your name?"

It's not a name at all, but no one bothered to tell my mother that.

"Yeah." I try to smile, as if I haven't heard all the *Maybe* one-liners in existence.

I'll take that as a Maybe.

Call me...Maybe.

Maybe she's born with it.

Maybe or Maybe not?

"Maybe Quinn." I stand taller. "Mind if I sit?"

With a nod, he sets down his beer, flashing a thick red line on his palm. I perch on the stool, trying not to stare at the scar.

"So, Maybe..." Jarret angles closer, his golden eyes poking holes in my bravado. "Which news network do you work for?

My pulse quickens. It's almost true, but not quite. I came here dressed like a reporter, hoping it would distract my real intentions. Evidently, I'm doing something right. But I don't want to appear too eager.

"Oh, that's not..." I school my features. "I'm just passing through."

That earns me a withering glare from Jake, who calmly says, "The only folks *passing through* this town are investigative journalists."

That title is above my pay grade, but he can think what he wants.

I glance down and spot a welted slash on his palm. Weird. They have the same scar?

Without being too obvious, I steal a peek at Conor's hand as she brushes a strand of hair from her face. Sure enough, another scar. They must've cut themselves on purpose? Like in one of those truth-or-dare games kids play?

"Who do you work for, Maybe Quinn?" Jarret tips back his beer, and a swallow slides down the strong column of his throat.

With a feigned sigh, I give him an answer that could be true. "Freelance. I write the story and sell it to the highest bidder."

I have the credentials to write and sell their dirty laundry. If they're as corrupt as I'm led to believe, I'll sell them out in a heartbeat.

"What's the story?" Conor narrows her eyes with distrust.

"Levi Tibbs is getting released tomorrow." I yank my hand from my hair, realizing too late I'm fidgeting. "What are you three planning to do about that?"

"What are we planning? Well, we're going to drink our beers." Jarret takes a hearty draw from his. "We'll probably warm up that dance floor. Then I'll work off some steam in a warm, feisty body." He checks me out again, a slow journey from north to south. "You're welcome to join the party. Particularly the last part."

On another day, in another life, I might've considered his offer. The deep rumble of his voice alone makes me feel blissfully warm and dizzy. I'm certain the rest of him would give me the ride of my life.

But my situation doesn't allow for indulgence. Especially not indulgence with *this* man.

"I think not." My tone is short, tolerating no room for argument.

"Then I expect you'll find your way out of town and back to wherever you came from."

"I'm gonna dance with my girl." Jake rises and cants the brim of his hat in my direction. "Ma'am."

He and Conor vacate the table, leaving me alone with Jarret.

"I'm not going anywhere." My stomach ripples with nerves, and I press my hands against my lap to keep my fingers out of my hair.

The silent space between us becomes the focal point, hovering like an awkward intruder. Jarret doesn't strike me as the quiet type. He's blatantly ignoring me.

"You were there the night Conor was attacked." I pull in a steady breath. "Yet you were unharmed. Were you in cohorts with Levi Tibbs?"

He moves his eyes slowly, deliberately, locking onto mine with lethal warning.

"Look at her." He tilts his head toward Conor without shifting his gaze from me.

My pulse stutters as I find her red hair in the crowd of cowboy hats. With her fingers curled around Jake's neck, she lifts on her toes and whispers to him. As he listens, his hands roam her tiny frame with intimate familiarity.

They're definitely back together.

"You may not see what I see." Jarret's voice yanks my attention back to him. "But you see her, and you know there's something extraordinary there. Something rare and priceless and worth protecting." His jaw flexes. "Here's a free tip for your bullshit story. I love that girl more than life itself. I can't even fathom playing a part in the brutality inflicted on her that night."

Crystal-clear sincerity sharpens his tone, his eyes glowing with devastation. I believe him, but I know he's involved in something. Something illegal. I just don't know how deep it goes. *Yet.*

In a blink, he's off the chair, breaching my personal space with his arms bracketed around me.

"She's been though more hell than you can comprehend in your privileged existence." He seethes at my ear. "If you exploit her suffering, I will *ruin* you."

"Don't you dare threaten me." My blood goes hot, burning my cheeks. "Step the fuck back."

His pupils swallow the golden hues of his eyes, and

his lips stretch into a humorless, wolfish smile.

"You got some fire beneath those prissy clothes." He returns to his chair.

I thought my clothes made me look professional. I'm either ridiculously transparent or he's really good at reading people. Unfortunately, I don't have any casual clothes among the few things left to my name.

"You just met me." I straighten my spine and meet his gaze head-on. "Yet you condemned me the moment I approached. You don't know a damn thing about my *existence*, privileged or otherwise."

"Fair enough." He rubs a thumb along his bottom lip, searching my eyes. "Enlighten me."

"What do you want to know?" I glance at Jake and Conor, where they burn up the dance floor with their eye-fucking, hip-grinding, disgustingly-in-love embrace.

"Which side of the bed do you sleep on?" he asks.

"What?" I whip my head toward him, expecting a taunting smirk.

"You heard me." He stares at me steadily, dead serious.

Last time I owned a bed, I slept on the right, snuggled up to the man I loved. But that's an ugly story, not appropriate for current company.

"I don't have a side," I say honestly. "You?"

"Same. Where is this bed of yours?"

"Chicago."

His gaze darts to Conor, eyebrows gathering.

"I know she lived there a few years ago, but it's a big city." I chew my lip and give him the truth. "None of you were on my radar until recently."

"How did you hear about us?"

Since he sees right through me, I won't lie to him again. So I answer with a non-answer. "I have my ways."

He continues to watch Conor dance with his brother, and a pinch of envy twinges in my gut. She's a lucky woman to be cared for so deeply by two protective, insanely attractive men.

"Are you in love with her?" I ask.

His eyes slide to mine, the only part of him that moves. "You're not very good at your job."

"What's that supposed to mean?"

"It means I've been straight with you, and you still don't get it." His stony expression chills me to the bone. "I consider her my sister, and I protect what's mine. It's time for you to leave."

"You don't own this establishment." I stare him down with the recklessness of a woman who has nothing left to lose. "Good luck kicking me out."

His silent glare confirms what I already assumed. He doesn't like me. That bothers me, but I don't blame him.

I'm a threat.

He rises to his feet and ambles away. Without speaking or casting me a backward glance, he effectively brushes me off.

My stomach sinks. The disappointment is made worse when he joins a table of smiling young women.

I remain seated, easily forgotten and replaced with the flirtatious giggles of his friends. Or potential bed partners. Or whatever those women are to him.

It stings. It shouldn't, but I'm hypersensitive to being cast away by men. It's like I'm wearing a sign on my forehead that reads, *Not worth the effort.*

Not even worth a goodbye.

As much as I want to tuck tail and flee, pride holds me in place through several songs. The music isn't bad. A little twangy. I like all kinds of genres, especially country pop. The folks in this town would probably roll their eyes at that.

Or so I thought.

Legends by country-pop singer Kelsea Ballerini trickles through the speakers, and the room gravitates toward the dance floor. At the center, Jake and Conor sway in an embrace that entrances the entire bar.

It's not just the seductive way they dance together. It's the passion that glows between them, like the rest of the world doesn't exist, and all they see is each other.

I thought I had that with someone once, and it was pretty amazing. Until it wasn't.

At the end of the song, Conor steps off the dance floor and heads into the bathroom. A few minutes later, Jake bypasses the line outside the door and shuts them both inside.

Across the room, the woman beside Jarret runs a hand up his thigh.

I've seen enough.

I make my way out of the Big Sugar. If Jarret's aware of my exit, he doesn't show it. He doesn't look in my direction once.

No matter. He'll see me again.

When I reach my ugly old sedan, I move it to an unlit corner of the parking lot and wait.

Jarret said he planned to *work off some steam in a warm, feisty body.* If that's the case, he'll leave with a woman.

Does he have a regular lover? Or does he play the field? If he has a confidant, someone he spends a lot of time with, I might have better luck coaxing information from her.

Thirty minutes later, Jake leads Conor out of the bar. Her smile screams *freshly fucked*, and following on their heels is Jarret.

He's alone?

The three of them pile into a big pickup truck, with Jake in the driver's seat.

It's only ten in the evening. Traffic on the main street allows me to tail them at a distance without being noticed.

Until they reach a dirt road at the edge of town.

They turn off, kicking up dust and leaving the Sandbank traffic behind. If I follow, they'll spot me.

I slow the car, creeping along the shoulder until Jake's truck disappears over a hill. Then I veer onto the dirt road.

Not wanting to catch up with them, I maintain a slow speed until I reach a private drive about a mile up.

I scoped out the route to their ranch earlier today and found a place to bed down for the night. There's a motel in town, but I didn't bother checking for vacancy. I can't afford to stay there.

Overgrown weeds consume the private road, surrounded by the seclusion of thick trees. The tire tracks are from my sedan earlier. Other than me, no one's driven through here in a long time.

I back in, park the car out of view of the dirt road, and shut off the motor. When I'm ready to sleep, I'll drive deeper onto the isolated property. There's a lake back there I can use to wash in.

For now, I'm content to sit here and watch the road for activity. Since Jarret rode to the bar with Jake, it's possible he went home for his own truck before heading out again.

If that happens, I'll follow him. I have nothing else to do and nowhere to go. Everything I own is in this car. How's that for privileged? Jarret would choke on his words if he knew how hard I worked for every penny I earned. *And lost.*

The large envelope on the passenger seat holds the solution to my homelessness. Once the documents are finalized, I'll get a piece of my life back.

But money isn't what brought me to Sandbank. I need to understand what happened. I need answers.

For now, I slide the envelope under the floor mat. From the backseat, I pull out a jar of beets and a bottle of water. Then I roll down the window and eat dinner beneath the soothing chirrup of night critters.

It's quiet here, so unlike the constant din of a big city. I could live in a place like this, away from the hustle and judgment of people.

There's nothing left for me in Chicago, and I won't be returning. I can write articles from anywhere. Hell, I can wait tables or bartend and be happy.

Happiness. I have that to look forward to. Starting over won't be easy, but I'm stronger this time. Less gullible.

But first, I need to right the wrongs that have been done to me.

Finished with dinner, I discard the containers in a trash bag and settle into a more comfortable slump behind the steering wheel.

Just as my eyes grow heavy with sleep, the sound of an approaching vehicle jerks me into awareness.

I crane my neck until headlights emerge on the hill in the direction of Julep Ranch. Grabbing the key in the ignition, I wait for the motorist to pass.

Tires crunch, followed by the blare of an unfamiliar country song. Then a pickup truck similar to Jake's rolls past.

An elbow perches on the window frame. Broad shoulders. Wide-brimmed hat. Sculpted profile.

Jarret Holsten.

Following him will be tricky until we get into town. I force myself to wait a full minute before I start the engine and speed off after him.

When I arrive at the main thoroughfare, he's nowhere in sight. I scan the passing trucks. Which way did he go?

I turn toward town center, hoping it's the right direction.

A few blocks later, I spot his truck at a gas station. My heart rate doubles as I park in the shadows of an adjacent lot and watch him stroll inside the convenience store.

Doesn't take him long to return to his truck with a small bag in hand. I'd bet the case of canned oysters in my backseat that he just purchased a box of condoms.

Oh God, I'm watching a man buy condoms. Of all the things I've done over the past couple of months, this is the first time I've felt like a bona fide stalker.

What am I doing? Am I actually going to follow this guy to wherever he goes to get laid? What if he sees me? What if I see something disturbing? Like freaky, fucked-up sex shit? Some things can't be unseen.

Considering the crimes I think he's involved in, this might not end well for me. He's not exactly the kind of man I want to piss off.

I'd rather focus on Jake instead, but he seems to be attached to Conor's hip. I need to keep some distance from her.

When this is all said and done, maybe I'll have my conscience examined. Until then, I need to stop second-guessing myself.

I have to finish this. If I don't, the mystery surrounding my total ruin will forever haunt me. I need an explanation.

I need closure.

With a tight grip on the steering wheel, I hit the gas and follow Jarret Holsten.

I trail three cars behind Jarret's truck, my shoulders tight and hands locked at ten and two, just like my mom in Chicago rush hour. *God rest her soul.*

I loosen my grip as he leads me through town. He swings onto a residential road lined with huge trees and tiny houses, in the opposite direction of the Big Sugar.

After several turns, he pulls into a driveway and kills the engine. I veer onto a side street and park on the curb, out of view. Then I sneak toward the house on foot.

Since I'm new at this stalking business, my attempt at tiptoeing is anything but quiet. Because I forgot to change my damn shoes.

I click-clack back to the car and consider my options. Heels or ballet flats? Neither would allow a fast getaway. I opt for no shoes and, after a moment a deliberation, grab the small hunting knife I keep under the driver's seat.

Untucking my shirt, I wedge the sheathed blade between my waistband and tailbone and creep barefoot down the inky, quiet street.

A dog barks in the distance, and my heart jumps. The humidity clings to my skin, and I tremble so violently my lungs seize, making it impossible to suck air without sounding asthmatic.

His truck comes into view, and darkness cloaks the front of the one-story house. Nothing moves. No sound. He must already be inside.

Curtains conceal the rooms within, but a spill of light casts a flicker over the side yard.

I head that way and find an uncovered, illuminated window near the rear. A bedroom?

Indecision holds me in place.

Can I assume he's in there with a woman? What else would he be here for? His only family in Sandbank is his brother. Is he visiting a friend? In a back bedroom? Maybe he's blackmailing or murdering someone.

If he hauls out a rolled-up rug, I'm out of here.

Keeping to the shadows, I slip between the houses, duck beneath the window, and slowly peek over the sill. The vantage point gives me a straight shot through the glass pane, into the bedroom beyond, and...

Oh my God, that escalated quickly.

A slender brunette climbs up Jarret's body, all legs and hands and frantic kisses.

He just stands there, letting her paw and lick him ravenously. She lifts his shirt, and he raises his arms so she can pull it off. Then she's on him again, clawing at his chest and eating at his mouth, as if he's the first meal she's had in days.

Is he returning her kisses? I can't tell. His profile's too fuzzy through the grimy glass. I wish I could see his full expression.

I wish I knew what he tastes like.

Ugh. What the hell's wrong with me? Yeah, he's insanely gorgeous, and the definition in his torso looks better than any airbrushed magazine. I would have to be in a coma to be immune to all that masculine sexiness.

But I learned the hard way male beauty is only skin deep.

I should go. He obviously knows this girl. I can come back later and try to talk to her.

Go.

Get your feet moving.

Step away from the window.

Rather than doing the logical thing, I linger, silently willing him to lower his jeans. I just want a glimpse. A forbidden eye full of Jarret Holsten in the buff. I bet he's hung like a stallion.

I know it's wrong. I'm invading his privacy, but he has it coming after being a jerk to me. I could do a lot worse than steal a peek at his package.

After a few more seconds of her groping, he grabs her shoulder-length hair and yanks her back.

My breath catches, and my skin heats. Christ, he's rough.

Using his grip, he forces her to her knees and stares down at her. His mouth moves, forming words I can't hear, and she blinks up at him, eyes heavy with hunger.

He shifts slightly, putting his back to the window and blocking my view of her and whatever he's packing in his pants.

I clutch my throat as her hands move to the vicinity of his fly. Then his jeans slide downward, just low enough to reveal two dimples on either side of his tailbone, the top of his crack, and the rise of sculpted butt cheeks.

She inches closer, and his back muscles flex. He tosses off his hat, unveiling thick, dark hair that's cut short enough to keep him cool in the heat, but long enough to tangle around fingers.

With her face hidden by his body, I can't see his cock sliding into her mouth, but he's definitely giving it to her, kicking his hips with his hands clenched on her head.

There's an edge to the way he moves. A sense of dominance and tantalizing power. It holds me in fascination and soul-deep longing to the point where I feel envious of her. Maybe even jealous.

I crave that kind of relationship, one where I can put absolute trust in a lover to fuck me however he pleases, to hurt me with pleasure-pain and take care of me afterward.

But that kind of trust has never worked out for me. Whoever said there's glory in love obviously doesn't know how that fantasy ends.

Fuck 'em and forget 'em. Now that's a motto that rings true, one I intend to adopt when I'm ready to move on.

Watching Jarret face fuck this girl makes me miss sex. I already missed it, but this plunges me into a whole new hell of lonesome yearning.

It takes about five minutes of plowing into her throat before he comes. His head falls back, and his hips grind erratically, ruthlessly, as he holds her face against him.

I clench my thighs together, imagining being taken that way by a man who wants me with mindless passion.

Christ, I really need to get laid.

He releases her, and she falls back on her butt, smiling. It surprises me when he pulls up his jeans and fastens them in place. Is he finished?

He slides the belt from his waistband and folds it in half while speaking to her.

Nope, not finished.

She jumps to her feet and strips her clothes, revealing caramel skin, voluptuous curves, and huge boobs. She's pretty. Absolutely stunning. And boy, do I feel inadequate.

I've always wanted a body like that. Instead, I've

been stuck with the same gangly limbs and tiny tits I've had since middle school.

The bag he brought from the gas station sits on the mattress. She crawls up beside it and sprawls on her back, giving me a full-on view of her Brazilian wax job.

He prowls around the bed, trailing a hand along her leg, her hip, the full curve of her breast. When he reaches the headboard, he loops the belt around her wrists and restrains her to the metal frame.

Of course, he does. Why wouldn't he play out all my fantasies while I stand outside the window like a creepy pervert?

My ability to leave has come and gone. I've never experienced the kind of raw, kinky sex I know this man is capable of. Watching might be as close as I ever come to participating in something like this.

He says something to her, tweaks her nipple, and steps into the adjoined bathroom.

Minutes pass, and I grow anxious. What is he doing? Fluffing his cock? Flossing his teeth? Maybe she keeps a bag of sex toys in there, and he's debating between a Baby Jesus butt plug or shock therapy nipple clamps?

She doesn't try to free herself from the shackle of his belt. Staring at the ceiling, she saws her legs together like a cricket calling for its mate.

Great. Now I'll be stuck with that visual while I fall asleep to the chirp of crickets tonight.

I return my attention to the bathroom doorway, watching for signs of movement. Where the hell is he? Something doesn't feel right.

As I turn away from the window, a hand claps over my mouth. Another wraps around my throat, pressing against my windpipe.

A chill grips my spine. My eyes throb, and my muffled scream vibrates in my ears.

I grip the fingers at my airway, scratching at the immovable collar of muscle and bone as my heart thumps out of control.

"Didn't realize you like to watch." Jarret's southern drawl caresses my ear from behind.

My nails bite into his skin as oxygen floods in and out of my lungs. He's not strangling me, but it feels like it. My stomach tenses with cramps, and fear rapidly exhausts my body.

"It's more comfortable inside." He nips at the shell of my ear, his breath hot and terrifyingly calm. "McKenna won't mind an audience." A trace of annoyance clips his voice. "She goes out of her way for attention."

His shirtless chest presses against my back like a hot slab of concrete. I force my hands to release his arm and twist my hips, reaching for the knife in my waistband.

He lets go.

I spin away, stumbling backward and wheezing for air. "Touch me like that again, and I'll cut off your fingers and shove them up your ass."

"How would you do that? Bite them off with your little kitten teeth?"

"Too much work." I pull the knife from its sheath and point it at him.

"No shit." He rubs his jaw. "Where'd you get that?"

"The knife store."

He stalks forward until the blade touches his chest. I snap my teeth at him, but he presses closer.

"How did you sneak out of the bathroom?" I hold the weapon steady, dimpling his pectoral with the tip.

"How did you not know the bathroom connects to the hall? It's a standard floor plan." He pushes against the knife, causing blood to well beneath the steel.

He's insane. Certifiable.

"Do you hear voices in your head?" I lift a brow.

He flashes a dark smile. "You hear them, too?"

Now he's just fucking with me.

"How did you know I was out here?" I edge backward, just a step.

He stays with me. "How did you know to find me at the gas station?"

He knew I was there?

Shit! I suck at this. "I figured you're the type of guy who buys condoms on his way to a family get together."

His smile falls. "You have a killer body, but you need a better workout routine for that mouth. I have something that'll help with that."

"What? A big dick? Too bad you have more of that in your personality than you do in your pants."

"You don't believe that."

His gaze lowers to my shirt, and I glance down. Several buttons popped free during the scuffle, and the fabric hangs open and off to the side, with the cup of my transparent bra in full view. And there's my nipple, hard and swollen and right out there for the world to see.

"Dammit." I yank the flaps of the shirt together, mortified.

"It's unfortunate."

"What?"

"How fucking beautiful you are, all fiery and worked-up with your teeth bared and nipples begging to be bruised. Can't remember the last time I was this hard."

I keep my eyes on his, refusing to acknowledge him with a glance at his groin. The brunette inside didn't have any issues making him hard. Doesn't exactly make me feel like a special snowflake.

"Doesn't matter what my dick thinks." He crosses his arms, and the movement flexes his biceps. "I don't fuck reporters."

"Oh well, good, because I don't fuck assholes."

He grins. I expect a vulgar retort about butt sex, but he leaves it alone.

"Sure you don't want to come in?" He nods at the window. "If your story includes details about my cock, you need to get the size right."

"Hmmm." I tap the flat side of the blade against my chin. "I just remembered. I have to be somewhere slash I'd rather scoop out my eyes with a rusty spoon."

I breeze past him and head toward the street with as much dignity as I can muster with a gaping shirt, no shoes, and a knife dangling from my hand.

"Maybe Quinn."

I pause at the call of his voice and glance over my shoulder.

"If you're thinking about harassing McKenna for information about my family, don't bother." He prowls to the front porch and rests a hand on the door handle. "In case you failed to notice, I don't come here for conversation."

My heart feels like it's shrinking.

"Get lost. That's my final warning." He enters the house and shuts the door behind him.

A sharp stitch of pain pulls through my insides, and I gulp air like I just got kicked in the gut. Self-disparaging thoughts slosh around in my skull, hazy and irrational. I can't swallow, because a lump has taken up residence in my throat.

This is what rejection feels like. It's nothing new, but this time it's misplaced and borderline manic. I don't know this guy. I have no claim on him. Yet I'm clutching the knife like I'm seconds from running into that house and cockblocking his good time.

The thought of him banging that woman makes my chest hurt.

He's under my skin, and I need to shake him off. Right now. This isn't who I am. I don't obsess over men. I don't swoon or buckle in the presence of washboard abs and flirty smiles. I'm not even tempted to look.

Until him.

A shadow passes through the glow of light on the side yard, and a second later, a shade lowers over the bedroom window, shutting me out.

I return the knife to its sheath and straighten my spine. A hard swallow dislodges the knot in my throat, and a good mental spanking forces my feet to the car.

He did the right thing by coming outside and confronting me. I shouldn't have spied on his intimate moment.

I screwed up, but that doesn't mean I'm giving up.

In the car, I start the engine and cue up a motivational song on my phone.

As *Hell On Heels* by Pistol Annies thumps through the old speakers, I roll down the window and hit the gas.

Tomorrow's a new day, and there's strength in that.

Tomorrow, I'll have my shit together when I show up at Julep Ranch.

Tomorrow, he won't be able to turn me away.

After a hot shower, I recline on the back porch with Jake and Conor and glide my fingers through the damp hanks of my hair. It's been a long day, and the silence between us hangs as heavily as the shadows over the field.

Restlessness penetrates my veins in surging fits, and the pasta from dinner sits uncomfortably in my stomach. I'm sure the leftovers were fine, but all I tasted was the dour mood in the air.

We killed Levi Tibbs tonight.

That's a damn good reason to celebrate, but none of us are feeling victorious. Conor seems lost in memory, no doubt mourning the night that bastard raped her.

I suspect Jake is brooding for the same reason I am.

For six years, we dreamed of drawing out Levi's demise and bathing in his blood. He deserved a more prolonged and gruesome end than what we gave him.

We decided against it for Conor's sake. Not that she isn't strong enough to handle violence and gore. Christ, the things she's survived would make a psychopath cry.

Nevertheless, Jake and I refused to expose her to more senseless depravity. She wanted to witness Levi's death, so we made it quick and efficient. I guess old habits die hard, because we can't give up our need to shelter her.

She curls up on the outdoor couch with Jake, burrowed against his side beneath the mantle of his arm. They look good together. Always have. But they seem stronger than ever now, their connection more balanced and immutable.

Despite the relapses she still has from her trauma, I know they're happy. The thought loosens some of the tension in my chest, but we won't know true happiness until we get Lorne back.

Without interrupting their quiet reflection, I collect the dinner dishes and step inside the house.

After I load the dishwasher, I head to the front door to spend the remainder of the night tinkering around in the stable. My project list is never-ending, and while most of the tasks are mundane, I love working with my hands.

Hard work is healing. Not in a magical way. It doesn't erase wounds. But it returns me to the person I was before—healthy and uncomplicated, focused and unjaded.

Outside, I hop off the front porch and stroll toward the stable in the dark. And stop.

What the almighty fuck?

Maybe Quinn steps out of a beat-up sedan and hurries toward me like a woman on a mission.

Oh, fuck no. This broad has the audacity to trespass on the ranch after I told her to get lost? Her ass will be glowing red-hot by the time I'm done with her.

I plant my feet in a wide stance and join my hands behind my back as she closes the distance.

A flowery, ruffled dress thing hangs by tiny straps

off her narrow shoulders, and white flats cover her feet. She looks like she dolled herself up for a tea party with the queen. It's kind of cute, in a nutty Alice In Wonderland way.

"Before you get all surly and dickish..." She points a finger at me and pauses a few feet away. "You want to hear what I have to say."

"I assure you, I don't." I pivot toward the stable and start walking, expecting her to follow.

"No cowboy hat tonight?"

"Sun ain't out." I measure my strides, outpacing the footfalls behind me.

"Trevor Pierson," she says out of the blue. "Grady Clark, Rogan Schroeder, Mike Zarda, Levi Tibbs."

A fist clamps around my heart. Thank fuck my back is to her, because I can't keep the anger from curling my lip. My legs keep moving without falter, but it takes great effort to not give her a reaction.

How does she know the names of the cocksuckers rotting at the bottom of the ravine?

A chill creeps over my scalp. What are the chances she shows up on the night of a fresh kill? What if she arrived just a few hours earlier while Jake was strangling Levi? What if she followed us from the shack where we trapped him?

If she knew we were murderers, she wouldn't have come here alone. She damn well wouldn't be hurrying after me in the dark.

What does she know exactly? That those men are missing? That they were criminal loan sharks, contract killers, and all-around worthless human beings?

I can't ask. Not without acknowledging I know them. Levi Tibbs is the exception. But the rest of them? All I can do is pretend to ignore her, as if I have no idea what she's jabbering on about.

"I met with your dad."

That stops me. My pulse thrashes in my ears as I slowly turn to face her.

"Why?" I want to roar at her and tell her how dangerous he is. "Stay away from him."

She crosses her dainty arms and sniffs. "Aren't you going to ask me what he said?"

"No." I storm away, rub a hand down my face, and spin back. "Where is he?"

"He lives with a young woman two hours from here. Holed up in northern Texas."

Fuck, that's not far.

A million questions run on a circuit in my head as I glare at her with unconcealed displeasure. She's on the cusp of stirring up a hornet's nest. I can't let her go until I find out what she knows.

Since she doesn't respond to verbal warnings, I'll have to try a more tactile approach.

Stepping into her space, I bend my knees and put my scowl in her pretty face. She doesn't flinch, doesn't so much as blink. She's either stupid or remarkably brave.

I grab a thick tangle of curls on the back of her head and yank hard, forcing her neck at an uncomfortable angle.

"No!" She scratches at my arm, her eyes aglow with blue flames. "Let go!"

"Are you concealing a knife beneath this dress?" I bat away her swinging arms. "If you don't answer, I'll search for it myself."

"No. No knife." She lifts a knee, aiming for my groin. Too slow.

I twirl her around by her hair, redirecting every kick, slap, and punch she attempts.

She's so lightweight it requires little effort to maneuver her where I want her. She might be taller than Conor by a couple of inches, but they're built the same. Short, fit, smallish tits, cute. *Fun sized.*

I love all shapes and dimensions of the female body, but I prefer Maybe's physique. While she's the right size to scoop up and haul around however I please, she's also sturdy enough to sustain a hard, savage fuck against a barn door.

What lies between her ears, however, makes her strictly off-limits.

"Let go of me, you fucking animal!" Her hands return to mine, uselessly trying to uncurl my fingers from her hair. "I mean it! Let go!"

I sweep a boot under her feet and release her in a single movement that dumps her ass-first in the dirt.

An *oomph* escapes her lips, followed by a breathy "Prick."

She shoves the dress over her thighs before I catch an enticing glimpse. As she starts to scramble back up, I straddle her hips and force her onto her back with a hand around her throat. Then I squeeze, just enough to scare her without causing pain or constricting airflow.

A normal woman would fall into hysterics right about now. The instinct is there, quickening her breaths and shining in her overly-bright eyes. But something else eclipses her fight-or-flight response.

The instant I sense it, my skin shivers, as if a cloud of electricity moves in and crackles the air. Is this what Conor meant when she talked about sparks and fireworks?

No way. I don't believe in that shit. But something strange settles over Maybe's flushed face, and it affects me, too.

Tingling currents ignite in my chest and spread through my limbs. A tiny gasp slips from her lips, and her eyes glaze beneath the hood of lashes. Am I cutting her airway?

No, she's breathing just fine, albeit shallow and fast. Her fingers rest against mine around her neck, but she doesn't try to dislodge me. It's as if I'm enthralling her, as if we're ensnaring each other.

She squirms beneath me. Actually rolls her hips to rub against the backs of my thighs. I let my weight rest against her pelvis and bring my face closer to hers, reeled in by an invisible string, drawn to her on a level I don't understand.

The scent of her hair reaches my nose. A natural aroma, pure and fresh like earthy moss and open air with notes of mint. Whatever it is, I'm addicted.

Her untamed mane fans out around her like a golden halo. Huge blue eyes glow in the moonlight, the rest of her features delicate and pixie-like. She might be as ferocious as a lioness, but she looks so damn soft and gentle. Everything inside me clenches to protect her.

What the hell is happening? There's attraction. There's sexual desire. Then there's *this*. It's curiosity and gravity and some kind of illogical magnetism that makes my heart beat with the impulse to claim and possess.

The thought pisses me off, and I tighten my hand around her throat.

Her lips part. Her eyes flutter, and she melts beneath my weight. Then she blinks. Her expression closes off, and every inch of her goes taut.

That's when it clicks.

She's different. So remarkably different from other women.

Small town girls want marriage, kids, the whole shebang. Throw in the huge estate on ten-thousand acres, and I'm the most eligible bachelor in Sandbank. When they're with me, they respond to rough play with squealing *Ahhhhs,* noisy gasps, and arched spines.

It's all fake. They kneel, suck, moan, and give me the reactions they think I want, all for a chance to score a ring and a commitment.

They don't stand up to me. They never say no. It's goddamn uninspiring. The exaggerated performance

McKenna put on for me last night was just more of the same.

Unlike the others, however, Maybe Quinn is positively kinky. No pretense about it. In fact, she's trying her damnedest to hide it from me.

Her pulse hammers beneath my palm, but she's muting her gasps and clenching her teeth. She despises me and wants me, and dammit, I'm fucked.

She's the one I've been waiting for.

Maybe I'm wrong.

God, I hope I'm suffering from temporary insanity.

I hover my face inches from hers, relishing the heave of her chest. "If I lift your dress, I bet I'll find the wettest cunt in Oklahoma."

She rears back a hand and slaps me with enough force to jerk my head to the side.

Momentarily stunned, I lose my grip on her throat, and she scurries out from beneath me.

I gotta hand it to her. She knows how to hit. My cheek throbs like a bitch, and I can't decide if I'm burning with anger or wildly turned on. Both, I think.

Crawling out of arm's reach, she leaps to her feet, loses her shoes along the way, and backs up.

"You should run." I rise and prowl toward her.

"You don't scare me." She squares her shoulders and stands her ground.

So bold and beautiful. Resting my eyes on her is deeply satisfying, and I'm gripped with a sudden sense of necessity. An urgency to keep her in my presence. It's an irrational feeling, but I can't let it go. It's already soaked into my bones and become a part of me.

I want her. Badly.

But I shouldn't.

I can't.

Maybe that explains my infatuation. She's the forbidden fruit. An enemy to my family and everything

I'm trying to rebuild.

That's all the more reason to keep her close.

Until I'm certain she's no longer a threat, I'll have to watch her like a hawk and prevent her from doing anything stupid. The best way to do that is to bring her into my inner circle and build a foundation of trust.

Luring her into my bed wouldn't just scratch this irritating itch. It would form a knot of togetherness between us. And let's face it. I have a long track record of growing bored with a woman after one night.

I won't get attached.

"You should be scared." I take a menacing step closer. "I know your weakness."

"What weakness?" Instead of retreating, she stays with me, circling with my steps and keeping me in front of her.

"One touch, and I know everything there is to know about your turn-ons."

"How is that a weakness? Unlike you, I'm selective about who I jump into bed with."

That's a damn good response. If she weren't trying to dig up my secrets, I would definitely keep her.

I focus on the challenge in her eyes. "Tell me what you hoped to gain by showing up on my doorstep."

"I want to offer you a deal."

"Explain."

"You need to know what I know, and vice-versa. I give a little. You give a little. Back and forth, until we both have what we want."

I want to tell her she has nothing I need, but that would be a lie. I need to know what she uncovered about the men we killed. I need to know every detail about her meeting with my dad. I need to hear her breathy pleas when I flog her with a crop, taste her tears when she begs me for release, feel how tight her pussy is when she clamps down on my cock.

"You're suggesting we use each other." My gaze

dips to her mouth.

"Not in the way you're implying." She narrows her eyes. "We need to talk. You know, *adult* conversation. Ever had one of those with a woman? Without getting an erection?"

I smirk. "My words tend to be more offensive than my *erections.*"

"That's good. It's great, actually. If you're verbally offensive, it means you're actually thinking and conveying those thoughts. It's a symptom of real communication." She anchors her hands on her hips and stares out at the dark landscape. "We want different things, and we're going into this on opposite sides. I'm willing to argue with you, make disrespectful claims, and *offend* you in the pursuit of truth."

Her pursuit of truth is what scares me. But that's not the only thing.

Everything she said is self-evident, but I never thought about it in such a succinct and intelligent way. She's smarter than me, and that scares me the most.

"I came here prepared for the backlash of your anger." She shifts her eyes back to mine. "I'm not an emotional bleeder or safe-space person." At the lift of my brow, she clarifies. "I'm not easily offended. I already know you give as good as you get. You won't hurt my feelings."

"Did you prepare that speech?"

"I'm kind of winging it as I go."

I like her even more. She's authentic and expressive and stimulating, and it has nothing to do with her physical beauty. I could pick her brilliant mind for hours and feel more fulfilled than a night of no-strings sex.

When was the last time a woman engaged me without trying to lock me into marriage?

Conor doesn't count.

"What do you say?" She juts her chin. "We'll talk. Exchange information. Then I'll leave. You'll never see me again. Do we have a deal?"

I'm focused enough to ensure she doesn't walk away with anything that could threaten my family. But she's sharp. Sharp enough to outsmart me.

What she can't do is physically overpower me.

"You think you have it all figured out." I drift closer, invading her space.

"I didn't say that." A head shorter, she has to tilt her neck back to meet my eyes.

"Did you factor in the possibility that I'm a coldblooded psychopath? Or that I'm bigger than you? Stronger and more aggressive?" I grab her jaw. "You should've run when you had the chance."

"I'm not running." Her swallow confesses her uncertainty. "But I *will* scream."

I lunge for her, catch her around her thighs, and haul her over my shoulder.

"Put me down!" She digs her nails into my back and kicks uselessly in the constriction of my arms. "Help! Help me!"

I live on ten-thousand acres. The only two people within hearing range probably went to bed. Even if Jake and Conor catch the sound of her screams, they won't interfere.

She struggles against me, wearing out the muscles in her tight little body.

"Give it a rest." I slam a palm against her ass. Hard.

She chokes on a shriek and elbows the back of my head. "What are you doing?"

"Demonstrating how I communicate."

"Keep your hands off my—"

I spank her again, and she really starts thrashing.

"This is illegal." She bounces her fists on my back and bucks up and down like a wild bronco. "I'll have you arrested for this."

"In Oklahoma, I have the right to use defensible force against trespassers on my property." I carry her along the dirt trail that leads to the stable. "You should learn the laws if you're going to write about a criminal case."

While I won't give her anything tangible to use against my family, I intend to offer her a deal she can't refuse.

If she wants juicy gossip, she'll have to work for it.

Except I'll be doing most of the work. The kind of single-minded, well-planned work that peels her open, layer by layer, until I penetrate every inch of her naked core.

It's a dangerous game, but I have to explore this. Not just the secrets she may or may not hold against me. I need to unravel whatever it is about her that makes me feel like I'm floating on goddamn sunshine.

She pushes her hands against my back, probably watching her car fade into the darkness behind us. "Where are you taking me?"

"To my office."

"I can walk there on my own. Put me down."

"No can do, sweetheart."

"This is bullshit."

"What you're smelling is horse shit. The bulls are in the west pasture."

She makes a frustrated sound in her throat. "How the fuck are you the sperm that won?"

"I can explain it to you, but I can't understand it for you."

"I really wish I had more middle fingers right now." Her arms flap angrily against my back, no doubt flipping me off. "What happens when we arrive at your office?"

"I'll lay out the terms of our deal."

I don't negotiate. I'll take what I want and give her what she needs, not what she *thinks* she needs.

Then I'll send her stubborn ass back to Chicago.

In the stable, I flick on the overhead lights and grab a bundle of rope from the wall. The blond hellcat in my arms gains a second wind, but her clawing and writhing only succeeds in exciting my heart rate.

"There's only one motel in town, and you haven't checked in there." I know the owner, who confirmed this for me this morning. "Where are you staying?"

"Wherever I want."

"Is this your idea of adult conversation?" I carry Maybe to the support beam at the center of the building.

"There's nothing *adult* about this situation." She pushes and jerks against me. "What are you doing with the rope?"

"I don't trust you."

Her muscles tense. "I haven't done anything to warrant—"

"You stalked me. Got your rocks off while watching me fuck—"

"I did not!"

"—another woman. You pulled a knife on me. Hit

my face. Trespassed on my property. And that's all in the last twenty-four hours."

"Well, you... You spanked me!"

There will be a lot more of that. I run a hand along the vertical beam, searching for nails, splintered wood, or anything that might hurt her.

A soft whinny drifts from one of the stalls, followed by the stomp of hooves. The horses don't like the commotion.

"I looked you up." I knot the rope around her squirming waist. "There are no investigative journalists under the name Maybe Quinn."

"I write under pen names." She shoves at the braided restraint. "Get this thing off me."

"Tell me the names you use."

"I'm not telling you shit until you..." She twists in my arms. "Get this..." Her breathing labors, and her body contorts with the effort to free herself. "Off me!"

I lower her to the dirt floor and cinch the rope tight as she finds her footing. She yanks on the binding, and I yank harder, forcing the length of her body against the post.

"Don't do this." She seethes. "I told you I won't run."

"I told you I don't trust you." I quickly lash her to the wooden beam, fighting down her arms and tying them against the support with several wraps around her torso. "How do I know your name is really Maybe Quinn?"

"If I had a fake name, do you think I'd choose *Maybe*?"

"I like that name. Is it short for something?"

"Maybelline. My mom really loved her makeup." A wince creases her makeup-free face.

Loved. She must've lost her mother.

"If you don't believe me, check my ID." Anger returns to her expression. "My purse is in the car."

"What else will I find in your car? Cameras? Binoculars? Listening devices?"

Her molars smack together, and she looks away.

"I can't have you roaming my stable, planting bugs, and invading my privacy." I check the bindings, making sure her circulation isn't impeded. "This allows me to focus on the conversation instead of where you're slipping your hands."

"I don't have anything on me. I promise."

"Your promise means nothing. If I release you, I'll have to strip search you for contraband. Or you can remain where you are and save yourself the humiliation."

During the tussle to secure her to the post, her dress caught in the rope. The lower half twists and bunches around her thighs, barely covering her panties.

A sheen of perspiration shines across her flushed cheeks. The dress straps hang off her shoulders, and her tits look amazing beneath the thin braless fabric.

Dirt smudges the white flower pattern from our tumble outside, and grass clippings stick out of her tangled hair. She's a hot mess of untamed beauty.

"Fine," she mutters under her breath. "I'll take the rope over your wandering hands."

By the end of this, she'll beg for both.

She flares her nostrils, as if reading my mind. "Does this mean you accept my deal?"

"On my terms." I hold up a finger. "No lies. I prefer silence over dishonesty."

"Same goes for you."

"Agreed." I extend a second finger. "You'll spend the evenings with me, doing whatever I say, when I say it."

A gasp parts her lips. "You think I'd sleep with you to get a story?" She bucks against the restraints. "I'm not a whore!"

"No, darlin'." I lean into her, so close I taste the possibilities on her breath. "You'll sleep with me because you won't be able to stop yourself."

"It must be exhausting."

"What's that?"

"Fending off horny women all day and night. I bet you have to use that big stick of yours to beat them away."

While my inner twelve-year-old appreciates the visual, the grown man in me won't touch that snarky comment.

"As a show of good faith..." I straighten, giving her some breathing room. "I'll allow you the first question."

"Gee, thanks." She scowls at the rope around her and directs that frown at me. "Why did your father leave the ranch?"

"Jake and I forced him out. He inherited the business from our mother and ran it into near-bankruptcy." At the crinkle of her brow, I pause. "What?"

"I don't know. I guess I expected a different answer."

Like the fact that he tried to have Conor and Lorne killed? If she knows about that, we have a serious problem.

She purses her lips, scrutinizing my carefully guarded expression. "So you're broke."

"My father's broke. Jake has a sound mind for business, and I replaced the ranch hands with a dependable crew. We're out of the red and will only improve from here."

None of what I told her is public information, but it won't hurt if she leaks it. Ranching is a tough business and a strenuous life. Very few make good money at it. We're the wealthiest landowners in Sandbank, but it's inherited wealth. Our fortune lies in the oil that runs beneath the pastures.

"My turn." I angle my head, marking the tension in her shoulders. "You said we weren't on your radar until recently. Explain how that happened."

"I was following a lead on a different project, and it led me to your father."

"What was the lead?"

"Someone you know."

"Who?"

She stares right at me and pins her lips.

Did she follow the trail of one of my father's dead cohorts? The answer could mean everything or nothing at all.

It's her turn again. Since her first question was easy, I bet she aims the next one at my throat.

That can wait.

"We've established how the Q&A will go." I stroll toward the tack room and slip around the corner, raising my voice. "Now I'll introduce you to the second part of our deal."

"I didn't agree to a second part," she shouts back.

"You will." I glide my fingers along buckled straps and metal bits and select a leather riding crop.

When I return to her line of sight, she spots the implement in my hand and flattens her back against the post.

"Don't even think about it." She flexes her fingers against the restraints.

"Do you know what this is used for?" I amble toward her, tapping the leather tongue against my leg.

"Not another step, Jarret." She kicks out a foot and grunts against the rope. "I'm not fucking around."

"The riding crop has many uses. Sherlock Holmes carried one as a weapon. On the ranch, we use them to discipline horses. But when you're with me…" I pause within striking distance. "This crop will be the liberation of your vagina."

"Oh my God." She shakes her head in disbelief. "My vagina does *not* need to be liberated."

"That so? When was the last time you had sex?"

A springy blond ringlet hangs in her face, and she blows it away with a huffed growl.

"When?" I press closer. "When was the last time Maybe Quinn spread her legs for a hard cock?"

Wide-eyed silence never felt so thrilling. I whack the crop against her bare thigh.

A sharp breath hisses past her clenched teeth. "Don't—"

I swat her again, harder this time, landing a nice sting high on her inner thigh.

"You're going to regret this, you sick, perverted, sick…sicko!" She goes crazy, jerking and thrashing and spitting fire.

All that does is bunch both ends of her dress toward her waist. If she wriggles much more, I'll have an unhindered view of her nipples. Not that I mind. Except that we're no longer alone.

The tread of boots sounds behind me, alerting me of Jake's presence before he steps into my periphery.

"Is this consensual?" His eyes tick between me and the seething ball of fury on the post.

I swat her thigh again, returning her focus to me. "I don't know." Stepping up against her, I brace a hand on the pole above her head. "Is it consensual, Maybe? Do we have a deal?"

"This is not what I had in mind." Her tits jiggle beneath the precarious slide of her dress.

"Yes or no." I grip her chin. "My brother's not going to leave until he knows you're willing. Do you want the story or not?"

Her eyes slide to Jake. "You can go. I'll deal with your brother."

I don't know how she thinks she'll deal with me, but she wins a gold medal for capturing my undivided attention. Her fighting spirit is a breath of fresh air.

Jake meets my eyes and wings up a brow. "You might want to bind her—"

A jolt of unholy pain slams into my balls and swallows my guts in fire.

"—legs."

I double-over, gasping from the kick to my groin. "I've got this."

"I see that." His footsteps retreat. "Good luck."

Bracing my hands on my knees, I take a few moments to breathe through the throb between my legs.

When the pain subsides, I straighten and lock onto Maybe's eyes.

The expression I find on Maybe's face hits me harder than the foot she nailed against my balls.

Tightness around her mouth, cheeks bloodless and ashen, lashes blinking rapidly—she's in full panic mode, shaking and terrified as if strangled by the very air around her.

The impulse to reach for her, to comfort her, pulls me toward her with my arm outstretched.

She flinches, sucking in a wheezing gulp. "Don't hurt me."

I yank my hand back before making contact. She thinks I'd retaliate because of that kick? It was my fault I let my guard down.

Fucking hell, I'm not an abuser. My chest constricts.

But I *am* a murderer.

Does she know that? Is that why she fears my reaction?

It doesn't help that I trussed her up against her will. I'm certain she's into this kind of play, but it's too soon. I pushed too hard, too fast, without a foundation of trust.

I fucked up.

"Listen to me." I lower my face to hers. "I would *never* hurt you out of anger."

"I don't know that."

"You're right." I grip the knot on the rope and loosen her restraints. "Let's back up and slow down."

As the rope falls away, her breathing slows.

I check her skin for rub marks and help her straighten the dress. "How long are you in town?"

"Until I have the story."

My jaw clenches. "Where are you staying?"

She runs her hands over the chaos of curls around her shoulders. "Doesn't concern you."

Why is she being so secretive about that?

I believe her about the listening devices, not that it matters. Jake and I don't discuss anything incriminating in the stable, where our crew could overhear.

I wind up the rope and return it to the wall, watching her as she wanders along the stalls.

She stops in front of Jake's stallion, and her eyes connect with mine over her shoulder. "Are any of these yours?"

"That one." I gesture at the black gelding behind her.

She turns, and her cheeks lift. "He's beautiful."

Not as beautiful as her smile. She should do that more often.

"What's his name?" She approaches the sliding grill door on his stall.

"Ginny."

"Oh." She cranes her neck, trying to look under his legs. "I thought..."

"He's a gelding." I join her side and hang an arm through the vertical rungs.

"Gelding?"

"He's castrated."

Grooves form on her brow. "Why would you do that?"

"When he bucked me off and almost trampled me to death, my dad deemed him too dangerous for a thirteen-year-old kid." I reach farther through the rungs and run a hand along Ginny's neck. "I fought to keep him, so Dad compromised by having him castrated. The procedure calms them down."

"Why does he have a girl's name?"

"That was Conor. She named all four of our horses." I move along the stalls, pointing to the critters that belong to Jake and Conor. "That's Barnabe and Ketchup. And this..." I pause in front of the white and brown dappled palomino stallion, who misses Lorne as much as I do. "This is Captain Undies."

Her lips twitch, and she bursts into laughter. It's a musical sound, dancing along my skin and penetrating me in ways it shouldn't.

"Holy shit, that's great." She composes herself but doesn't lose that smile. "How did she come up with that name?"

"Her brother had a flair for superhero underwear. She used to tease him for that." My throat thickens in memory. "We all did."

"Why did he go along with the name? And you, for that matter? I mean, you let her name your *male* horse Ginny?"

I shrug. "We love to indulge her."

Then *and* now. After abandoning her for six years, there's nothing I wouldn't do to make it up to her. If I could only expedite her brother's return home...

Captain lowers his head and nudges the gate with his nose. I gladly answer his request for attention with a vigorous ear rub.

Every horse has different boundaries and

preferences for affection. I try to handle Captain the same way Lorne did, but the horse knows it's not the same. My stomach hardens with regret. Nothing's the same without Lorne.

Maybe rests her arms on the gate, studying me. "You miss Conor's brother."

"Yeah."

"Can we talk about his incarceration?"

"Nope." I pat Captain on the shoulder and turn to the blue-eyed intruder beside me. "What about you?"

"What about me?"

"I shared something personal. My employees don't even know the story behind Ginny's name."

"Thank you for telling me." Her gaze flicks away and takes its time returning to mine. "I don't really have anything to share."

"Likes? Dislikes? I know nothing about you."

"I love animals."

"That's not an answer." I grunt. "Anyone with a heart loves animals."

"Okay, well, let me elaborate." She shifts from one foot to the other. "Sometimes when I drive past a chicken farm, I dream about plowing through the gate with an eighteen-wheeler. When the owner runs out, I shoot him with a shotgun. Not a fatal shot. Just some buckshot in the leg, enough to give him a terrible limp and unbearable pain for the rest of his life. Then I gather all the chickens and usher them into the truck. There's soft bedding and food and soothing music to make their journey comfortable. I take them to a sanctuary. You know, like the chicken version of an all-inclusive resort, where their little chicken hearts overflow with happiness. They're surrounded by people who love them and pamper them with affection, and oh my God, it's the best place on earth." She blinks the shine from her eyes and looks at me expectantly. "What do you think?"

"You're serious?"

"I mean, yeah. It's a dream, but it can happen. Don't you ever want to do something like that?"

"No." I stare at her, incredulous. "I eat chickens. Breaded and fried, skewered and grilled—"

"Enough."

I grimace with realization. "You don't eat meat."

"What's wrong with that?"

"You realize I raise cattle to be butchered, right?"

"Yes." She hardens her eyes.

"Don't ever ask me to go to a chicken farm with you."

"Fine."

"And I'm hiding all my shotguns."

"Geez. Now you're just making me feel like a crazy person."

"You're a vegetarian. 'Nough said."

She looks down at her bare feet and smiles to herself.

The emotion on her angelic face isn't easy to decipher. Mystery lurks in that smile. Something deep and contradictory. Like pain. That's it, I think. There's a sadness about her I'm just now noticing. A lonely, lost look in her eyes.

That's where her soul shines the brightest, in those vast oceans of restless blue. All the beauty in the universe can't compete with the allure in her eyes. Vivid layers of complexity burn like fire, and when she lifts that gaze to mine, I ache to be incinerated by it.

I remain still, not wanting to stir the sliver of calm between us. "Tell me what you're thinking."

"I like this... Talking with you."

"If you trusted me, you'd like that, too." I nod at the support beam I tied her to.

She follows my gaze to the post, pulls in a deep breath, and slowly releases it. "I should go."

"Not until I know where we stand."

"You're asking me to let you use me, under uncertain terms, to work out your kinks or whatever you—"

"No. I'm offering an exchange that benefits both of us. I'm attracted to you. I want to know you, in every way. And you want to learn about me and my family. Isn't that why you're here? To seek the truth?" I harden my tone. "Spend your evenings with me."

I'll open her eyes to all kinds of truths. She can write a story on my devious sexual proclivities, for all I care. My livelihood rides on the price of cattle. What I do in the bedroom has no impact on that.

On the other hand, if another one of us goes to prison for murder, it would crush our family.

She chews on her lip. "I need to see a contract."

"That's not how I work. No contracts or safe words or any of that crap. Maybe I won't lay a hand on you. Or maybe we'll explore every fantasy you've ever conjured. But that's for me to decide. I lead, and you follow."

"That sounds safe," she deadpans.

"It's not." I rest a knuckle under her chin and lift her gaze to mine. "There's a delicious sort of thrill in taking risks. I see the excitement in your eyes."

"That might be true." She pulls away from my touch. "Doesn't mean I jump on every thrill that comes along."

She heads toward the door, and I trail behind her, admiring the abundant mass of curls that hang damn-near to her waist.

"I need to sleep on it." She steps outside, her face aglow in the moonlight. "I'll give you an answer tomorrow."

I'm not a patient man like my brother, but I find I'm willing to wait for this woman. "I'll walk you to your car."

The five-acre hike to the lot passes in silence. It's the kind of silence when I would reach for a woman and caress her soft skin. When a woman would drift closer to my side, seeking a kiss that would lead to a not-so silent night.

But none of that happens. Maybe Quinn isn't easy. Not when it comes to sex or anything else. That only makes me want her more.

We pass the spot where I dumped her on her ass, and I change course, searching the ground.

"What are you doing?" She stands where I left her, watching me pick through the tall grass.

"You lost..." I spot her shoes and scoop them up. "These."

"Oh, right." She sighs. "Thanks."

I follow her to the car and open the rear door to toss her shoes inside. The dome light flicks on, illuminating cases of canned food piled on the backseat.

I squint at the labels. "Is that...?"

"Would you like a can of oysters?"

"That's a lot of oysters."

"I start every day with three cans."

"You do?"

"No." She opens the driver's door and bends to slide in.

"I thought you were a vegetarian."

"I am." She leans back up, facing me. "Oysters don't have eyes."

This woman is a trip.

"Let me get this straight." I rest my hip against the car and cross my arms. "If a chicken is born without eyes, it's okay to eat it?"

"No! That's not..." She stares at the cans and sucks on her bottom lip. "We're talking about oysters, not chickens."

"Sounds discriminatory. What about equal rights? Oysters have families, feelings, reasons to live—"

"All right. You made your point." She grips her

temples. "I'm never eating another oyster again."

Chuckling, I return my attention to the car. More food clutters the floorboards—cases of canned beans, meatless spaghetti, beets, granola bars, and bottled water. Blankets, matches, and random hygiene products fill the backseat.

No luggage. Maybe it's in the trunk or at the motel? If that's the case, why are her toiletries littered throughout the car?

"What are you doing with all this?" I pop the cap on a bottle of mint shampoo and sniff. *Smells just like her hair.* "Expecting an apocalypse?"

"Or surviving one."

My gaze snaps to hers. "What does that mean?"

"Nothing." She pushes on the rear door, nudging me back. "Enough snooping."

"This car isn't a rental."

"It's mine. I drove it from Chicago."

As old as it is, she probably paid fifty bucks for it. I can't believe it made the nine-hundred-mile journey.

I shut the door. "Open the trunk."

"Why?"

I give her my hardest glare, and she tosses one right back.

The soft lowing of a nearby herd echoes in the dark. Lightening bugs flicker above the grass, and Maybe Quinn grinds her teeth, realizing I won't back down.

With a huff, she reaches under the dash to pull the lever. The latch clicks behind me.

Circling around the back, I lift the lid and find what I expected. Instead of luggage, a few boxes line the cargo space. I rifle through them. All clothes.

She's living out of her car.

"Be careful." Her footsteps pause beside me. "You're going to get my *privileged existence* all over you."

"Is this everything you own?"

She sweeps her gaze over the car and the meager supplies within. "Pretty much."

"How long have you been living like this?"

"A while." She raises her chin, not a trace of embarrassment on her face.

I already know the answer after her apocalypse comment, but I ask anyway. "Is this a lifestyle choice or a financial necessity?"

"It's a consequence of bad judgment and rotten luck."

"Explain that."

"I'm homeless until I get this story. That's all I'm saying."

A news story won't pull her out of poverty. There's more she isn't telling me, and she won't until she trusts me.

I make a decision. She'll fight me on it, but I won't be able to sleep knowing she's conked out, alone in her car, where someone could sneak up on her and hurt her.

Digging through her clothes, I look for something casual, like jeans, t-shirts, sneakers... There's nothing practical here. It's all pants suits and dresses and nonsense.

"Where are your regular clothes?" I ask.

"I sold everything except..." She gestures at the boxes. "I kept the nice things that would help me find work." She crosses her arms. "I realize that was stupid and tried to find a second-hand store today to pick up some jeans."

"We don't have anything like that in town." I turn over one of the boxes and dump the contents into the trunk of the car.

She gasps. "What are you doing?"

"Grab what you need tonight." I carry the box to the backseat and drop the shampoo bottle in it. "I have a spare room."

"I don't want your charity."

"This isn't charity. I work long days. There's endless shit to do. You can help me with the workload, earn your keep, and we'll get to know each other in the process."

She pinches her bottom lip. "There's room in the bunkhouse?"

That would be the ideal place to put her, but… "No one lives there. We shut off the utilities to that building to save money."

"I don't need—"

"You need a shower and A/C in this heat. You'll stay in the main house."

Her gaze shifts to the estate, expression pensive.

I'm offering her a journalist's dream. She wants the seedy truth about Julep Ranch. Here's her chance to nose around in our home.

What she doesn't know is she won't find anything to use against us. We destroyed all documents and evidence *after* we digitalized and uploaded it to a secure location.

But she could plant bugs in our living space, which means Jake and I will have to guard what we say.

"Don't make me wait." I push the box into her hands.

"I haven't agreed to the second part of the deal."

"All we're doing tonight is sleeping."

"I feel like there's a catch."

"No catch. I'm going to put you to work. Out there." I point toward the fields.

"I don't have the right clothes."

"I'll take care of that." I reach into the front seat and grab her purse. "Is this coming in?"

At her nod, I rummage through it, searching for weapons and offending electronics. Her lips tighten, but rather than complaining, she packs the things she needs for the night.

I pull out her wallet and glance at her driver's license. Her name, her Chicago address, everything checks out.

That done, I take the box from her and lead her into the house and through the dark foyer.

"That wing belongs to Jake and Conor." I tilt my head at the door that closes off their quarters. Pivoting in the opposite direction, I face the Holsten wing. "My room is down that hall. It's the largest of the two wings, but I remodeled it into two master suites. The second one will be Lorne's."

"Where am I staying?"

"In Lorne's suite."

I lead her through an abbreviated tour of the common areas—formal dining room, sitting room, and a gaming area that's never used.

When we arrive in the kitchen, I give her slender body a once over. "Are you hungry?"

She shakes her head, looking around the open floor plan. "It's all very masculine."

Our fathers installed the reclaimed hardwood and rustic accents and filled the spacious rooms with dark, timeless furniture.

"I've been thinking about updating it." *When I have enough money.*

"No, I like it. It suits you." She searches my eyes. "Who's older, you or Jake?"

"I beat him into the world by fifteen minutes. Do you have siblings?"

"Nope. Just me."

"Living parents?"

Another shake of her head. "Mom passed last year."

"I'm sorry." My fingers twitch to touch her. "Were you close?"

"Yeah. She, uh... She had cancer. I was with her at

the end, and…" Pain mars her pretty features. "Let's change the subject."

"I'll show you to your room."

I guide her through the estate and into the Holsten wing.

"My rooms are just through there." I motion at the end of the corridor. Turning back, I open the door to the vacant suite and flip on the lights. "It's not furnished. Just a bed and—"

"Wow." She enters, taking in the bare white walls and enormous spread of interconnecting rooms. "It's huge."

I gave him the larger of the two suites because he's the oldest, and for some reason, I've always imagined him marrying before I do.

"The bathroom is around the corner, and you'll find a closet full of towels and shit for the bed." I set the box of toiletries on the mattress, glancing at the scarcity of its contents. "You don't have much here. Do you need anything?"

"No, I'm just going to take a shower and go to sleep."

I give her a nod and stride toward the door.

"Jarret?"

"Yeah?" I pause on the threshold and glance back, sinking into her deep blue eyes.

"Thank you."

I doubt she'll be thanking me tomorrow. With another nod, I close the door and make my way to the wing on the opposite side of the estate.

By the time I knock on Jake's door, I've prepared myself for every argument he'll hurl at me.

The door cracks open, and he pokes his head out, his hair tousled and eyes heavy with sleep. "What?"

"We need to talk."

He opens the door wider and moves to step out.

I stop him with a hand on his bare chest. "In your

room."

His entire body goes rigid, his voice an angry hush. "You brought her into our house?"

I don't answer him. He sees the adamancy in my eyes.

"Dammit." He glances behind him at the bed and squints. Then he opens the door all the way.

I follow him through the dark and veer off to sit on the couch near the fireplace. His silhouette moves to the bed, where he adjusts the covers over Conor's still form and kisses her on the head.

A moment later, he joins me, lowering into the chair, wearing only boxer briefs. "What the fuck are you doing?"

Despite the absence of light, I feel his glare and know it well.

With a deep breath, I recap my evening with Maybe Quinn, detailing the names she listed, the meeting she claims she had with our father, her financial situation, every word we exchanged. Then I outline my plan to keep her close and gain her trust.

He sits back with a grunt. "You're thinking with your dick."

"No, I—"

"So you don't want to fuck her?"

"I didn't say that."

"Get rid of her."

"I know what I'm doing. I just need you to—"

"I'm not participating in this madness."

"Shut up, Jake." Conor's drowsy voice drifts from across the room. "Stop being such an asshole and let him talk."

A smile tugs at my lips. "I'm sorry I woke you, Conor."

"It's okay." Her shadow stirs in the bed, rising to a sitting position. "Your brother's snoring was keeping me up anyway."

"She's full of shit," Jake mumbles.

She turns, reaching for something, and the moonlight glances off her nude back.

I avert my gaze. "Until I know more about this woman, I have to keep tabs on her. What better way than to have her working with me all day and spending time with me at night."

"In your bed."

"Does it matter?"

"No, it doesn't." Conor approaches, dressed in a t-shirt three-times too big for her. "Keep your enemies close. Isn't that what they say?"

Jake holds out an arm to her.

She slides into his embrace and onto his lap. "Is she crafty enough to hide cameras around?"

"I don't know." I rub a hand through my hair. "She's smart. We'll have to monitor our conversations, but we should be doing that anyway. This will keep us from becoming complacent."

Jake releases a slow breath, exposing a crack in his resistance. "You need to talk to Lorne."

"I'll email him tonight."

Even though he's in prison, we run every decision by him as if he were still here.

"Don't be a jerk to her." Conor leans forward, green eyes shining in the dark. "She's on her own, doing her job, and if what she said is true, she has no family. She doesn't have what we have. Don't punish her for a crime she hasn't committed yet."

Jake's silence tells me he agrees with her.

"I won't." I'll play with her, but I won't treat her unfairly.

"Good." She relaxes. "Now how is she going to help on the ranch?"

"I have some ideas." I smile inwardly. "I'll keep her away from the ravine, while the concrete pad is poured tomorrow. But there's a small issue."

"What's that?"

"She needs work clothes."

A bright light and sudden loss of warmth wakes me from the best night's sleep I've had in months. I reach for the blanket, but it's on the move, racing down my bare legs and off the bed.

"What the—?"

"Get dressed." Jarret stands over me with the bedding clutched in his hand. "You're going on an adventure."

I don't like the sound of that. Not with his eyes glimmering and his powerful body all decked out for a hard day's work.

Faded brown cowboy hat, tight blue t-shirt, low-slung jeans, wide leather belt, and I stop there. It's too damn early to be checking out his bulge.

What time is it anyway?

The overhead lights are what woke me. I roll over, and darkness greets me beyond the window.

"Get a move on." His footsteps retreat. "We're burning daylight."

With a groan, I sit up and shove the frizzy rat's nest

out of my face. "The sun isn't even up."

"Exactly." He ambles toward the door. "I brought you some of Conor's clothes. You're taller, so the jeans won't cover your ankles. But the boots will take care of that. Breakfast is served in five."

"Five...?"

"Minutes. Oh, and..." He turns in the doorway, and his eyes drop to my chest. "Wear a bra."

I cover myself with my hands, realizing too late he can probably see through my thin tank top. At least I had the right mind to sleep in cotton shorts.

"I'm not trying to embarrass you." He hooks a thumb under his belt buckle. "Since you'll be in a saddle today, Conor asked me to pass along the advice."

"Okay. Thanks."

He shuts the door, and I slump on the bed. I've never been on a horse. There's a lot of bouncing involved with that, I guess. So chest support makes sense, even for *B* cups.

I don't know the first thing about riding or ranching, but I agreed to stay here and earn my keep. With regard to his other offer, however, I'm still leaning heavily in the direction of *No fucking way.*

But I can't leave, either. If what John Holsten told me is true, his sons know exactly where I'll find what I'm looking for.

What am I willing to give up in exchange for answers?

I turn toward the pile of clothes and boots on the chair.

Pride. That's what I'm sacrificing. The instant I put on borrowed clothes and step outside, I'm on their turf, in their world, completely out of my league.

I'm going to make a fool out of myself.

"Let's get on with it then."

I clean my face and teeth and plait my hair into *Laura Ingalls Wilder* braids. Then I change into Conor's jeans.

They fit a little too loose through the hips and fall just above the ankles, but they'll work. I slip on a bra and opt to wear the pink tank top I slept in.

The boots don't look like the kind Conor wears. These have a shorter, wider heel, and the etched design has a masculine feel. They're definitely used, given the deep scratches and stains.

I slide a foot in and wiggle my toes. A little roomy but surprisingly comfortable.

When my five minutes are up, I take a deep breath and make my way to the kitchen.

The aroma of pork grease and coffee saturates the air. I don't mind the scent of cooked meat as long as I don't think about it too much.

Jake stands at the stove, frying eggs while Conor carries a sizzling pan of bacon around the small breakfast table near the window. Outside, a whisper of light touches the pasture, beckoning the sunrise.

"Mornin', Maybe." Conor waves a tattooed arm and pauses beside Jarret to drop some meat on his plate.

"Morning." I linger on the perimeter, feeling awkward and out of place.

"Sit." Jarret pulls out the chair beside him and fills the glasses with ice water from a pitcher.

His hat rests on the table, his dark brown hair all tousled and lustrous around his ears. He watches me with eyes the color of wheat fields, his face strong and smooth, as if chiseled from granite. His perfect lips are his softest feature. Not that I've felt them, but my God, they look ripe for kissing.

He lifts a strong hand, the skin calloused from rugged work, and summons me with the crook of a finger.

Despite the blush tingling my cheeks, I don't care that he caught me staring at him again. As ridiculously handsome as he is, he must be used to the attention.

Conor finishes loading up the place settings with bacon. I sit at the table and glance down at the rotting pieces of flesh on the plate in front of me.

Jarret leans in, and his mouth brushes my ear. “You look good enough to eat.”

A swallow lodges in my throat.

Conor lowers into the chair across from me. “Looks like my jeans are too big for you.”

“No, they’re fine.” I rub a palm along the worn denim. “Thank you for loaning them to me.”

“Don’t mention it.”

She smiles a lot. Considering everything she’s been through, I didn’t expect that. She’s obviously here willingly. Maybe Jarret and Jake aren’t the bad guys. Or maybe Conor is involved in the corruption.

“How do the boots fit?” Jarret angles his neck to see my feet under the table.

“Really well. Whose are they?”

“Jarret’s.” Conor smiles at him. “You wore those when you were what? Twelve? Thirteen?”

Jake steps to the table with a skillet of eggs. “He wore them during his Britney Spears phase. She’s the reason he started playing with his dick. A habit that would later be known as *Oops!... I Did It Again.*”

I can’t stop the amusement from twisting my lips.

“You know, Jake, this is why everyone talks about you as soon as you leave the room.” Jarret reaches over and snatches the bacon from my plate.

“Don’t steal her food.” Conor launches across the table to smack his hand.

He dodges her, holding the crispy strips out of her reach. “She’s a carrot muncher.”

“Oh.” Conor drops back on the chair and stares at me like I have a terminal disease. “I’m sorry.”

My eyebrows lift. “You’re sorry I’m a vegetarian?”

“Well... Yeah.”

Jake hovers the skillet in front of me. "No eggs, then?"

I shake my head.

"I'll take her baby chickens." Jarret shoves the bacon into his mouth and holds up his plate. "Survival of the fittest and all that. My stomach is a graveyard for the weak and helpless."

If he's trying to gross me out, he'll have to do better than that.

Jake divides the eggs between the three of them and sets the skillet aside. "What does she eat?"

"Oysters." Jarret grins.

I die a little inside.

"What does she have against oysters?" Conor stabs her eggs with a fork.

"Maybe she was wronged by one in a previous life." Jake sits and digs into his food. "Can't blame her for that. I like to double fist my enemies before I eat them. Especially if they're Kentucky fried."

"Kentucky fried death." Conor laughs.

I reach for my glass and guzzle the water to drown out a string of ungracious retorts.

"A person can't live on oysters and rabbit food." Jake shovels in another forkful. "No wonder she's so skinny."

I chew on the inside of my cheek. People in Chicago don't blink an eye at vegetarians or vegans. I'm not even an extremist or health-food fanatic. I just choose to not eat animals that have been twisted and crushed with cruelty.

The microwave dings, and Jarret leaves the table. I silently beg him to hurry back and save me from this bigotry.

Conor waves around a strip of bacon and bites into it. "Doesn't she realize pigs would eat her if they could?"

My face heats. "You know, I'm sitting right here."

"Wasn't Hitler a vegetarian?" Jake asks.

Was he?

"Yep." Jarret returns to the table. "And lesbians. They don't eat meat."

"Straight men don't eat meat, either," I mumble. "Your logic is flawed."

He sets a bowl of oatmeal in front of me, and it almost makes me want to forgive him for letting this conversation continue.

"She could never be an Eskimo." Conor carries her plate to the sink. "I mean, how would she grow her food?"

"Here's what I want to know." Jake swallows his last bite and looks at Jarret. "If you start eating her out on the regular, does that mean you're on a vegetarian diet?"

My jaw clenches. Teasing is one thing. This is crossing the line.

"Enough." I place my hands on the table and temper my voice. "I know I'm a guest in your home, but this discussion is about as stimulating as a big bag of tiny dicks."

Silence blankets the room.

I twist in the chair, meeting each pair of eyes. "You think eating meat makes you tough? Good for you. You want to put mechanically-separated animal parts in your bodies? After it's been ground up and squished through a sieve—bones, beaks, eyes, guts, and all—and comes out looking like your *Kentucky fried* nuggets? Be my guest. I won't stop you. But when you harass me for my dietary decisions and ethical views on killing, I *will* stand up for myself. I'm skinny because of my genetics. But I'm *healthy*, not that it's any of your concern. As for your decision to eat meat, it should be within your own logical interest to save the fluffy chickens of the world. Not only is it a moral responsibility, the mass consumerism of animals is destroying the environment with its deforestation, pollution, water depletion, and species extinction. By supporting that, you're basically confessing the worthlessness of your own feeble mortality."

I have so much more to say about this, but I won't. Raising cattle is their livelihood, and preaching is *not* mine.

I turn back to my plate and wait for the backfire.

Conor steps beside me, drawing my gaze to hers.

"Welcome to Julep Ranch." A grin spreads across her face. "You'll do just fine here."

She strolls out of the kitchen, leaving me stunned and staring after her.

As Jake follows her out, he claps a hand on Jarret's shoulder. "I like her."

When he vanishes around the corner, I dare a peek at Jarret. "What just happened?"

"No one here cares what you eat." He folds his arms on the table. "They were just feeling you out. Seeing what you're made of."

"That's fucked up." My eyebrows pull in as my mind spins with curiosity. "What do *you* think I'm made of?"

"Backbone." He reaches out and yanks on one of my braids. "And now they know it, too."

"Why does that matter?" I straighten my spine.

"They were concerned I might take advantage of you."

"Is that a habit of yours?"

"Only with meddlesome reporters." He pushes the oatmeal closer. "Eat."

"Thank you for breakfast." I grab a spoon and start eating. "You don't need to cook special meals for me. I have food in my car."

"Oysters?" He grins and nods at the bowl. "It's microwaved oatmeal. Nothing fancy. Since our moms died when we were young, none of us learned how to cook."

"As much as you work, I'm surprised you don't have a personal chef."

"We're running the ranch on a bare bones crew to trim costs. We'll hire more cowhands before we invest in a personal staff." He stands, slides on his hat, and starts clearing the table.

He's already done?

I eat faster, scraping the bottom of the bowl. "How did you guys scarf down everything so quickly? Did you even taste your food?"

"We were raised to eat efficiently. It's a way of life here. Meals are fuel and nothing more. After a couple of days, you'll get used to it."

When I finish the oatmeal, I help him with the dishes and try not to dwell on how domesticated all this feels. Moving around him in the tight space by the sink, bumping arms, brushing hands, sharing air—it's more intimate than the live-in relationships I've had.

Jarret starts the dishwasher and grabs a hat from the back counter.

"This is a Stetson." He sets it on my head and adjusts the roll of the brim. "The felt is made from the fur of various critters, and before you get all self-righteous—"

"I didn't say anything."

"Good, because we use a lot of leather and hide around here. It's durable and lasts a long time. I wore this hat through most of my teens." He lifts my chin with a finger, inspecting my face. "Do you burn easily?"

"Sometimes."

"Conor!" His booming voice makes me jump. "Where's your sunblock?"

"Mudroom," she shouts from somewhere in the house.

The finger beneath my chin becomes a hard grip, and something flashes in his golden eyes. "Let's get started on that adventure.

Butterflies erupt in my stomach as I follow him to the mudroom.

"You want me to put my hand *where*?" I curl my fingers in the long-sleeved glove that Jarret lubricated to my shoulder.

"The rectum." He pats the rear flank of the cow in front of us, and she returns a cheeky snort.

After I lathered up with sunblock, he led me to this cowshed on foot. During the five-minute walk, he could've prepared me. He could've said, "Hey, so that adventure I mentioned? It's a trip down a dark tunnel of shit. Literally."

But, no. He walked ahead of me, as fast as those long legs could carry him, without saying a word.

I close my eyes and breathe deeply, but not too deeply because the air reeks of manure.

When I open my eyes, I find the rich amber of his waiting inches away.

"I'm not qualified to do this." I frown at the cow's twitching tail. "What if I hurt her?"

"I won't let you."

"You still haven't told me what *A.I.-ing the cattle*

means."

"Artificial Insemination. Explaining why we do this is more complicated than explaining how to do it."

I make a grudging sound in my throat and release a breath. "Okay, just tell me what to do."

"That's par for the course." The insinuation in his deep voice vibrates through me. "What's your experience with anal?"

"Jarret, I swear to God, if you make this sexual, I'll believe everything I've heard about rednecks and their farm animals."

"Let's set one thing straight." He puts his face in mine. "If I ever spit without opening my mouth, mow my lawn and find a household appliance, get a farmer's tan while watching NASCAR, name a son after a Southern Civil War general, or take a seventeen-year-old bride in my fifties, *then* you can call me a redneck."

He's so serious and intense it's hard to keep from laughing.

I narrow my eyes. "What if your porch collapses and kills five dogs?"

"Since I don't have dogs, I didn't include that one."

"Fine, but if I find a stuffed opossum in your bedroom, you're gonna wear that label with pride."

"Shut up and put that lubed hand to work."

"Ugh." I shift toward the cow's rear and fortify my resolve. I'll do this because he gave me oatmeal and a place to sleep, but that's not why I'm here. "Tell me about those men I named last night."

"Levi Tibbs attacked us six years ago. You already know what he did to Conor."

"Where is he now?"

"You'll have to ask his parole officer." He steps behind me and guides my gloved arm. "When you go in, you'll feel the reproductive tract through the rectal lining. You're looking for the cervix. It feels like a turkey neck."

Not exactly helpful, since I've never touched a turkey neck. "What about the other men? How do you know them?"

"I didn't say I did."

"You're hedging."

"You're stalling." His breath caresses my ear, his broad chest like a branding iron against my back.

I let him move my hand closer to the cow's poor butt, and my mind takes a disturbing detour. "Please tell me you're not into fisting."

"Haven't tried it, but if that's your thing, we can discuss it."

"Nope. Forget I asked." I glance around the barn, finding nothing related to impregnating a cow. "Don't we need a turkey baster with semen or whatever?"

"We use a semen gun, and we're not ready for that. You need to practice."

Why do I get the feeling this is another test to *see what I'm made of?*

I lift her tail with my glove-free hand and wince. "What if she poops while I'm in there?"

"It happens."

"Oh God." With a groan, I extend my hand the final few inches.

"Stop!" Conor shouts from the doorway.

I yank my arm back, pulse spiking. Did I do something wrong? I haven't even made contact yet.

She storms toward us, takes off her hat, and whacks Jarret over the head with it, knocking his Stetson to the ground. "What the hell is wrong with you?"

He backs up, hands in the air and laughing his ass off.

"That's a first-calf heifer." Conor points at the cow, glancing between us.

"I don't know what that means." I glare at Jarret.

"It means she's already pregnant." She gives him another smack with her hat.

"I was going to stop her." He rubs a hand over his smirking mouth. "I just wanted to see how far she'd go."

I guess the joke's on me. I meant what I said, though. I'm not a sensitive person. What he doesn't know is I'm a firm believer in retaliation.

As Conor gives him a good ass chewing, I calmly step away and search the dirt floor. When I spot a fresh, wet mound of cow shit, I scoop it up in my gloved hand, hold it behind me, and casually walk over to him.

His gaze slides from Conor to me. A smile stretches my cheeks, and his eyes narrow. He starts to look down, but I'm already swinging.

Manure splatters his chest, followed by my palm. I rub it in from his neck to his stomach, feeling up all those hard ridges through the shirt.

He stares down at the filth with a half-groan, half-grin. "Shit."

"Yep." I give his jaw a sloppy pat, leaving behind a smudge.

Conor presses the back of her hand against her mouth, her green eyes alight with amusement.

At the sound of her chuckle, I head to the utility sink, discarding the glove in the trash along the way.

"There's a calf—" Jake charges into the cowshed and slams to a stop, taking in the scene. "What did I miss?"

I stroll past him. "When your mom went to the bathroom, she forgot to flush your twin."

"I feel like that insults me as much as it does him."

"She's a proponent of verbal offensiveness," Jarret says, joining me at the sink.

I wash my hands, not looking at him.

Until he strips off his shirt.

He wets a towel and runs it over his bare chest and neck, his biceps twitching and pulsing with the movement. No man should have a body like that. It's criminal.

Stacks of muscle form a rippling terrace for water to travel as he squeezes the rag against his pecs. His sun-kissed skin is hairless perfection, his physique a flexing, breathing trove of strength and masculinity. I've never seen anything like it.

"If you wanted me to take off my shirt, all you had to do was ask." He tosses the towel in the sink and stares down at me with his hands resting on trim hips.

"Is that right?" I trail a finger along the corrugated wall of his abs, testing him with no intention of following through. "Take off the jeans."

He grips my wrist, stopping my journey to his belt buckle. "Tonight."

Heat rises up my neck.

"While you're in here fucking around," Jake says behind me, "another calf fell into the creek."

"Figures." Jarret releases me to collect his hat from the ground a few feet away. "Is Randy working on the fence today?"

"Yeah. Should I pull him?"

"No." Brushing off the Stetson, Jarret sets it on his head. "We need those posts fixed. I'll help with the calf. Same spot as last time?"

"Yep." Jake looks at Conor.

"Go ahead." She rummages through a shelving unit of tools. "I'll start cleaning the corrals."

"Meet you there," Jake says to his brother and leaves the barn.

Jarret turns to me and scrutinizes my face. "I expected a tantrum after the heifer incident."

"Sorry to disappoint."

"You're really not mad." He looks surprised.

"Not even a little." I run my gaze down his shirtless chest. "I got a nice view out of it."

"You'll be punished for that."

"For what?"

"Being a cock tease." He walks to the exit, gesturing at me to follow. "You promised me an answer today."

An answer to the second part of his deal.

You'll spend the evenings with me, doing whatever I say, when I say it.

That's not going to happen.

I hurry after him and catch up with his long strides outside. "My answer is—"

"Don't say no."

He must read it on my face or maybe he knows what he's demanding is completely insane.

"Submit to a kiss." He advances on me, forcing me to shuffle backward until my back hits the outside wall of the cowshed. "A kiss without resistance. If you're not affected, I'll drop it and tell you what you want to know."

It's tempting. My God, just to experience the feel of that beautiful mouth against mine. But I would lose. There's no way I wouldn't be affected.

"Don't you have a calf to pull from a creek?" I push against his immovable chest.

He pinches his lips together, his eyes etched with frustration. Or maybe that's determination. I don't know him well enough to decrypt the nuances in his expression.

He pulls away and hikes toward the stable to saddle his horse. As I trail behind him, he gives me a crash course on horse riding.

I absorb his instruction, but my thoughts keep returning to the conversation we left unfinished. He's going to kick me out tonight without giving me answers. I need to find a way to compromise.

Ten minutes later, he sits in the saddle and stretches a hand toward me, where I stand with my arms crossed.

He already explained where I'll ride, how my legs will press against his, and the necessity of keeping my arms wrapped around him. It's the best and worst place for me to be right now.

"Come on." He gives me a come-hither gesture. "Ginny won't bite."

"Ginny's not the one I'm worried about."

The grin he unleashes has the power to melt panties within a ten-mile radius. "I know you're as attracted to me as I am to you. Why are you fighting this?"

"You mean, why won't I just fall on my back and let you rut between my legs?"

He leans forward on the horse and drapes an arm over the saddle horn, staring at me.

I'm reminded that he probably spends an hour at most with a woman before he has her on her back or tied on her knees or whatever he does with them. I suspect this is the most time he's spent with someone he wants to fuck, without actually fucking her.

If he knew the real reason I was here, he wouldn't want to fuck me or talk to me or have anything to do with me.

"I have a counteroffer." I reach a hand toward him.

He clutches it and swings me up into the saddle behind him, as if I weigh nothing. Then he takes the reins and guides Ginny out of the stable.

Ruining his shirt was a terrible idea. No matter where I put my hands, I touch warm, tight, bare skin. His abs are obscene, all sculpted bricks, flexing grooves, and zero body fat. I realize I was wrong about him being hairless when my fingers brush against the dusting of hair that dips beneath his belt.

His back muscles twitch so close to my face I see freckles. Not many. Just a faint dot here and there across his defined shoulders. And his scent… I don't know if it's his shampoo or the soap he uses, but his skin emits a raw, outdoorsy, manly aroma that begs me to bury my nose in it.

"Your counteroffer?" He nudges Ginny into a faster pace across the field.

I clench my thighs around the outsides of his to remain upright. "Since I have a high tolerance for pain, I'm willing to let you restrain me and swat me with your crop. I'm saying I'll try it, but if you push my boundaries—"

"I'll push them."

"Okay, when you push my boundaries and I tell you to stop, I need to know that you will. If you can't do that, there's no deal."

"You want a safe word."

"I want equal power in this."

He steers Ginny past the quiet bunkhouse, over a hill, and across another meadow. I assume his silence means he's thinking about my offer. Or maybe he just likes to make me sweat.

About fifty yards up ahead, his brother stands beside a brown stallion and stares over a ledge.

Jarret slows Ginny to a crawling halt and meets my eyes over his shoulder. "If you say stop, it's over. It doesn't just end the scene. This, us, your pursuit of truth—all of it ends. You'll get in your car and drive away."

"Deal."

He twists around to face me, angling slightly off the horse with only the strength in his legs to hold him on. Then he grips the back of my neck and yanks my mouth to his.

A current of hunger sparks across his lips as they brush against mine. I splay a hand against his shoulder, intending to push him away, but instead I leave it there. Dear God, I can't even fight the thoughts rolling through me. His scent, his minty taste, everything about him is consuming. Persuasive. He floods my senses.

His tongue slides along the seam of my lips, demanding entry, and I grant it. My heart flutters. His breathing quickens, and we fall into a kiss that ruins me for all others.

I press closer, crawling halfway onto his lap, clinging to him as he devours my mouth softly, deeply, so deliciously unhurried and nothing like I expected.

My borrowed hat bumps his, and his twisted position in the saddle feels precarious, but I don't want him to stop.

His hand rests below my ear, his thumb caressing my cheek. His tongue explores mine, communicating a story worthy of more. A story I will never write but will always remember.

Because I love this—the hungry taste of his mouth, the skillful way he controls mine, the bunch of his muscles around me, the perfect fit of our lips, the ease in which I relent as he wraps my braid around his fist, pulling tighter, harder.

Then he leans back and opens hooded eyes.

"Maybe." He prolongs each syllable and licks his lips.

I don't know if he's saying my name or answering a question I didn't ask. I'm so damn dizzy. Tangled in sensations. Thoroughly seduced.

He rights himself in the saddle and guides my limp arms around his waist. As if he didn't just kiss the wind out of me, he kicks Ginny into a fast gait and steers us to where Jake waits.

That's when I realize my mistake. He gave me the power I asked for, but it's all or nothing. If I stop his devious game, I'll lose access to him. I won't do that unless I absolutely have to.

If a safe word ends a relationship, it isn't a safe

word at all. It means I'll allow more with the hope of keeping this going than I normally would. It's dubious, and he knows it.

But he already said this won't be safe.

I have no one to blame but myself.

When we reach the creek, Jarret helps me dismount the horse and follows me down. His demeanor is all business, and that excites me. It'll be kind of cool to experience a real-life dilemma on a working ranch.

I follow the sound of throaty, agitated mooing to the edge of a fifteen-foot sandy bank. At the bottom, a white calf kicks along the creek bed, water sloshing halfway up his legs as he searches for a way out.

There's no shoreline or beach. Just steep walls of mud and roots on both sides in either direction. The poor thing must've tumbled all the way down.

"How old?" I ask.

"Six days." Jarret unties a bundle of rope from the saddle.

He's just a baby. Every inch of him is white, except for those big black ears and adorable black nose and mouth and oh my God, are those black eyelashes? He looks like a little lamb.

I'm instantly and utterly in love.

"How will you get him out?" I press a hand against

my chest, aching with each scared cry he bellows at us.

"We'll rope it and shimmy it through the water to where the bank levels out." Jake points downstream.

Jarret knots the end of his rope like a lasso. I step out of the way as he throws it. The noose lands around the calf's neck, but the instant Jarret pulls, the calf goes crazy and bucks free.

Jake laughs. "Slippery sucker."

"How many times have you tried?" Jarret glances at his brother.

"'Bout a dozen times."

"He's so scared." I crouch on the ledge, searching for a path I could slide down. "There must be an easier way."

"They're always frantic in this situation." Jarret gathers the rope to prepare another throw. "It's like trying to catch a wild dog that's attacking with everything it's got."

Because he doesn't want to be roped. He's down there all alone and traumatized and just wants to find his mother.

I stand and pace behind the guys. They intend to drag this terrified baby kicking and screaming down the creek, only to sell him off and turn him into hamburger.

My chest constricts. "If I rope him, can I keep him?"

"Jarret or the calf?" Jake arches a questioning brow.

I roll my eyes and point at the calf.

"First off," Jarret says. "He is a *she.* Secondly, you don't know how to rope cattle."

I hold out my hand for the rope. "Challenge accepted."

He laughs and tosses me the bundle. "This'll be fun."

Jake steps back and folds his arms across his chest, wearing a bored expression.

I coil the rope into a wide circle and drape it across my body. A dead tree clings to the edge a few feet away, its thick roots dangling midway down the creek wall. I make my way there and step on a low branch. Seems sturdy enough.

"Maybe..." Jarret shakes his head.

"It'll hold her weight," Jake says, as if my demise has suddenly made this more interesting.

"You'll get covered in mud." Jarret prowls toward me.

"Are the boots waterproof?" I edge onto the trunk and rappel down a few feet, gripping slimy roots and knocking away spiderwebs.

"I don't care about the boots. That calf weighs more than you do, and there are snakes—"

My handhold slips, and I make an ungraceful plunge down the muddy wall, landing in the creek with a splash.

The calf skitters back, screaming in fear. *Shit.*

"What kind of snakes?" I clamor to my feet and frantically search the water.

"The kind that bite." Jarret squats at the ledge fifteen-feet above me. "You okay?"

My ass throbs where I landed on a rock. I'm soaked head to toe and standing in brown, snake-infested water. "Yep, just dandy. Are we talking poisonous snakes? I really don't want to die today."

"I got bit by a water rattler and survived." Jake grins from the safety of his perch.

"That makes me feel so much better." I turn toward the splashing frenzy behind me.

The calf scrambles in and out of the water against the opposite embankment, determined to scale that wall.

"It's okay, baby." I make shushing noises and slowly wade through the water. "I'm here to help you."

The calf goes still, and those huge brown eyes own

me instantly, completely. Yep, I'm a goner.

With careful movements, I lift the rope over my head and hold the knotted end like a hoop.

This will be just like the ring toss game I played when I was a kid. Except the target is a scrambling, spinning ball of cuteness.

Movement sounds above me, followed by Jarret's voice. "You don't have to do this, Maybe."

My boots are so full of water a snake could slither in. I'm going to flip the fuck out if that happens. But I have to save her. She and I just need to get over our fears and work together.

A few feet away, I toss the rope and lasso her neck. My sigh of relief is short-lived when she jerks free and snorts at me.

"Don't be such a chicken." I move closer. "I won't hurt you."

She arches her back with her butt in the air, looking all fierce and brave, like she's going to charge me.

I throw the rope, catch her around the ears, and she shakes it off.

Laughter sounds from the ledge, only fueling my determination.

Five more attempts and I finally toss a ring that sticks. I move quickly, scrambling toward her while pulling tight on the rope. The wrestling match that ensues submerges us to our necks in filthy water, but I have her in my arms, both of us bellowing like crazy.

I manage to loop the rope around her shoulders like a harness. Then I slump against the muddy cliff, winded and worn out.

"Well done." Jarret stands on the edge and smiles down at me.

"Thanks." I smile back with pride and climb to my feet, gathering the rope. "Now what?"

"Can you climb back up those roots?"

"No way. I can't even reach them."

"You'll have to walk out with her." He motions to the right. "The creek levels out about a mile down. Throw me the rope."

"I'm sorry? Did you say a mile?"

"Yep."

Fuck me sideways.

The soggy jeans slide down my hips, and I yank them back up.

"Looks like you two have this under control. I'll leave you to it." Jake mounts his horse and trots off.

"All right, Chicken." I adjust the rope around her squirming body. "We can do this."

"Did you just call her Chicken?" Jarret squints at me.

"That's her name." I toss the wet rope up to him.

He catches it and removes the slack. "Rule number one on the ranch. Never name cattle you plan to sell for slaughter."

Panic grips my lungs. "You can't sell her!"

I know I'm being irrational. It's not like I can keep her. I don't even have a place to live.

Raising cattle to be butchered is what he does. I didn't come here expecting to change that, but dammit, it hurts. Maybe I'm an emotional bleeder after all.

He knots the end of the rope on the saddle horn and swings up onto the horse. "Ready?"

"Yeah." I nudge Chicken forward, helping her navigate the rocks.

Jarret leads the way, guiding Ginny along the ledge with the rope connected to the saddle.

A few minutes into the water-logged hike, he leans down and nudges up his hat. "Why Chicken? If you're going to name her, it should be Big Mac or Tenderloin or Angus."

I shoot him a glare. "She represents all the

chickens that need to be saved."

With a grunt, he straightens and focuses on the path ahead of him.

It's a long goddamn walk. Not because I'm wearing wet jeans that won't stay up. Or because the sun beats down on my shoulders like a furnace. Or because Chicken stops every few feet to fight the rope that pulls her forward.

It's long because every time I run a hand over the little white cow licks on her head, my heart bleeds. I can't bear the thought of her ending up in a cardboard box tossed out a drive-through window.

When the walls of the creek give way to sloping banks, Chicken runs up the dirt ramp and bounces through the tall grass around Ginny's hooves.

"That was longer than a mile." I shuffle out of the creek and collapse on my back in the mud, eyes closed.

"It was closer to two miles." Jarret's shadow falls across my face. "I can take you back to the house if you need to rest."

I crack an eye open. "Is there more work to do?"

He laughs and folds his arms across his bare chest. "The day just started."

I might not have his physical stamina, but I'm not quitting until he does. "What's next?"

"Fence repair."

"I thought you had a guy on that?" I push myself to a sitting position and fight a bout of lightheadedness.

"You need water." He retrieves a sports bottle from the saddle and offers it to me. "With ten-thousand acres to fence in, there are more repairs than we can keep up with. It's the second worst job on the ranch."

I drink deeply, savoring the cool refreshment. "What's the worst?"

"Paperwork."

I try to smile, but I don't have the energy to make my cheeks move.

He glances back at the frolicking calf. "I need to take Chicken to her mother."

My heart swells. "You called her by her name."

"You like her." His brows knit.

"It was a harrowing journey of bonding and friendship. I love her."

"You're serious."

"Look at that cute black nose. It can't be helped."

"She won't be weaned until winter." He shuffles his boots. "We can work something out after that."

I gasp. "You won't sell her?"

He shakes his head, frowning.

"No way!" I leap up and tackle him in a hug. "Thank you!"

"Just *this* one." He frames my face with his hands and gives me a stern look. "You can't save them all."

"I know."

"Stay away from the other calves."

"Okay."

"Don't even look at them."

I nod my agreement.

"You're a mess." He swipes a thumb across my cheek. "A beautiful mess."

"Thank you."

His gaze dips to my mouth, and I'm certain he's going to kiss me. My body aches for it, pulsing in places that haven't been touched in so long. I've forgotten what it feels like to lose myself in another person.

"This is the first time I've ever considered missing a day of work." His hands lower from my face.

"You love it that much?"

He nods. "Not as much as I love the look in your eyes."

I glance away. "I'm ready to earn my keep and…" I wave a hand at Chicken. "Whatever it'll cost to keep her happy indefinitely."

His chuckle slides across my skin like velvet. “You have a lot of pliers and stretchers in your future.”

“I really hope those are tools for fence repair.”

He gives me a wicked wink and hoists me into the saddle.

Crouched beside a mangled portion of the fence, I wipe the sweat from my brow and sit back on my heels. We've been repairing barbed wire for hours in the heat, and Maybe hasn't tuckered out yet.

Not only is she a fast learner, she doesn't fill the silence with empty chatter. While I prefer to work alone, I find I actually enjoy her company.

A few yards away, she rises from the section she's fixing and stares along the fencing that goes on for miles.

"There's not enough daylight for everything that needs to be done." She pulls down the brim of the hat to shade her eyes. "No wonder you inhale your food."

When we stopped for lunch, she gave me hell for wolfing down my sandwich. Meanwhile, she nibbled on cheese and lettuce between slices of bread, as if it were a normal thing to eat.

"Take a break." I tilt my chin at the shade beneath a nearby tree.

"Not until you do."

Stubborn woman. I'm accustomed to grueling

work. She's not.

Every day, I use wire, leather gloves, fence clips, staples, pliers, and splicers. I smile at the fence stretchers in my hand, loving where her mind went when I mentioned them.

"Snowdrifts destroyed a lot of this over the winter." I gesture at the fence. "Some of the wire is older than I am and it—"

"You're two years younger than me."

I squint at her. "You're twenty-six?"

"That surprises you?"

"A little."

I hadn't given any thought to it, but with her hair in braids, dirt streaked across her face, and that tiny tank top hanging off her shoulders, she looks barely legal.

"What were you saying about the fence?" She props a hand on her hip.

I shift back to the wire in my grip. "See how barbed this is? It's so industrially well-made most of it hasn't needed repairs until now."

"Why are you fixing it instead of replacing it?"

"Wire isn't made like this anymore. It's dangerous to work with, but the cattle won't go near it."

"There must be miles of it on the property." She scans the horizon, taking it all in. "I noticed some of the fences are made with wooden railings, too. Do you have someone who runs the perimeter every day, checking for breaks and holes?"

"There's no way to do that when the land goes on forever. We check the problem areas regularly and rely on the cattle to let us know when the fence is down. Because they'll find a way out. Same with kids. When the four of us were little, we disappeared all the time. Our dads would have to send out search parties."

"I bet."

She returns to her section of wire, her hands protected by heavy leather gloves as she works. She appears focused, but at the mention of my dad and Dalton, something shifted in her mood. I anticipate what's coming before she opens her mouth.

"John Holsten and Dalton Cassidy borrowed money from people outside of financial regulators. You know who those people are."

I know who those people *were*. But she used present tense.

"Where's Rogan Schroeder?" she asks, confirming she doesn't know he's buried at the bottom of the ravine with his truck.

"Why do you assume I would know?" I watch her profile out of the corner of my eye.

"Your dad told me you and your brother know where to find all the men on my list."

My stomach hardens. I should be happy Dad didn't tell her they're dead. But instead, he sent a suspicious reporter to us armed with potentially incriminating information.

"Why would you believe anything John Holsten told you?" I infuse my tone with boredom.

"Instead of denying his claims, you answer my questions with questions. That's telling, Jarret."

We agreed to speak honestly or remain silent. My silence would've been *more* telling. I can't stop her from making assumptions about what I'm not saying. But when she leaves here, assumptions are all she'll have, and that doesn't make a worthy news story.

"I know Rogan Schroeder has been here." She keeps her gaze on her work. "When was the last time you saw him?"

Of all the men she named, Rogan is the only one who met with my dad on the ranch. The others worked for Rogan as hired killers or loan sharks.

I don't know how much she's uncovered, but I understand why she's not telling me. If she reveals what she knows, she loses her bargaining power. Maybe she knows nothing, but the fact that she has that list of names makes me hesitant to call her bluff. She knows *something.*

"Did my dad explain his relationship with Rogan Schroeder?" I ask.

"He confirmed what I already know."

"And that is...?"

"You and Jake are involved in bad business."

I chuckle. "Define *bad.*"

"Illegal." She lowers her chin, avoiding my eyes.

"Do you believe that?"

She breathes in deeply and releases a sigh of uncertainty. "I would be naive to ignore the evidence."

"Evidence of what?"

"You tell me, Jerry."

"I'm not answering to that."

"You just did."

We're talking in circles, and it's giving me a fucking headache. The suffocating heat only heightens my aggravation.

"Look at me." I shift toward her and wait for her gaze. "You have a place to stay and food to eat. There's no urgency to get your story, right? Nothing pressing?"

"That's not..." Her brow pinches. "I don't know. I mean—"

"You either have a deadline or you don't."

"There's no deadline."

"Then forget the interrogation for now." I tilt my head, studying her as she studies me. "Work with me during the day. Relax with me at night. With time, we'll get to know each other and *trust each other* enough to have this conversation."

She rolls her bottom lip between her teeth, scrutinizing me with tapered eyes. "If you have nothing to hide, why not just answer my questions?"

"I want you. I've been clear on that point."

"Are you saying you're pretending to hide information so you can get me in bed?"

"In a bed, on the kitchen table, against a wall..." I shrug. "Sounds like a plan."

I'd rather her believe that than suspect me of murder.

"There's more going on here than scratching an itch." She huffs. "You can have any woman you want."

"None as challenging as you." I turn back to my work.

"So that's it? *Hard to get* is your flavor of the week?" At my silence, she mumbles under her breath, "I should just fuck you and remove that from the equation."

"That's *my* call to make. I *will* fuck you. You'll get what you need. Then we'll go our separate ways."

That night, I sit beside Maybe on the back porch. The outdoor couch we share feels like heaven beneath my tired muscles. The drizzle of rain beyond the overhang reduces the evening heat. Jake and Conor recline across from us, quiet and content.

Evenings like this center me. If Lorne were here, it would be perfect.

We grilled T-bones and potatoes for dinner. Maybe sliced a cauliflower head into steaks, brushed olive and steak seasoning over the tops, and tossed them on the grill like meat. We teased her about it, but she shrugged it off with a smile.

I love that about her. She might've come here to wheedle information out of us, but not at the risk of losing her self-identity. As gorgeous as she is, she could resort to seduction to get what she wants. She hasn't, and I respect the hell out of her for it.

"I want to hear you play before I pass out." She motions at the harmonica in my hand.

Her hair, still wet from the shower, winds down

her chest and around her hips. Pink colors her cheeks—from a sunburn, the warmth of the evening, or something else… I'm not sure. Her blue eyes glimmer in the dim porch light, her dense lashes dipping lower and lower with each blink. She's fading quickly.

I lean back, resting my shoulder against hers. "I wore you out today."

"You, Chicken, Ginny, the whole menagerie." She yawns. "I'm not cut out to be a ranch hand."

Conor and Jake heard all about Chicken during dinner. What I didn't tell them is how impressed I am with Maybe's work ethic.

"You did really good out there." I angle toward her. "I didn't go easy on you, yet you caught on quickly and never complained."

She groans. "Flattery isn't necessary. I know I slowed you down."

"Jarret might have a charming smile." Conor reaches for the guitar beside her. "But he doesn't give a compliment unless he means it."

"Good to know." Maybe arranges her lips in a tired smile. "I'm glad I could help."

I gave her one of my t-shirts to sleep in, and it swallows the little shorts she wears for modesty. Seeing her in my things today—my boots, my hat, my shirt… It stirs something indescribable inside me.

I've never shared my clothes with anyone. I don't do overnights. I've never slept beside a woman. But before she returns to Chicago, I intend to do all that and more.

Because she's different. She's not desperate or clingy like the women I've been with. She doesn't bend at my every command. She has convictions, and she stands up for them with fire in her eyes.

It doesn't help that I get hard every time I look at her. She's easily the sexiest woman I've ever encountered. Those perky tits, long legs, and fuck me, that smile… She's a goddamn knockout.

"What made you decide to play the harmonica?" She twitches her fingers where they rest beside my leg.

"Conor and Lorne play guitar. Jake sings. I wanted to jam with them when we were kids, but I don't have a musical bone in my body. The harmonica seemed like the easiest to learn."

"He's being humble." Jake props a boot on the coffee table between us. "Play something by The Wild Feathers."

"Which song?" I ask.

"You have to do the harmonica piece in *Wine & Vinegar."* Conor plucks the strings, already rolling into the intro.

I cup the instrument against my lips and direct air in and out, vibrating the notes. When Jake begins the vocals, Maybe's chest rises and falls with a happy sigh.

Conor leads us through the country rock song, singing along with Jake and tapping her foot. We flow together without effort, the music rushing in and around the back porch until my sore muscles give way to a comfortable purr in my chest.

It's not the beats that assuage my heart and pump liquid energy through my veins. It's us. My family. Our togetherness. I lose all sense of everything except for my connection with the people who mean the most to me.

And the woman at my side.

Maybe might be an intruder, but I can't stop myself from soaking in her reactions and savoring the lift of her cheeks. She feels it—the elevation of spirits, the harmony between us, and the rightness in simply enjoying one another's company.

When the song ends, she presses a hand against her breastbone, her sleepy eyes blinking up at me. "Wow. You're really good. Will you do another one?"

I rest a hand on her bare thigh. "You should get

some sleep."

"Nope. I'm good." She slips deeper into the couch, the last ounces of strength draining from her body.

"This one will wake her up." Conor flashes an impish grin and strums the chords of *Whips and Things* by David Allan Coe.

All three of us belt the lyrics, because it's one of those songs that should be bellowed as loudly and obnoxiously as possible.

The raunchy words send Maybe into a fit of laughter, and by the time we finish, we're all laughing, just like we did when Lorne introduced it to us in our teens.

"I'm going to play that song at our wedding." Jake grins.

"You do that." Conor tweaks his nipple through his shirt. "Because when I play it at your funeral, I'm bringing a date."

He grips her wrist and yanks her close. "Put the guitar away. I have something else for you to play with."

With a defiant look, she twists her arm free and strums the chords of another song.

I scratch the stubble on my jaw. "You're losing your touch, Jake."

"We'll see about that when she comes to bed begging for a punishment."

"So it runs in the family," Maybe mumbles beside me. "Whips and things..."

"Whips are overrated." I give her a wink and raise the harmonica to my mouth.

We play a few more songs before her head rolls on her shoulders, and her mouth parts in a quiet snore.

"We lost her." Conor sets the guitar aside and crawls onto Jake's lap.

"I'll be right back." I lift Maybe's slack body and carry her into the house.

She stirs during the walk but doesn't fully wake.

Eyes closed, she curls against my chest and saturates my inhales with the minty scent of her shampoo.

As shadows dance along the soft curves of her hips and legs, I'm not above checking her out. The perfect shape of her heats my blood and awakens a primitive urge to keep her close just to prevent other men from touching her.

I wish I wasn't attracted to her. This would be less complicated if she were more of an adversary and less of a fascination. But she seduces me without even trying. The silky feel of her skin, the sweet taste of her mouth, the fight she gives me at every turn—she's a mysterious dream wrapped in the promise of sex. No single man could've turned her away.

I didn't just demand that she stay. I gave her a well-bred, papered-up British White Park calf, for fuck's sake. What was I thinking?

I wasn't. This goes beyond fascination and headlong into insanity.

The door to my suite emerges at the end of the hall, and I consider it for a span of several seconds before forcing my feet into Lorne's room. As I lower her onto the bed, she rouses.

"I fell asleep." She peers up at me with heavy-lidded eyes and touches my face. "God, you're handsome. I bet you hear that all the time."

I usually find those words trite and unctuous, but on her lips, they sound genuine.

"I almost carried you to my bed." I turn my head and kiss her fingertips. "But I want you there on your own accord."

"I won't—"

"You will." I crawl over her and lower my body between her legs. "I'll wait."

"Is *this* waiting?" Her hands fall to my hips and clench.

"You have no idea."

The impulse to grind against her is overwhelming, but if she says stop, this ends. I would lose her, and I can't risk that.

Instead, I wait for her to push me away.

She doesn't.

An inner battle tightens her expression, her body stiff and resistant beneath me. Then her gaze lowers and parks on my mouth. That's all the invitation I need.

I swoop in and draw her bottom lip between my teeth. She gasps, and I bite, forbidding her from jerking back.

A startled noise sounds in her throat. Then a heartbeat of hesitation. And another.

She lifts a hand to my hair. The other slides along my jaw. Her mouth closes over my upper lip, and she presses closer, leaning up, breaths accelerating, fingers curling and pulling at my roots.

She wants this. Christ, I feel the need vibrating through her. But I hold still, forcing her to come to me.

Give in, baby.

With a groan, she suckles my upper lip, softly at first, then harder, hungrier. Her jaw unlocks. Her tongue darts out, and she liquefies beneath me in irresistible submission.

I dive in, taking over the kiss and claiming her with urgent strokes. My cock wakes up, and my breaths escape in bursts. I grip her thigh around my hip and dig closer, rubbing my zipper against her core and seeking relief. Fucking hell, I want her so badly this is torture.

Her hands hold my face to hers as I plunder her mouth, preventing her from forming words. Each lash of my tongue is an order to accept, every bite a demand to surrender. My grip on her thigh commands her to let go, to give into my desire, to join me in the urgency.

"Jarret." She pushes against my shoulders, panting. "I can't. I'm not..."

Blood throbs along my shaft, my thoughts a cloud of need, need, need. “Not what?”

“I’m not like the women you sleep with.”

“I know.” That’s precisely why I’m all tangled up in her.

With great effort, I roll off her and sit on the edge of the bed, dropping my elbows on my knees.

She pulls the covers to her shoulders and settles on her side, watching me. “If I wasn’t here tonight, would you be in town?”

“Yeah.” I run a hand through my hair, unnerved by the fact that at some point over the last twenty-four hours, I lost all interest in other women.

“I don’t know how you work twelve-hour days and find the energy to pick up girls at night.” An acidic undertone sours her voice. “Don’t let me stop you from going out. It’s been two whole days since you got laid.”

She’s jealous, underlined by the scowl she tries to hide behind the fold of her hand on the pillow.

It’s fucked up, the conflicting feelings pulsing inside me. Satisfaction, because I affect her. Guilt, because it upsets her to think of me with someone else. The latter makes me want to drag her onto my lap and assure her she’s the only one I want.

But I’m not in a monogamous relationship with this woman. She’s on an errand to expose my family, and I’m certain she’s harboring her own secrets. I respect her, but I don’t trust her.

I need to work her out of my system, convince her I have nothing to hide, and send her home. At least I don’t have to worry about her getting attached.

“I’ll let you sleep.” I rise from the bed and head toward the hall, denying the urge to give her a parting glance.

Until I reach the doorway.

I can’t help it. There’s something so striking and

addictive about her it draws my gaze and makes me twitch to put my hands all over those soft curves in a way I've never considered touching a woman.

I want to hold her without the anticipation of sex. I want to learn where she's ticklish, what makes her toes curl, and how to coax a smile with the caress of my hand. More than anything, I want to capture the flame inside her and keep it burning between us.

Her full lips flatten, and her bright blue eyes narrow over a pert nose as we remain locked in a stare. I don't know what she knows about me or the things I've done, but whatever it is, she isn't afraid. Perhaps all she has is that list of names and a head full of assumptions.

Is that enough to compel a homeless journalist to drive nine-hundred miles to investigate?

Six years ago, Sandbank crawled with reporters from all over the country. With Lorne's trial and the disgusting attack on Conor, there were enough lurid details to fill newspapers. But that's in the past. The parade of news vans and fancy cameras rolled out as quickly as they rolled in.

Maybe Quinn might dress like a reporter, but she doesn't behave like one. She's tough, but not in the pushy, aggressive way I expect. I haven't seen her with a recording device or even a memo pad. She has a phone, but she's not connected to it or the outside world. Aren't journalists obsessively passionate about the hustle of life and capturing it all for public consumption?

She doesn't fit that persona at all.

I cast her a hard look. *Why are you really here?*

She glares right back, and damn if I don't want to kiss the attitude off those pouty lips. Instead, I flick off the light and shut the door.

On my way to the back porch, I stop in the laundry room and switch her clothes to the dryer. Before dinner, I washed the things she wore today. She'll have to wear them again tomorrow and the next day and so on until I figure out a solution. I draw the line at going shopping.

As I toss her wet clothes into the dryer, my fingers slide against a thin scrap of satin. I pause with my hand in the machine, bending down to stare at the pair of black panties in my hand.

I glance back at the door where I left her, imagining the look on her face if she walks out and catches me.

Don't be that guy.

Too late.

I lift it to my nose by compulsion, not by choice. The laundry soap erases any scent of her, but my cock reacts anyway as I visualize the fabric rubbing against her pussy all day.

"Are you sniffing her panties?" Conor's whisper drifts from the entrance of the hall.

In an attempt to embarrass her, I hold them up, dangling by a finger, and arch an eyebrow in her direction. "If you think my brother doesn't smell yours—"

"I know he does." She strolls toward me and hops up on the dryer. "What are you doing, Jarret?"

The loaded hush of her voice tells me she's not asking about the laundry.

"I have no idea." I toss the panties in, push her legs aside to shut the dryer door, and reach around her to power it on. "What do you want?"

"You were gone a while. Jake and I took bets on whether you and the reporter were getting busy. Then he got tired of waiting and went to bed."

"Who won the bet?"

"I did." A smile softens her eyes. "She's not one of your buckle bunnies."

"No, she's not." I turn away and head toward my room.

"If she's staying, she needs more work clothes."

Conor's footsteps follow on my heels, down the hall, and into my suite.

"I'm working on it."

"We both know you don't shop." She shuts the door behind her. "Want me to order some clothes? I know a few online stores that—"

"Yes." I pull a wad of cash from my wallet and hand it to her. "That would be really helpful."

"Consider it done." She pockets the money and climbs across my bed to root through the drawer of my nightstand. "Do you still keep your—?" She yanks out the tin box. "Yes!"

"Don't even think about it." I snatch the box of weed from her hand and return it to the drawer.

I smoke to mellow the aches and pains of hard labor. When we were younger, Conor used to sneak out and get stoned with me. Until Jake and Lorne found out.

They let me know what they thought of that by rearranging my face.

"Jake's not the boss of me." She crosses her arms.

"Try telling *him* that."

She makes a growly noise and flops onto the bed. "I talked to Lorne about your house guest."

"He responded to my email this morning." I tug off my boots and sprawl on my back beside her. "He wants to meet her."

"Do you think that's wise?"

"It's not like he'll say anything incriminating. The prison monitors everything."

"Shh!" She slaps a hand over my mouth and whispers, "What if she planted something in here? She could be listening right now."

I push her arm away. "She hasn't had the opportunity."

"You can't watch her every second of every day. Aren't you worried about her spying?"

"No."

"Jarret, this is important. If I lose another one of you to prison..."

The worry in her voice prompts me to turn on my side and face her. "Her mind doesn't work like that. I can't put my finger on it, but I know she's not as manipulative or conniving as she wants me to believe."

"What do you mean? Like she's not a reporter?"

"No. Yes. Fuck, I don't know. Something led her to my dad. She said it was a lead on another story. That's plausible, but..."

"But?"

"This feels personal. She's homeless because... How did she put it? *Bad judgment and rotten luck.*"

Her green eyes flare. "Do you think she was involved with the moneylenders? Or someone in her family? What if one of those men was her father or brother...?" She gasps. "Oh God, Jarret."

"Slow down, Watson. *It is a capital mistake to theorize in advance of the facts.*"

"Was that Sherlock Holmes?" Her gaze flicks to the steel bookshelf, where my favorite childhood books reside.

"Yeah, and the facts are these... She has no siblings or living parents."

"That's if she's telling the truth. Are you listening to your gut or something else?"

"All of it."

I roll to my back and launch into a rambling diatribe about my conflicting feelings regarding the woman in the other room.

Conor settles in on her stomach. Resting her chin atop her folded hands on my chest, she absorbs every word just like she did whenever I vented about girls in high school.

When I fall quiet, she makes a humming sound.

"What?" I peer down at her.

"She's going to fall in love with you."

I release a startled grunt. "That's not even in the realm of possibilities."

"If you believe that, I feel sorry for you."

"What the hell's that supposed to mean?"

"You're a good guy. A *great* guy. I know you've done things you're not proud of, but it doesn't define who you are."

My stomach cramps. "Abandoning you for six years makes me the worst brother—"

"Jarret." She lifts her head and grips my t-shirt. "That's not what I'm talking about. I forgave you for that. Let it go."

I can't let it go, but I ruffle her hair until she relaxes on my chest.

If she's referring to the bodies in the ravine, I don't feel an ounce of remorse about that. Those men threatened her, and I did exactly what Lorne would've done. I protected her at all costs.

"I missed this." She flips to her back with her head propped on my torso. "We used to have the best girl talks, didn't we?"

I chuckle. "Yeah. How are *you* doing?"

"Better. Jake's kind of a bear, but I need that. He makes me write down every feeling and memory and…" She groans. "It's awful. But then we rehash it over and over until it's not so awful. He has the patience of a saint."

"I need some of his patience to rub off on me."

"You know, it's nice to see you working for a woman's attention for a change. You'll appreciate her more."

I already appreciate her. Every insatiable, infuriating inch of her. That's the problem.

Conor laughs to herself. "Remember Stacy in high school? The girl who gave you a scrapbook album of your future life together? It included your wedding with her and random things about you, like your favorite food, color, songs, and there was a whole page dedicated to the shape of your lips."

I shudder. "The longest conversation I ever had with that girl was, *What's up? Nothing.*"

Conor highlights a few more stalkers from my past, and we slide into easy conversation about everything and nothing at all, laughing and reminiscing and losing track of time.

Until the door creaks open.

Jake fills the doorframe, shirtless and scowling.

"You said you were going to grab a glass of water." He folds his arms across his chest.

Conor sits up and shoves the auburn tangles from her face. "Jarret needed help with his girl problems."

"She came in here to bum a joint." I give her a kick off the bed.

"That, too." She lands on her feet and sashays toward the door, smiling back at me. "Same time tomorrow?"

"You'll be too tired for conversation."

Branding season starts tomorrow, which means no downtime for a week.

"Good point." She pauses beside Jake. "Can I have a piggyback ride?"

"No." He pops her on the ass. "Get to bed."

Her laughter follows her out of the room and down the hall.

He turns back to me and hardens his eyes. "Don't get her stoned."

"Chill out. Her lungs are safe."

He studies me for a moment, measuring my mood. "If you need to talk about...whatever's going on..."

"That's what I have Conor for."

We share a grin. Communication between us doesn't require words. Sometimes we use our fists, but that's not needed tonight.

With a nod, he steps into the hall and closes the door.

I sink into the mattress and consider rubbing one out before the evening is spent. The bed frame creaks as I shove the jeans down my legs and yank off the t-shirt. Exhaling, I grip the base of my cock through the briefs and close my eyes.

The image of blue eyes and blond curls flickers across the backs of my eyelids. I creep my hand along my swelling shaft, and the air thickens with a craving that goes beyond a quick release.

My heart hammers just thinking about her. I know she wants me. I sense it every time our eyes connect. So why am I lying here alone when she's right down the hall?

This is madness.

I swing my legs off the bed, fasten the jeans, and walk with purpose to the door. I don't stop until I reach Lorne's suite and step inside.

My body tingles as I approach the bed, and I become painfully conscious of my breaths.

And hers.

Soft and feminine, the sound of air flowing past her lips gives me pause. The depth of her slumber is a testament to how much I overworked her today. As I perch on the edge of the mattress, she doesn't even stir.

Why did I come in here? I knew she'd be asleep, and I have no intention of waking her. I just needed to check on her. I needed to see her.

The hallway light slants through the partially open doorway, painting a gentle glow across her face. She's a side sleeper, her arms tucked against her chest and hands folded around the pillow. The perfect position to back up against me, side by side, in the center of my bed.

Ringlets of gold splay around her shoulders and arms, engulfing her small frame. Her full lips, slightly parted, emit a small puff of sound with each exhale.

What holds my attention the longest, however, are her lashes. Long and thick, they aren't clumped together with the black goop most women wear. I don't think she even owns makeup.

What I wouldn't give to trace a finger along those lashes. I bet they feel like feathers against the apples of her high cheekbones. Someday soon, I'm going to kiss each of her eyelids and let those sexy lashes caress my lips. I never want to see them wet. Unless it's on the cusp of pleasure.

She's going to fall in love with you.

That's not the danger here.

It's me. I'm slipping, and I fucking know it. I need to pull back.

I don't even know her.

Except every breath in my body demands that I do.

Reaching toward her face, I carefully sweep the soft curls away from her cheek. The simple touch comes with startling realization.

I want to take care of her. It's not just a desire. It's instinct. Whether I've earned that right is negligible. She's my responsibility.

I don't know what that means exactly, but it feels like I could run forever, search forever, and end up right back where I'm at.

I'm destined for this, whatever *this* is.

The third week of every June is our date of brand. The next six days consist of long, miserably hot, back-breaking hours of sorting, branding, vaccinating, and castrating cattle on little sleep. It's also an excuse to blare music, barbecue meat, and talk a ton of trash.

We have to bring in extra guys, and they haul in their horses and trailers. Everyone has their own job—a gate, corral, chute, panel, electric prod. Each person knows to stay in position to keep things running smoothly.

Except Maybe.

"Why are they screaming like that?" She shouts above the bellowing cows and chases my boot heels around the corral.

"Cattle are smarter than they look. They know they're going to get shots and be separated from their calves, and they're fightin' mad about it." I scale the railing of a steel pen and grip her arm, stopping her from following me over. "Where are you supposed to be?"

A scowl mars her pretty face, and she points at the

chute behind her.

"Get there and stay put." I turn away, focused on the next task, but her tiny hand catches the back of my shirt.

"Where's Chicken?" Her wide eyes scour the pens filled with calves.

One of the older guys ambles by and tilts his hat at her. "Ma'am."

Her gaze snags on the branding iron in his hand, and she gasps. "Oh my God, Jarret. You can't—"

"I put Chicken in the stable this morning. No reason to brand her."

"Why do you have to brand any of them?" She presses a hand to her forehead and spins around. "It's barbaric and cruel and—

"It's necessary."

"Jarret!" Jake calls from the other side of the pen. "Did you get a head count yet?"

I hold up a finger and return to Maybe. "The brand inspectors at the sale barns won't let us sell the critters without our brand. That's just the way it is, darlin'. If you can't stomach it, sit this one out."

Sadness brightens her eyes as she scans the restless, bellowing calves. I half-expect her to do something irrational, like open the gates and try to free the herd.

But she's an intelligent woman. And tough. If she can rope a terrified hundred-pound calf in a creek and psyche herself up to shove her arm in a heifer's ass, she can handle the stench of burning cow hair or the sight of a calf losing its manhood to a dull Buck knife.

"What's it gonna be?" I nudge up my Stetson and wipe the sweat from my brow.

A decision settles in her expression and seems to take over her entire demeanor. My God, it's a beautiful thing to watch. She shoves her shoulders back and lifts that chin, exposing the graceful lines of her neck. Strong posture, strong jaw, and even stronger eye contact, she moves into my personal space and grips the railing between us.

"Stop gawking and get to work, cowboy." Her lips hover a kiss away.

"Jarret, goddammit!" Jake shouts behind me. "Hurry up."

The cows bellow louder, and somewhere nearby, a pickup truck blasts *Get Along* by Kenny Chesney through crackling speakers.

The chaos fades around me as I lean in. Or maybe she leans in. I'm not sure who moves first, but the caress of her warm mouth against mine sets my brain on fire and spreads warmth from my lips to my boots.

It's a long-lasting kiss, not in duration but in memory. It becomes my salvation and my torment over the next week as I replay it through the endless cycle of shots, castrations, and brands.

When each day ends—eight, nine, ten o'clock at night—we eat in exhausted silence and sleep like the dead, only to wake before dawn, rinse, and repeat.

Since the ranch stretches twenty miles, we use the trailers to haul the cattle to and from the pastures. From round-up to finish, the work is nonstop and physically taxing. As much as I want to pick up where I left off with Maybe, I barely have the energy to carry her to bed. Which I do, every night, when she falls asleep during dinner.

At the end of the week, I wake with a start and find myself sprawled on the living room sofa. Rubbing a hand down my face, I stare into the blue eyes of an angel. She floats above me, her thin frame engulfed in one of my t-shirts.

I glance around, dazed. "When did I—?"

"You passed out about an hour ago. I wish I could've carried *you* to bed for a change."

She slumps onto the cushion beside me, as if every muscle has given up its fight against gravity. Her shoulders hang limp with fatigue, her freshly-showered hair dripping down her arms. Bleary-eyed and sleep-deprived, she's so damn gorgeous it's arresting.

I can't bear the thought of spending another night away from her.

"Come on." I drag my dog-tired body off the couch and clasp her hand.

She doesn't try to pull free as I lead her through the dark house and into my wing.

Jake and Conor must've already gone to bed for the night. That's where I'm headed, only this time, I won't be alone.

"Jarret." She digs in her feet as we pass her room. "Where are you—?"

I tighten my grip on her hand and pull her the rest of the way to my suite.

"I'm too tired to fight you." I release her outside my door and amble to the bed. "I'm too tired to do anything but sleep. But I want you beside me."

She lingers on the threshold as I lower onto the mattress and bend to remove my boots. My hands, my back, every joint in my body aches so deeply and thoroughly the smallest movement clenches my teeth.

If I can just get out of these clothes, a good night's rest will take away the pain. I tug on a boot, grunting with frustration.

Her silhouette stirs in my periphery, and the soft pad of her footsteps approaches. She's been at the ranch for eight days, and this is the first time she's entered my suite.

"I'll do this." She kneels before me and removes my boots and socks with a gentleness that makes me moan.

I collapse on my back, legs dangling off the bed, and fight to keep my eyes open. "I can't move."

Buckled

"I like you like this." She stands between my knees and rests her hands on her hips. "A big, harmless baby."

I try to formulate a response, but my brain isn't working. The next thing I know, she's crawling over me, attempting to remove my shirt.

"You fell asleep again. Lean up." She pushes the cotton up my chest and works it off my head with little help from me.

Her eyes dip to my belt buckle, and she blows out a breath.

"I'm going to remove your jeans. Don't get any ideas." She tackles my belt and zipper. "We're just sleeping."

"Sleep sounds great," I mumble.

She tugs the denim down my hips, keeping my briefs in place as I lift and arch with the last of my strength.

The jeans drop to the floor, and she steps back, chest heaving, lips parted, and greedy eyes devouring my useless, half-nude body.

She likes what she sees. Too bad I don't have the energy to do something about that.

"Jesus, you're..." Her breath catches. "Really hard."

I glance down at the semi in my briefs and shut my eyes. "Only way that's getting any action is if you fall on it. I couldn't move my hips if I tried."

"No, I mean, you're hard *everywhere*. Sorry, I just... I've never seen a man who looks like you."

My nostrils flare. I don't want to think about the *men* she's seen. "Come to bed."

"I think I'll just..." Her retreating footsteps crack open my eyes. "I'll sleep in the other room."

"No, you won't." I drag my ass to the center of the bed with clumsy movements and yank the sheet over me.

"I won't be another notch in your bedpost."

"I've never slept beside anyone." I lift the covers in invitation. "Please."

"Never?" Her eyebrows jump.

"Not once."

"I'm the first?"

"The *only* one."

Her bottom lip rolls between her teeth, and she releases it with a stern expression. "No sex."

"Get your stubborn ass over here."

"Say please again." She crosses her arms.

"You're going to be the death of me." I drop the covers and sink into the pillow. "Please."

Biting down on her smile, she shuts the door, flips off the light, and tiptoes through the room.

"You have an urban modern decor thing going on in here." She slides in beside me, keeping several feet between us. "Very monochromatic with the gray and black color scheme and steel furniture."

Whatever that means.

I hook an arm around her waist and pull her across the mattress until her back is flush with my chest. She squeaks, stiffens against me, then relaxes.

"You expected stuffed opossums?" I run my nose through her soft, damp hair, savoring the feel of it against my face.

"Yeah. And a wall of shotguns, thermal long johns, riding crops..."

"Long johns are in the closet."

"Only you could wear those and still look hot."

"Stick around until winter and you can see for yourself."

She clears her throat, fading into a whisper. "What's on the agenda tomorrow?"

"We'll sleep in till six."

She releases a lethargic snort.

"I have some work to do in the morning." I slide a hand over her hip. "In the afternoon, we're going to visit

Lorne."

I have plans for her during the two-hour drive to the prison. If she's still around after that, I'll put some miles on the riding crop tomorrow night.

She remains quiet, her body soft and slack against the front of mine. The even tempo of her breaths feathers the air, her skin unresponsive as I caress her bare thigh.

She's already out, wrapped in exhaustive sleep.

I start to drift along with her, fighting it with everything I have. I want to savor this—the warmth of her flesh, the scent of her hair, the rhythm of her heartbeat. She's a dream I ache to remain awake for, an erotic canvas to be explored and appreciated.

As I trail a hand along the curve of her thigh, unconsciousness falls like an ax.

Before dawn, I wake just as abruptly, my groggy mind luxuriating in the remnants of a dream, reluctant to let it go.

I blink against the darkness, realizing the dream is very real, curled up in my arms, breathing against my neck, with a leg tossed over my painfully hard erection.

The clock on the nightstand tells me I have twenty minutes before I need to be in the saddle. Twenty minutes to take a tour of the curves and valleys molded around me.

I start at the back of her knee, shifting her leg from my groin to my stomach. With featherlight fingers, I trail a path along her thigh to the hem of her cotton shorts.

She moans in her sleep and nuzzles her face deeper against my neck. My breathing accelerates, my body heating and tightening against her.

I can't remember the last time I went longer than a week without sex, but it's not just that. It's *her.*

Everything about her feels right, from her argumentative spirit to the innocence that radiates from her pores. Her open-mindedness and ability to adjust is refreshing. She's a vegetarian, but she doesn't push her dietary choices onto others. She wants to save all the chickens, but she isn't here to sabotage my business.

She doesn't sleep around, yet her eyes illuminate with so much sexual curiosity and interest it makes my balls throb.

I want to learn her fantasies, break them in, and spank them into something she'll only ever experience with me. But for now, I'll just be content with a twenty-minute taste.

She's taken to wearing my shirts to bed, and this one hangs off her shoulder and halfway down her arm, creating an enticing plunge across her breast.

I dip my mouth there, ghosting my lips across the rise of supple flesh. Inching a hand along the back of her thigh, I slip beneath the loose shorts and palm the firm muscle of her ass. *No panties.*

A stretch shudders through her, and she wriggles closer, arching against my mouth with her fingers in my hair. Her dusky nipple pops free, and I latch onto it, drawing it between my lips with a groan.

She tenses. "Jarret?"

"I'm just tasting." I lave my tongue over the taut bud, flicking and nibbling. "You're so fucking sexy."

Her backside flexes beneath my palm, but instead of pushing me away, she edges closer, shifting restlessly with shallow breaths. "What are you doing to me?"

Ruining her for all other men.

"You're sleeping in here from now on." I palm her round butt cheek and glide my fingers down her crack.

"I might be more receptive…" She shoves at my arm and squirms to escape. "If you were less bossy and more imploring."

"Imploring?" I grip her waist and drag her on top of me to straddle my hips.

"Please and thank you would be a good start." She

stays where I positioned her, staring down at me in the dark.

The shadow of her hair curls around her face and torso. Soft and tousled, there's so much of it I could use it like rope to bind her arms.

"How did you sleep?" I reach up to pluck her exposed nipple.

"Surprisingly well." She knocks my hand away and adjusts the shirt to cover herself. "Thank you for behaving yourself…until this morning."

Now that I'm rested, *behaving* isn't an option. "Have you ever slept beside a man?"

"I've had some failed relationships. Men I lived with." Her expression darkens. "Mistakes I don't intend to repeat again." She pushes away from me and climbs off the bed. "I need to get ready."

One question and I completely soured the mood.

As she flees the room, I burn to chase her down and demand answers. Answers about her past relationships. Answers about her knowledge of the corruption and murder at Julep Ranch. Those are two areas that seem to shut her down the fastest.

But I won't get anywhere until I earn her trust. The best way I know how to do that is with my hands and mouth, pain and pleasure, surrender and dominance.

If she learns to trust me with a crop in my fist, she'll open up. I'm certain of it.

Later that morning, I put Maybe in the saddle and ride out to the pasture to let her visit Chicken.

Her face lights up so magically at the sight of the calf I feel a twinge of jealous resentment for the critter. But since I can't deny her this happiness, I'll bring her out here every damn day until the calf is weaned.

Except that'll be six months from now. Maybe will be long gone by then.

My chest constricts, and I shove the feeling away.

"I'll be back to get you." I lean down in the saddle, meeting her eyes where she stands near the fence. "Might be an hour or so."

"Take your time." She stares across the pasture at the calf and rests a hand against her heart. "Thank you so much for this."

"You're welcome."

A ribbed tank top clings to the high round globes of her breasts. Jeans mold to her slender hips and dip tantalizing low, revealing her flat midriff. Conor spent my money well, and Maybe was humbly grateful when the clothes arrived.

I could watch her all day, taking in her expressions, her sexy sounds, and her beauty, while committing everything to memory. If I don't peel my gaze away now, I'll never leave.

Nudging Ginny into motion, I steer him in the direction of the main road. There's a vulnerable spot along the fence line there that requires regular monitoring.

It's a ten-mile ride on flat land, so I let Ginny loose into a full gallop. His smooth, even strides glide over the dirt at a velocity that lifts me out of the stirrups. As his weight shifts from back legs to front legs, I lean forward and adjust the angle of my hips to compensate for the momentum and maintain my center of gravity.

Nothing feels closer to flying than riding a horse at this speed. Heart thundering, wind blasting past my ears, the vibrations of hooves through my body—it's an indulgence that's as warm and real and sentient as sex. And almost as pleasurable.

When I reach the fence, I make a quick pass, and everything checks out. On the other side, the dirt road stretches over the hill. Off in the distance, the main house and stable look like hazy mirages in the heat.

Urgency pulls me away. I need to clean the stalls before I return for Maybe. As I turn in that direction, the sound of an approaching engine gives me pause.

The only traffic on this road are employees and visitors of the ranch. We're not expecting visitors.

A black SUV emerges over the hill in a plume of dust. The light bar on the roof glints in the sun.

Son of a bitch.

Sheriff Fletcher doesn't come around unless there's trouble. It could be any number of things, but I suspect Levi Tibbs' failure to report to his parole officer tops the list.

Exhaling a heavy breath, I guide Ginny closer to

the fence.

Fletcher slows to a stop beside me in his swanky SUV, one the Sandbank police department could never afford. No doubt the drilling on Julep Ranch helped pay for the hunk of metal.

"Morning, Jarret." He bends an elbow out the window and fiddles with his silver mustache. "How's the cattle business?"

"Busy. What can I do for you, Sheriff?"

"Oh, well..." He leans his head out and spits in the dirt. "I expect you haven't heard about the manhunt for Levi Tibbs?"

"No, sir." I widen my eyes a little, playing dumb.

"He went missing within hours of his release. I heard Conor's back in town, and I wouldn't want anything to happen to her."

The lying fuck doesn't give a shit about her.

"Jake's always a half-step behind her," I say. "But I appreciate the heads up."

"I also hear there's a pretty little reporter staying with you." He twitches his bulbous nose. "Unless she's gone missing, too."

The bastard stares at me with beady eyes, knowing damn well Levi Tibbs is dead and I'm the reason. But to imply I'm capable of killing Maybe heats my insides to boiling.

"Maybe Quinn is working here for a while, learning the business. I'm sure you'll see her around town at some point."

"Is she digging a story out of you?"

That's the real reason he's here. He wants to make sure I don't feed her details about his unlawful activities. While he doesn't have evidence against me, I have plenty to send *him* to prison.

"Our agreement hasn't changed, Sheriff. You just stick to writing parking tickets and you have nothing to worry about."

"Good to hear, boy." He pats a hand against the car door. "Good to hear."

"You take care now."

"Same to you." He motors away.

The sheriff will always be a liability, but not one I lose sleep over. If anything, he serves as a buffer between the ranch and other law officials. It's in his best interest to prevent anyone from snooping around on our land. Including reporters.

The rest of the morning rolls by achingly slow as anticipation builds in my gut. For over a week, I kept my hands to myself. I've been a respectable, proper gentleman.

It grates on my nerves.

By the time I load Maybe into my pickup truck, every muscle in my body is coiled and vibrating.

She wears the dress I instructed her to put on, the flowing white one from the night she arrived at the ranch. Her hair tumbles around her bare arms, her skin flushed and glowing from the shower. The fact that she chose to wear my boots with the dress only fuels the desire sliding through my veins.

I climb behind the wheel and narrow my eyes at the wide space between us. If she sits any closer to the passenger door, she'll be eating the window.

"Move to the middle." I point at the center of the bench seat.

"Why am I wearing a dress while you're in jeans and a t-shirt?"

I shift toward her and give her the truth. "I want access to your pussy."

Her mouth falls open on a breathless gasp, and she whirls toward the door, fumbling the handle in her attempt to escape.

"Maybe." In a tone I've never used with her, my voice cuts through the cab, sharp and deep. "Turn your ass around and look at me."

She turns and shoots me a withering glare.

I give her one right back. "We don't trust each other. You think I'm hiding something. I *know* you're hiding shit. We both have walls up, and I'm going to change that."

"By shoving your hand up my dress?"

"Yes."

"Unbelievable." She gapes at me. "You're such a... I don't know what you are, but I bet it's a thirteen-syllable word in a psychiatric ward! I can't even believe—"

"Shut the fuck up and listen."

Her teeth clack together, her eyes fuming with blue smoke.

"It would be so easy to learn everything I want to know about you." I soften my tone. "One call to a private investigator and I'd have a full report in my hands by morning."

Her breath hitches. "That's invasion of—"

"I won't do it, Maybe." I clench a hand on the steering wheel. "I want more than your secrets. I want those, too, but I'm not going to *take* them. I want you to give them to me when you're ready. I want to earn your trust."

"Sex doesn't earn trust. It destroys it."

A sinking feeling hits my stomach. "Who hurt you?"

She averts her eyes to the window and rests the back of her hand against her mouth.

Tension knots in my shoulders. "Who?"

She shakes her head, robbing me of her gaze.

"Let me be frank with you." I drum my fingers on my thigh. "I'm not good at this."

She casts me a questioning look.

"This..." I gesture between us. "I don't do this with women."

"You don't do what? Conversation?"

"Yes. I talk to Conor, but she's... *Conor.*" I twist in the seat to face her. "When I'm with a woman, I communicate with my eyes, my touch, my body."

She makes a disgusted face. "I'd rather not hear about–"

"I'm talking. Isn't that what you want?"

"You're right." She straightens. "Go ahead."

"I've spent my entire life out in those fields." I motion at the landscape beyond the windshield. "It's solitary, physical work that involves my body. *Not my voice.* I'm hands on when I complete tasks and communicate with others. When I talk to my brother, we use our fists. When I'm interested in a woman, I tell her with my eyes. When I want to talk to her, I tie her to a support beam and express myself with the lash of a crop." I give her a knowing look. "Sex is communication at the deepest level."

"For a tactile guy, you explained that fairly well with words."

"I can explain myself a whole lot better with my hands." I rest a hand on the seat between us, palm up.

"That sounds like a pick-up line."

"I've never used a pick-up line in my life."

"Because you don't have to," she mutters. "Women throw themselves at you."

"I'm willing to work for this. I *want* to. But I need you to work for it, too. Meet me in the middle."

She stares at my hand, where it waits between us. After a moment of hesitation, she reaches out and slides her fingers along the scar on my palm.

"Thank you." I close my hand around hers. "I'm going to touch you for the next two hours. I'll push against your boundaries, but I'll stop before you say the word."

"How will you know?"

"It's what I'm good at, Maybe. I know how to read

a woman's body."

"Really?" A bark of laughter. "What's mine telling you?"

I give her a once over. Darting gaze, tense neck, excessive swallowing, clammy palm, and a subtle bounce in her foot.

"You're annoyed. Conflicted. Apprehensive." I return to her eyes and absorb the pain she tries so hard to conceal. "Lonely and lost."

Her head jerks back, and she swallows again.

I pull on her hand, a silent command to sit where I instructed.

She yanks free of my grip and straightens the dress over her knees. Her fingers go to her hair, fidgeting with the tangles. A nervous habit.

Then she lowers her hands. "I'll give you the benefit of the doubt as to whether your methods build trust. But I'm not just falling in line because you growled an order. I'm *choosing* to give it a try."

A thrill jolts through me. She's wonderfully, beautifully, remarkably perfect. Stubborn as a mule, but damn, I wouldn't change a thing about her.

She scoots over, adjusting and smoothing the dress. I help her buckle the lap belt and start the engine. Then I hit the road.

We ride to town in silence, and I stop at the gas station to fill up the tank. Now would be a good time to buy condoms since I don't keep any at home. But I decide against it when I catch her staring at the convenience store with enough fire in her eyes to burn the place down.

Back in the truck, I connect my phone to the stereo and cue up my playlist.

The Cowboy in Me by Tim McGraw starts the drive. The tires hum on the pavement, and Maybe sits motionless at my side.

I wait until we're out of Sandbank before I give her my full attention. Her knees squeeze together. Her hands lie flat against her abdomen, and her shoulders bunch near her ears. Not the body language I hoped for.

"You're uncomfortable." I rest a hand on her locked knees.

"I'm, uh..." She drags in a long breath and releases it. "I get queasy when I'm nervous."

Nervous is better than scared.

"I'll go slow. So slow you'll accuse me of being cruel." I squeeze her knee. "Put your hand on my leg."

Since I have to watch the road, the twitch and flex of her fingers will help me monitor her reactions.

She doesn't move. No surprise. I'm prepared to push as hard and long as it takes until her reluctance crumbles.

I clench my fingers tighter around her knee, tighter, tighter...

She makes a noise in her throat and slams a hand down on my thigh.

I loosen my grip and glide my palm around her clenched knees, keeping the fabric in place as a barrier.

That's where I linger for the next thirty minutes. Stroking, kneading, I touch her through the dress until her hand falls slack on my lap and her knees relax.

I inch the material up, just enough to bare her lower thighs. Her fingers dig into my leg, and I hold still.

Since she had live-in boyfriends, I know she's not a virgin. This has nothing to do with prudence, and everything to do with distrust. She tenses as if I'm going to wrench apart her legs and stab my fingers inside her.

After I restrained her to a wooden beam, I guess I can't blame her.

Eventually, she takes a few breaths and uncurls her claws.

Over the next hour, I focus on her thighs, caressing the velvety skin, memorizing the slender shape, and coaxing the toned muscles to contract and loosen, all while edging carefully, subtly closer to her panties.

It's an hour of delicious discovery.

Featherlight touches make her ticklish. A gentle massage sinks her deeper into the seat and turns her body to butter. But it's the bruising press of fingers and my restrictive grip on her leg that revs her breaths and causes her hand to curl and uncurl on my thigh, as if subconsciously pleading for more.

She enjoys being worshiped and adored with affection, but she gets off on rough, unyielding domination.

As long as it's with the right man. A man she trusts.

If my instinct is correct, she's never had that kind of relationship, which means she's never experienced the total and complete submission she longs for.

She's already so pliable beneath my hand—her legs partially open, muscles loose, breaths deep and wanton. I could slip my fingers past her panties and inside her cunt before the word stop crosses her mind.

But I want her at my mercy during the visit with Lorne. I want her thinking about the drive home, aching for more, needing, and imagining as she twists herself into a creature of ravenous hunger.

So I spend the remaining thirty minutes playing with her. Teasing fingers along the edge of her panties, brushing against the seam of her pussy, and caressing the insides of her thighs, I work her into a state of trembling, panting desire.

The mood shatters the instant we arrive at Oklahoma State Penitentiary.

I park in the lot, surrounded by two-story, anti-cut metal fencing, barren grass, and suffocating gates. I've been coming here for six years, and I still succumb to skin-tightening, throat-burning, lead-in-my-stomach guilt every time I see it.

Lorne killed one man the night Conor was raped, and he was sentenced to ten years in this hellhole.

I've killed many. Premeditated. Coldblooded. Yet I haven't served a single day behind bars. If I have any regrets, it's that Lorne is locked in there instead of me.

"This isn't easy, is it?" She slips her hand from my leg and pushes the dress over her knees.

"Lorne's the strongest guy I know. If anyone can survive this place, it's him."

She nods slowly, staring at the guard tower. "I know he killed an innocent man, but it wasn't intentional. Ten years seems too long a punishment."

One day would've been too long, but Dalton Cassidy and Sheriff Fletcher made sure Lorne was put away long enough to drill on his land.

She looks down at her lap. "We just spent two hours together and didn't exchange a word."

"But we communicated more during that time than we have in the past nine days."

Her lips pinch and relax, curving into a small smile. "Maybe so."

"I knew I'd find it."

"What?"

"An agreeable bone in your body."

She huffs a laugh. "Let's go see your brother."

Even though Lorne isn't really my brother, I consider him one. This isn't something I told her, and she hasn't witnessed my interactions with him. Yet she's paid close enough attention to *me* to understand how I feel. It engenders a tenderness for her I've never felt for anyone outside my family.

For the next hour, she sits quietly beside me as I catch up with Lorne. These visits never give me a sense of wholeness or reunion. We're separated by a metal table. Our conversations are monitored and surrounded by chattering, often tearful families. But I can read a lot in his eyes, and today they seem darker than ever.

Incarceration hasn't just paled his complexion and toughened his appearance. It's slowly sucking away his spirit, leaving behind a ghost of the boy I grew up with.

He's aged faster and harder than Jake and me. Only a year older, he scowls more, speaks less, and moves in a cagey, shielded manner that concerns me. No matter how many times I ask about his life within these walls, he refuses to discuss it. He won't even hint at his misery. But I know. I know that whatever is happening to him in here has jaded him, reshaped him, and I fucking hate it.

"You're pretty." He stares at Maybe, his expression as unreadable as his tone. "Way too pretty for this guy."

"Thank you, but why would you assume...?" Sitting a foot away, she turns to me. "Did you tell him we were together?"

I look at Lorne and announce, "We're together."

"No, we're not." She pushes her shoulders back.

"I told him about our deal."

"All deals aside..." Lorne rests an elbow on the table. "The tension between the two of you is stifling."

She shifts in the chair and averts her eyes. I bet her panties are wet and her mind's sprinting through the possibilities that await her during the drive home.

I wish I had a better feel on Lorne's thoughts. He's been in here since he was eighteen, without his family, without the ranch, without sex. On the outside, he appears put together. If he's dealing with internal shit like I suspect he is, he'd never show it.

"Why are you here?" He levels her with a look that spurs her to sit taller.

"Jarret invited me."

"Jarret isn't the kind of man who's led around by his dick."

I curl my fingers against my lips, concealing a grin. Lorne has the ability to wield a glare like a hammer, and he's wearing that glare now to intimidate her. But she's already nervous, given the twist of her fingers in her hair.

"I know." She forces her hands onto her lap.

She also knows I'm not the only one who will come after her if she fucks with my family. Lorne wasn't a forgiving guy before prison. Now, he's downright frightening.

"We have more in common than you think." She lifts her chin, her soft blue eyes clashing with Lorne's hard green.

I shoot her a curious glance as Lorne growls, "I seriously doubt that."

I'm with Lorne. They're nothing alike.

"What do you mean by that?" I ask.

She gives me a sad smile and looks away. "I'll tell you someday."

Damn her fucking secrets.

Lorne meets my eyes, silently reprimanding. *Get control of this.*

I stare right back. *I'm working on it.*

We slip into conversations about the ranch, and too soon, the hour is over. I hug him as tightly as possible and force myself to let go. I force my boots out of the room, out of the prison, and into the truck with Maybe at my side.

She sits in the middle without being asked. "There's some good breeding on Julep Ranch, and I'm not referring to the horses."

I pull out of the parking lot and toss her an inquisitive glance.

"You all are insanely good-looking," she says. "Lorne's no exception. He's also intimidating. And kind of scary."

"Prison will do that to a person."

"I'm sorry."

"Me, too." I slide a hand across her thigh for no other reason than to be close to her warm softness.

"I can't do this." Her fingers curl around mine instinctively, as if her body is on a different trajectory than her mind.

Can't do what? Hold hands? Let me between her legs? Be in a relationship? I don't ask, because I want all those things and refuse to settle for anything less.

"That's okay." I pull out my phone and select a song. "I'll convince you that you can."

"That's what I'm afraid of." She cocks her head, listening to the lyrics of *From The Ground Up* by Dan + Shay. Then she laughs. "I never would've pegged you for a romantic."

"I don't know how this got in my playlist."

"I just watched you choose this song."

"And?"

"I like it." She slips deeper into the seat and rests a hand on my lap.

This time, she doesn't stop my fingers from sliding along her thighs, molding, rubbing, and easing up her dress. She whimpers as I stroke higher, deeper into the crease of her leg, teasing the edge of her panties.

Her knees part, just enough to welcome me. But I don't need the encouragement. I'm set on a course to take this slow, to savor the quivers in her thighs and the shallow gulps of her breaths. With a steady hand on the wheel, I use the other to cup her mound and finger her through the material until she becomes damp to the touch.

Halfway through the drive, I still haven't breached the barrier of her panties.

"You're cruel." She moans, even as her muscles tighten, ready to fight me.

"You're not the only one suffering, darlin'."

I've swelled so tightly and painfully against the

zipper I'm distracted by the urge to adjust. But I only have two hands.

"We should stop this." She rocks against my touch, such a beautiful contradiction.

I hook a finger inside the crotch of her panties. "Open wider."

"Jarret."

"Let me in."

"If I don't?"

Stallions are easier to break than her resolve, but I'm undeterred. "You will."

I grip her thigh and force her to spread. She clenches, and I pull, digging in my fingers with a snarl.

"Don't growl at me." She shoves at my hand. "And keep your eyes on the road. You're going to cause an accident."

I jerk the wheel to the side, roll onto the shoulder, and slam the truck into park. Then I release my seatbelt and turn to her.

She stiffens, breathless, trembling. "What are you—?"

I fist her hair and capture her mouth, ravaging her lips with a need that's bigger than my skin. It scratches and expands inside me, trying to get out, to get to her, to devour her whole.

Pulling her leg across my lap, I yank at the soaked satin that's tormented me since we left Sandbank. Removing it requires coordination and patience in this position, neither of which I have at the moment. So I slide my fingers past the obstacle and slip one inside her.

She moans against my tongue, and I groan with her. The warm, tight channel around my touch clenches so hard I stop breathing.

"Oh, God." She rakes her hands through my hair, knocking off the hat. "Please, Jarret."

I add a second finger, and she gasps. I thrust deeper, and she chases my kiss with fire, biting and sucking with greedy pulls of her lips.

"This is what you needed." I rub my tongue against hers, controlling the rhythm and pressure as I stroke the hot depths of her pussy. "You needed my fingers in your cunt, destroying it, owning it, you dirty, filthy girl."

"No, I'm… I can't." She rears back her head and drags in a breath.

"If I hear *can't* one more time—"

She attacks my mouth, licking and feasting and grinding against my hand.

Finally. Fucking finally, I have her. Wild and molten, wet and volatile, her fight is beautiful, but her surrender is goddamn exquisite. I consume it with everything inside me, feeding on it and fueling a desire that has never felt this out of control.

Heat gathers at the base of my spine. Blood surges along my shaft. My balls tighten. My tongue plunders, and I sense the rise of orgasm from the friction of grinding against the leg across my lap.

I'm humping her like a damn dog.

I need to pull back, just enough to drive us home. But I'm not stopping. I have no intention of snuffing out this inferno now that it's roaring.

Holding onto her leg, I break the kiss, remove my fingers from her wet heat, and slowly draw them into my mouth as she watches, panting and dazed.

She tastes like sweet innocence and wild beauty. Blond curls tangle around her flush cheeks and heaving chest, her body loose and primed, trembling for release.

We have time.

I return the hat to my head, straighten behind the wheel, and pull back onto the road.

"That's it?" Anger and hurt spark in her eyes.

"Not even close." I grip tight to her leg, preventing her from pulling away. Then I return my hand to her pussy.

The last hour of the drive is pure torture. With my fingers curling inside her, I bring her to the edge repeatedly. She pleads and writhes. My body throbs and protests the eternal wait.

We both need relief, but I'm determined to make it home, where I can take my time, tease her kinkiest desires to the forefront, and introduce her to the dark edges of pleasure.

When the night ends, there will be no distinctions between her cravings and my needs. She said we want different things, but she's wrong.

We want this, *us*, with matching intensity, and tonight, I'll prove it to her.

Clearing my head of filthy, thrusting, flogging thoughts, I'm left with an earth-shattering revelation.

I don't care about her secrets. I don't even care about the sex. Not in the way I care about *her*.

She isn't some gold-digging, narcissistic, faceless woman seducing her way into my bed. She's everything I've been waiting for and nothing like I expected.

I made a deal with her that I have no intention of honoring.

Because I can't fathom going back to a life without her. The notion is so bleak and horrifying it fills me with desperate rage.

I will *never* let her go.

By the time Jarret parks the truck at Julep Ranch, I'm in a panting, shaking frenzy of yes and no, stop and go, can't and will and *holy fuck*.

He didn't just spend four hours touching me. He spent four hours telling me *with just his hands* that he loves the texture of my skin, prefers the spot where my inner thigh meets my groin, and intends to control when, where, and how I come.

He can sense my approaching orgasm even when I stifle the signs. He has enough restraint to pull back, no matter how hard that tent in his jeans strains his zipper. The man has the power to reduce my body to ravenous starvation and rebuild me into whatever he desires—all while operating a vehicle at high speeds.

It's terrifying.

I've never felt so desperate, vulnerable, reckless, and *alive*.

I need to get a grip on this unraveling, out-of-control free fall. At the same time, I yearn for it. I crave everything he's promising to the point of self-ruination.

How can I pass this up? A journey in sexual discovery. A door that opens to a world of real-life fantasy. An aggressive, attentive, trustworthy man who knows what he's doing. He offers all this with a determination that shakes the ground beneath my feet.

It's just... The timing. I had a life, *a good life*, and it vanished before I realized what was happening. I can't move on until I understand why.

Jarret Holsten holds the key to that. I so badly want to explain my circumstances and tell him everything, but if I do, I'll never find the answers I'm looking for. I'll never know the full story.

Because he's involved, in a precarious, illegal way. All evidence leads to his doorstep, and my meeting with his father confirmed it.

People are missing. I don't know if they made themselves disappear to escape their crimes, if they were threatened and forced to flee the country, or if something much worse befell them.

I can't fathom Jarret or Jake participating in that *something worse*, but their father would. Are they loyal to John Holsten? Enough to protect his crimes?

I've asked Jarret to explain his relationship with his father, as well as the disappearances of his father's business partners, but he refuses. If I tell him what I know or why I'm here, he won't just refuse to give me answers. He'll kick me out of his life faster than he roped me into it.

"You're thinking too much." He turns off the engine and releases our seat belts.

The deafening clicks of the metal latches should instill a sense of freedom. Freedom from the confines of the truck, the overwhelming press of his masculinity, and the probing examination of his eyes.

Except an entire evening with him awaits.

Shadows lengthen across the field, chasing the sun to sleep beneath the horizon. But sleep isn't on Jarret's mind. Not with that smoldering look on his face.

I clutch the mess of curls around my chest, restlessly twisting the strands into knots. "I don't feel well."

It's not a lie. I'm sick to my stomach with fear, but not for the reasons I should be. I should be worrying about the secrets he's hiding and things he's done. Would he make me vanish like the others? What if he considers me such a threat he snaps my neck and dumps my body?

He won't.

I trust him to protect me from himself and anyone else involved in his corruption. I trust him to not hurt me in an irreparable way, and *that's* what scares me.

Instead of running for my life, I'm compelled to stay, to seize the attraction between us with both hands and hold it close. I want to foster it and mold it into something deeper, stronger, and longer-lasting than a make-out session in a pickup truck.

I want this man at a level that disregards logic, self-preservation, and mental health.

"You need to eat." He opens the door and unfolds his powerful body from the truck. "And Maybe..." He grips my hand and helps me out. "Silence that noise in your head."

"I get the feeling everything you do is a ploy to distract me." I follow him into the house, my fingers held prisoner in the unbending shackle of his.

Without comment, he leads me into the kitchen and points to a chair at the table.

I sit as he ambles toward the fridge. The tight fit of denim across his ass, the thick muscles flexing along either side of his spine, the thin shirt that cleaves to his massive torso and reveals every chiseled dip and indention beneath—all of it holds me in a trance.

There's something so intrinsic and captivating

about the way he moves. I can actually see his strength flowing beneath all that golden skin. Even the taut cords in his neck add to his appeal as he ducks his head into the fridge and removes a plate of hamburger patties. If he would only lift his shirt so I can properly ogle his tapered waist and sculpted abs.

To think, I slept against all that mouthwatering virility last night. God help me, I want more. More closeness. More kissing. More nights.

There I am again. *Distracted.*

I'm no closer to finding answers than I was nine days ago. He's definitely distracting me, probably on purpose, and I'm letting him. Because he's holding this shiny, rare gift in front of me, this opportunity to experience the grittier side of pleasure at the hands of someone who's mastered the art of delivering it.

It's risky. I'm already losing myself in this gorgeous, overbearing, mysterious man. Yet I feel the justification of it down to the kernel of my soul. If I don't explore this, the chance will slip away and I'll never know if it was a risk worth taking.

When dinner is ready, Jake and Conor join us. As the three of them inhale burgers and oven-baked French fries, I eat the spinach salad Jarret prepared for me with beets and walnuts.

Between hurried bites, they manage a conversation about today's visit at the prison and their concerns for Lorne's mental wellbeing.

I suspect Lorne is the glue that holds them shoulder to shoulder, moving forward as one. He's not physically here, but he's always in their thoughts. The depth in which they miss him blackens their voices, etches their faces, and stiffens the air. But they endure this ache together and seem stronger as a result.

As an outsider, I'm content to listen without speaking. That said, I feel a twinge of envy for the bond they share. They know one another so well they don't need words. Instead, they rely on the familiarity of body language and eye contact to transmit the colors of their thoughts.

I find myself collecting the nuances of their expressions and mannerisms to piece together what they're not saying. In the gloom of Lorne's absence, one would expect sadness to radiate off them. It's there, but they also project feelings of hope, anticipation, and unbreakable unity. The energy between them is galvanizing.

After dinner, I clear the table and decline Conor's offer to help me. She and Jake already put in a long day in the fields, and I want to earn my keep, not leech off their generosity.

They head to their room, and I stand at the sink, finishing up the dishes, lost in thought.

A few minutes later, I sense him. Footsteps creaking the floorboards, heat at my back, breath against my neck, he closes in and traps me between the sink and the force of his presence.

"Place your hands on the counter." The rumbling authority in his voice shivers through me, spurring me to obey.

When I do, a satisfied sound reverberates through him. He dips his head and puts his mouth against my neck, his lips gliding along my prickling skin, heating, teasing, tasting. My knees tremble, and he grips my waist, guiding my backside to his groin and letting me feel the swell of his hunger.

I drop my head back with a sigh as his tongue travels along my throat. Every lick is a brand of intent, every groan an assertion of his need. My mind gives way to instinct and gluttony, fanning flames that have less to do with sex and more to do with my longing for a connection with him.

The hands on my waist shift, caressing my

hipbones through the dress. They inch higher, over my stomach, my ribs, and pause to cup my braless breasts.

I fill his palms just barely. The rest of me feels so small and fragile in the hulking embrace of his body against my back. He's easily twice my size, a head taller, and packed with bulging hardness... *everywhere.*

He continues to nibble on my neck, kissing and biting as his fingers pluck my nipples into tight buds. Every point of contact—his mouth, hands, chest, erection—ignites deep, throbbing waves of heat between my legs.

I've never been this quick to arouse. With previous lovers, I had a pre-heat setting that required coaxing and touching before sensation stirred below my waist. Even then, I never felt this hot and sexual.

Jarret only needs to look at me and my entire body catches fire.

His mouth traces my neck with so much passion and reverence I wouldn't remain upright without the support of his arms. Cupping a breast in one hand, he lowers the other between my thighs, unerringly locating my clit with the roll of a finger.

I can't catch my breath or form words, but I don't care. Swaddled in a haze of skin and sultry energy, I don't want him to let go or slow down.

His assertive mouth moves along my bare shoulder, his teeth grazing and nipping. "If I take you to the bedroom, I'm going to fuck you."

I tense. I don't mean to, but my brain is a damn cockblock, sounding alarms and firing off protests. I try to relax, but he senses my reluctance and pulls back.

Disappointment tightens my face, which is stupid. I shouldn't be flirting with this man or even with the idea of him, no matter how much I justify it.

I'm keeping a secret from him, and it's going to destroy us.

"Maybe." He turns me to face him and lifts my

chin with a finger. "I'm going to play with you tonight, and I need you to trust me."

"That's the problem, isn't it? We don't trust each other."

"You trust me with this." He leans in and brushes his mouth against mine. "And this." He lowers a hand to my thigh and slides it upward, beneath the dress, and strokes the crotch of my panties.

My heart hums, and I sink my teeth into my lip, drawing his eyes to it. The space between us is so alive with electricity I struggle to breathe through the static. It charges with clawing potential, uncertainty, excitement, and guilt.

My guilt.

"I'm keeping something from you." My chest heaves with an erratic breath. "Something personal."

"I know." He removes his hat and sets it on the counter.

My throat closes.

"Are you ready to tell me what it is?" His gaze slips to my mouth.

"No."

"Then we'll focus on the things you *are* ready for." He twines our fingers together and guides me out of the kitchen, out of the house, and into the darkness.

With his palm pressed against mine, my attention hones in on the scar he shares with his family.

"All four of you have the same cut on your hand." I noticed Lorne's during the visit today. "Will you tell me about it?"

"It's an oath we made as kids." Glancing at me sidelong, he doesn't slow his gait. "*Something personal.*"

The message in his tone is clear. He won't share that story until I share mine.

"Where are we going?" I navigate the tall grass in borrowed boots, stumbling to keep up with his strides.

"We're going for a ride." His deep, melodic voice resounds with double-meaning.

My lower body quickens with desire, at odds with the panic crashing through my veins. He said he would play with me, and I can guess what that entails.

I can also end it if he crosses the line.

The question is where do I draw that line? I'm not sure, which is why I'm following him, driven by curiosity and foolishness.

He leads me into the stable and saddles up his horse.

Twenty minutes later, I sit behind him, arms hooked tight around his rock-hard stomach as he steers Ginny deep into the night.

Fireflies blink across the pasture, the only light in the starless, moonless landscape. It's so dark and muggy I feel as though I've slipped through the seam of an unknown world, with a rugged, broad-shouldered, unpredictable outlaw as my only companion.

Blood pumps from the trepidation in my heart as safety descends farther behind me. I look back, the silhouette of the stable slowly shrinking toward oblivion.

I face forward, where blackness and uncertainty reign, beyond the deep breaths and masculine scent of the man carrying me toward a nebulous future, with only one thing on my mind.

Him.

In the most intimate way possible.

A lightning storm amasses in my stomach as Jarret lowers me to the ground and ties Ginny to a fence post. I don't know what he expects from me or how far I'll go, but it's too late to turn back. Not that I want to.

But I *should* want to. I should be running hard and far away.

What am I doing?

The lowing of cattle alerts me of their proximity, but I can't see them in the darkness. Shadows billow over the fields in every direction, creating a backdrop for the nocturnal opera of croaking and twittering creatures.

"Why are we here?" I turn toward the dark towering mountain at my side.

Nightfall shrouds his eyes, but I feel them pressing and probing so intensely the ground threatens to slope away from my feet.

"I want you comfortable." His hand drifts to my hair and pulls, angling my head back. "But not too comfortable."

I shiver.

"It's dark enough to give you a sense of modesty." He twists me toward the wooden fence and guides my hands to the railing. "The absence of light will also serve as a blindfold, forcing you to concentrate on sound and sensation. There are no doors out here, nothing to hide behind. Nowhere to run. It's just you and me and—"

"The cows."

"—the sound of my voice." He squeezes my hands against the wooden rail. "Don't move."

His footsteps amble toward Ginny. Leather creaks, followed by the rustle and scratch of whatever he removes from the saddle bag.

I remain where he put me because I'm addicted to this, to the way he makes my pulse shake and my mind dance. It's scary and thrilling and everything in between.

I'm not the kind of woman who takes orders, but whatever this is soothes the deepest parts of me, the parts that long for romantic adventure without the burden of decision.

Of course, it was my choice to come here, and it's my choice to keep going. But he's constructed an illusion around me, one that has the ability to trick my brain into believing I'm confined by his will and not responsible for my actions. It's the illusion that enraptures me. *He* enraptures me.

He returns to my position at the fence and sets a few things on the ground. My heartbeat tumbles into a pounding flurry, suspicious and eager, turbulent and exhilarated.

"Arms up." He clutches the hem of the dress at my knees and gathers the material, slowly sliding it to my thighs.

My muscles quiver, and my stomach coils. I knew my clothes would come off, but knowing isn't the same as standing in the presence of a potent, sexually-charged man who's intent on stripping me bare in every way.

I ache to do this. For me, not for him. But I can't

contain my nerves. "If I tell you to stop—"

"I'll stop and take you back to the house."

"And you'll make me leave the ranch."

"That was the deal."

Disappointment hitches my chest, but I agreed to this deal on day one. I gambled my need for answers on the outcome of a kinky game.

Getting answers, however, isn't the only thing at stake now. If I tell him to stop, I'll lose access to him and this captivating thing between us.

Can I call it a relationship? Is there even a name for the feelings I harbor for him? I like him, but I don't trust him. I want him, but I'm terrified of him. He frustrates me, arouses me, captivates me, and fills me with equal parts dread and joy, vulnerability and fire, doubt and sin. There isn't another person on the planet who affects me like this.

"Would it be hard for you to make me leave?" I despise the insecure crack in my voice.

"It would destroy me." He lifts the dress to my ribs, exposing my lower body to the evening heat. "I won't let it go that far."

Relief surges, girding me with courage. I raise my arms.

He yanks the dress over my head, leaving me braless and clad in only panties. My back is to him. It's pitch black outside, but I feel more naked than I ever have as his hands roam over me. I can't stop trembling like a damn virgin.

"Christ, you're beautiful." His exhale stirs my hair and trickles a chill down my spine.

"You can't see me."

"I feel you." His hands follow the lines of my collarbones and around the outer swells of my breasts. "You're exquisitely shaped. Every curve." He caresses the dip of my waist. "Every bend and toned line." He palms my backside and hooks his thumbs under the waistband of my panties. "Every soft, sexy inch of you begs to be eaten."

He slides that last scrap of fabric down my legs, crouching to work it past the boots. Then he steps back and groans.

I glance over my shoulder. Is he holding my panties to his nose?

"Oh my God." My pulse lurches. My cheeks flush, and a rush of heat spirals between my legs.

He stuffs the satin into his pocket and grabs something from the ground. Then he slings himself over the fence and approaches me from the other side.

The bundle of rope in his hand quickens my breath, but he doesn't give me time to think. His arm hooks around my back. His head lowers, and his hot mouth seals over my nipple.

I squirm against him, overcome by the stimulation. His arm holds me in place, and his teeth dig in, replacing the suck of his lips with deliciously harsh bites. I stab my hands into his hair, yanking at the strands as he abuses my breast with savage expertise.

He drags me closer, feasting. I curl my fingers against his scalp, scratching. The wooden railing rubs against my stomach, separating us, preventing us from climbing into each other.

He releases me, and blood rushes to my nipple, throbbing, aching. God, I need more.

"Hands on the fence." The gruffness in his voice summons images of hard, wet fucking.

My body throbs for exactly that as my mind panics. *I can't. I shouldn't. Don't do it!*

I grip the railing, boots braced apart, knees locked, and nipples erect. I've never felt so wanton and reckless.

He ties my wrists down with practiced efficiency, looping and knotting in swift movements.

"You've done this a lot." I search the shadows of his gorgeous face.

Without responding, he drops the excess rope and hops the fence to return to my side.

"How many times?" My stomach hardens. "How many women?"

"I've been sexually active since I was sixteen." He crowds my back and feathers his fingers up the fronts of my thighs.

My skin prickles beneath his touch. "Do you have regular lovers? Friends with benefits?"

He makes a sound of irritation. "No."

"You always restrain them?"

"Yes." His fingers bite into my upper thighs.

He's twenty-four, so that's... I close my eyes. Eight years. Different women every week. I don't need to do the math to know he's a manwhore.

"I'm just a number." I twist my neck to glower at him. "One of hundreds, I'm guessing."

His heat vanishes from my back, the only warning he gives me before slamming a palm against my bare bottom. The impact lifts me onto my toes, and I gulp as the sting deepens, spreading fire through tissue and muscle.

"You will *not* judge me for enjoying sex with willing women." His voice is unruffled velvet as he strikes me again.

"No, I'm—"

He spanks my other cheek and smooths his hand over the hurt. "Nor will you cheapen what's happening here."

I tighten my fingers around the railing, swaying against the burning pleasure in my backside. Every swipe of his palm reignites the throbbing heat. I feel it everywhere—in the gust of my breaths, the tingling in my muscles, and the molten spasms between my legs.

I want him to hit me again before the pulsing ache fades. At the same time, I don't want him to stop caressing my hot, sore flesh.

I'm losing my mind.

"What's happening here?" I hope he can explain it, because I'm at a loss.

"Something different." He lowers his hand, depriving me of his touch.

"Different?" Anger leaks into my voice. "I saw you with McKenna. You were rough with her. You restrained her. How is this different?"

He grips my jaw and wrenches my neck around, imprisoning my gaze in the black cage of his.

"I fucked them." He shifts closer to my side, fingers pressing against bone as he glares into my soul. "They took from me. I took from them. When it was finished, I walked away."

I've spent nine nights with him, and he hasn't fucked me. I've slept beside him when no one else has. He gives me more than he takes, and he isn't bored yet.

My lungs expand. *This is different.*

"I can't walk away from this." His fingers loosen, gliding across my cheek and into my hair. "Can't walk away from *you.*"

"Same." A knot forms in my throat.

He ducks under my restrained arm and slides up the front of my nude body. The sheer size of him makes the space between me and the fence terribly cramped. But he fits, his chest pressed against mine, his hands meandering along every part of me he can reach, and his mouth...

The instant our lips connect, my back arches and my insides crackle and fizz. His fingers slip between my legs, and my knees buckle. One long digit curls inside me, and my breath sprints away.

"Goddamn, you're wet." His tongue brushes against mine, and he lifts his hand. "The spanking did this." He trails a sticky finger across my mouth.

"You did that." I close my lips around his touch, tasting the tang of my arousal.

"You're authentic, Maybe. So fucking real and dirty and stunning from the inside out. Jesus, look at you." He clutches my shoulders and stares down the length of my naked body. "You're everything I never dared to hope for."

His words have the power to slay me. The kiss that follows is a filthy, unhinged, catastrophic confirmation that I will never be able to walk away from him. Not if I want to remain whole.

Time stands still as he lavishes me with the seductive pleasure of his tongue and hands until no oxygen remains in the atmosphere. Then he teases that skillful mouth down my neck, my chest, my stomach, covering every inch of skin with licking, sucking kisses as he fingers my pussy.

I shiver and moan and fall apart beneath his aggressive attention. My brain fries. My blood sings, and I wring my wrists in the rope, trying to reach him.

"I want to touch you." I shudder against the diabolical stroke of the fingers inside me.

"Not yet." His voice is gravel and smoke.

"Take off your shirt."

"Stop talking." He kicks my boots apart, forcing me into a wide stance.

I bite his lip. "Don't be a dick."

"If you don't shut up, I'll gag you with my dick." He lowers his knees to the ground between my feet and clasps my hips.

"If you're going to threaten me, make it—"

He buries his face in my pussy, stealing my voice and deleting my thoughts.

A deep groan vibrates against my clit, and his tongue joins in, flicking and lashing. He kisses my sex the way he kisses my mouth—deep and penetrating, hot and vicious, open jaw, lapping tongue, bruising lips, no holding back.

No one has ever eaten me with such obsessive, crazed enthusiasm, and damn if he doesn't know the right spot, the exact pressure, the precise rhythm. It's a perfect storm of talent and passion, executed by the sexiest, most dominating man I've ever met.

Sparks of an impending orgasm flicker to life, building and strengthening in my core. My nerve endings multiply, spread out, and strain toward his mouth, wired and greedy.

Just as I reach that blissful crest, he pulls back.

"No." I shamelessly arch toward his face, trembling and desperate.

He spanks me again, not as hard as before, but the bite he inflicts on my hipbone tears a scream from my throat. His teeth break skin, and holy shit, that hurts. I jerk away and glance at the wound. No blood.

"You left a mark!" I gape at him.

"Exactly." He ducks around my leg and rises to his full height behind me. "By the end of the night, you'll be covered in my marks."

"Unless I say stop."

"You won't." He sinks his teeth into the tender part of my shoulder.

My moan shudders through the darkness, laced in pain and reedy with pleasure.

"Please, Jarret." I crane my neck, unable to capture his gaze behind me. "I was seconds from coming."

"I know."

His hand returns to my drenched heat, stroking and tormenting as the other lifts to my chest, tweaking my nipples with ungodly pinches.

He's a torrent of brutal force and sensual precision, fluctuating between violent bites and gentle kisses, rough hands and expert caresses. His passion is explosive, his touches methodical. Nothing about him is tame.

While I'm uncertain about my limitations, he seems to be fully aware of them, never pushing me too far and always easing back when pain overrides enjoyment. But there's a wildness about him, a feral wolf trapped beneath his skin, snarling and clawing to escape. Just when I think he can no longer contain it, he sweetly tucks a curl behind my ear or peppers a tender trail of kisses along my jaw.

"I want you," he murmurs against my lips. "I've never wanted anyone or anything this much. What are you doing to me?"

My gasps deepen, stretching my ribs. If he shoves his cock inside me right now, I won't stop him.

That scares the crap out of me. I need to untangle my feelings, compartmentalize, and separate. I need to remember why I'm here.

How do I do that when it's no longer clear what I want? I need the truth about my past. I need Jarret in my future. Which do I need more?

Because I can't have both.

The sky lights up in the distance, a bolt of white ripping the utter blackness like paper. A moment later, thunder peals.

I shiver against the electricity in the air, and the tiny hairs on my arms bristle beneath the static.

"Have you ever watched a summer storm roll across a field?" He swirls his tongue along my neck, short-circuiting my thoughts.

"No."

"Keep your eyes on the horizon."

He steps back as another flash of lightning cleaves the night. Thunder booms, and a second later, a sharp crack slams against my backside.

A guttural scream bursts from my throat, and I bow beneath the burn.

That's not his hand.

Before I can look behind me, another strike comes. Then more and more, one on top of the other in rapid succession.

I didn't see him pack the riding crop, but the deep stings laddering down my thighs could only be from the whip of a leather tongue.

It's an acute pain, barbed and merciless. Each whack leaves behind the sensation of branding, one that awakens me emotionally, mentally. The torment is so horribly and wonderfully strange I don't know whether to fight it or sink into it.

Brilliant shocks of white fork across the graphite sky, and the rumble of thunder arrives sooner, closer, announcing the storm's approach. He seems to be timing his hits with the crackle of lightning, flogging my butt and legs in sync with the jagged strobes of light.

This can't be safe. We're standing in the middle of a pasture, like targets begging to be struck. But the danger heightens the thrill. I'm naked and restrained to a fence, staring down an imminent tempest as another violent storm slams against my back.

Each searing lash of leather magnifies the soreness of its predecessor. But beneath the flames of discomfort lies a tingling, all-consuming realization.

I love this.

The restraints on my wrists, the futility of struggle, the stabbing pain, and Jarret's unwavering attention on my body—all of it enables me to connect to my sexual self in a way I've never connected during actual sex.

It's like I'm crossing a bridge between what I've experienced and what I've only dared to fantasize about.

Desires are dangerous, and I've suppressed so many in my life, never permitting myself to act on submissive tendencies. I feared my cravings would make me needy and weak and turn me into a doormat. As a result, I became sexually anorexic and lost my appetite for pleasure. When I engaged in sex, all I felt in my body was panic.

I've never even had an orgasm with a man.

But I hoped. I still hope. With the right person, I know I can give him total control over my body.

Like now.

Jarret broke through my misgivings. He's the only one who has ever restrained me, spanked me, and made me so damn aroused I can't think straight. When I'm with him, I actually feel like a sexual being, with none of the hesitation and disconnect I've experienced during conventional sex.

And his dick hasn't even left his pants.

Lightning crashes and breaks apart the inky night, reminiscent of what sex would be like with him. Stormy and powerful, combustible and dramatic, white-hot, perilous, and electrifying, with thundery flashes of radiance that burn into my retinas. Just thinking about it charges my pulse and floods my pussy with wetness.

Behind me, his breathing accelerates with each ruthless swing of the crop, the lashes growing faster, harder, until a strange illumination flickers across the field.

"Did you see that?" I hold still, straining my eyes through the dark.

"St. Elmo's Fire." He drops the crop, and his sweat-damp chest slides against my back. "Keep watching."

A few seconds later, an eerie glow dances through the pasture, accompanied by the bright white of electrical zig-zags high above. The lightning illuminates the meadow and the herd of horned cattle standing in the stillness.

"St. Elmo's Fire?" My mind trudges through the

sensations firing in my body. I can't focus with him all hard and hot against me.

"It's the discharge of electricity from the storm."

Spiky bolts endlessly protrude from the sky, sprinkling an incandescence of light along the silhouettes of horns.

"Why is it glowing on the tips of the bull's horns?"

"They're steers." He nuzzles my neck. "When the electrical field strength reaches a high level of volts, it gravitates to pointed objects, like the long horns."

"Does it hurt them?"

"No." He glides talented fingers around my breast. "They probably feel the static."

"I've never seen anything like it."

"Me, neither." His lips feather down my neck, making me moan. "Nothing compares to you."

He shoves a hand between my legs and sinks his fingers inside. The roar of thunder clashes with the panting sounds of his groans. I melt against him, gasping as his clothes rub against my sore backside.

My orgasm has been building since the drive to the prison. With the thrust of his fingers and the raid of his lips on my neck, I'm seconds from detonation.

"Don't come." He grazes his teeth, followed by the ravishing slide of his tongue.

"Jarret." I moan. "I have to. It's too much."

"Not until it rains. When you feel the first drop, you can let go."

My gaze darts to the dark canvas of sky as jolts of light flash like a camera. He continues to fuck me with his hand, curling those sinful fingers along my inner muscles as I shake and wheeze uncontrollably.

His other hand fondles my chest, kneading and cupping my breasts. "I fucking love your tits."

"I need to come." I quake with the effort to hold it back, but I'm falling fast. "Oh God, Jarret. I'm right there."

"Wait." He rolls his tongue around my earlobe. "Just a few more seconds." His thumb finds my clit, thrumming and torturing. "Three... Two..."

"Jarret, I need..." Everything inside me tightens and squeezes.

"One."

The sky opens to a deluge of rain, and I come. Fucking hell, I come violently, wildly, screaming and writhing, throbbing and panting. My vision blackens. My legs give out, and my insides shatter into a million fiery sparks.

He holds me up, grinding his erection against my welted flesh as I choke and laugh beneath great sheets of rain.

"Holy fuck." I tilt my face to the sky, relishing the cool shower on my heated cheeks.

"My thoughts exactly." He removes his hand, slowly scraping his fingers through the trimmed hair on my mound. "You can't be real."

"Untie me and I'll prove I am."

I might be the only one warring between right and wrong, but in this moment, wrong is winning. Against all reasoning, I need to see this through.

He unleashed something inside me, something demanding and overwhelming, and he's the only one who can satisfy it.

"We need to get to shelter." He moves to the rope and loosens the knots, peering through the drenched strands of hair dripping across his brow.

Good lord, he's gorgeous. The surrounding darkness writhes around him, clinging to his menacing edges, making him appear bigger, badder, more threatening. He's a shadowy, lethal pulse of energy and allure.

The instant the restraints fall away, I attack him. Arms and legs around his formidable frame, I feed on his lips with a fury.

It's exactly what McKenna did the night I watched through the window, but this is different. He doesn't just stand there. He rivals my frenzy and competes with my urgency, battling my teeth and fingernails with fangs and claws.

Hoisting me up his chest, he stumbles backward through the downpour and dominates the kiss with firm, aggressive lips. "There's a barn."

"Where?" I reach between us, tackling his belt buckle.

"Quarter mile." He groans against my mouth, fingers digging against my backside, in my hair, tongue colliding and wrestling with mine.

I manage to release the belt, then his zipper. The denim is stiff, sopping wet, and unmanageable, but I'm too far gone to let that stop me. I wedge my fingers beneath the waistband of his briefs and slide through his patch of short hair. So close...

"If you touch my cock," he growls, "we won't make it to that barn."

We're soaked to the bone, surrounded by lightning bolts and endless grass, muffled by thunderclaps, and I don't care about any of it.

I shove my hand in deeper and grip the thick length of him.

"Ahhhh, Maybe!" His head falls back, and he thrusts his hips, stroking himself in the clench of my fingers.

His mouth returns to mine, hungrier, harder, all control gone. The world spins and lifts, and in the next breath, I'm on my back in a bed of watery grass with a rutting, grunting pillar of muscle and testosterone between my legs.

"I need you." He thrusts against me, grinding his zipper along my swollen flesh. "Fuck, I don't have a condom."

I have an IUD, but I don't want to shout over the rain about disease and sexual histories. Instead, I push against his shoulder, rolling him to his back.

Lying beneath me, he holds an arm over his eyes and squints through the downpour. I can't make out his expression in the dark, but I feel his need. It vibrates through him, shaking his limbs, tightening his fingers, and hijacking his breaths.

I wrangle his soaked t-shirt up and off and scoot down his body, splaying my hands across his magnificent chest. I ache to trace every indention along the cut of his abs, but I'll do that later when I can take my time.

When I reach his jeans, I yank and wrangle and grunt until his huge, swollen cock lurches free. Sweet mother, he's gloriously hung. The silhouette alone is intimidating as hell.

My hands go to it instinctively, fingers wrapping around the base and sliding up with ease, lubricated by the pouring rain.

His body bows and stiffens as I rub up and down his length.

"Goddamn, Maybe." His eyes squeeze shut, and his hands dig into the grass. "Feels so fucking good."

The intensity and the volume of the storm increases, but it's no match for the tumultuous sight of Jarret Holsten on the cusp of climax. His hips kick and jerk. His hands claw the earth. Muscular twitches move his legs, and his boots drag through the grass, as if he's struggling to hold still, trying to rein himself in.

Then he snaps. His fist clamps around mine, and he arches his lower body, slamming into the sheath of our hands. Three thrusts later, he roars into the rain, shaking and pumping and spurting across his abs.

It's the most erotic sight I've ever witnessed.

I intended to suck him to completion but miscalculated how close he was. I lower my head anyway, attempting to catch a taste of him before the rain washes it away.

The flared head of his cock pulsates between my lips as I suck him clean. Then I move to the carved terrain of his stomach and swipe my tongue along the bumpy grooves, lapping at the salty blend of come and rainwater.

"Killing me." He groans and pets my hair, shifting restlessly beneath me. "Come here."

He hauls me up his chest and takes my mouth, plunging his tongue past my lips and licking my depths.

Having just found release, we should be sated. We should be slow and purposeful and thinking about getting out of the rain. But we're not. If anything, we're even more worked up, grunting wildly and grinding together.

His cock bounces and strains against my pussy, nudging forcibly, intending entry. How is he still hard?

He rolls me to my back and hovers over me, lips swollen, eyes black, and the heavy, engorged length of him hanging between us.

I no longer feel the pelt of rain, hear the clap of thunder, or see the violent illumination in the sky. The storm has suddenly passed.

But something else churns the air.

Anticipation.

Hunger.

Inevitability.

He grips his shaft and rubs the head along the seam of my pussy. "Let me."

"We don't have protection." A swallow sticks in my throat.

"I'm clean."

"But—"

"I want children with you."

"What?" My heart stops.

"You heard me."

"Children? Have you lost your mind?" I scramble out from beneath him.

"I don't mean right now." He stands and tucks himself into his jeans. "I just... With you, I want marriage and kids and all of it. You're it for me. Today, tomorrow, and all the tomorrows after."

I feel like my eyes are going to pop out of the sockets.

"Stop looking at me like that, dammit." He stabs a finger in my direction. "I'm fucking serious. If you're not ready, I'll wait. However long it takes."

"You'll wait for what?" I hug my bare chest, trembling and soaked.

"For you to accept this."

"I can't believe we're having this conversation." I thrust my arms out to the sides, agitated and baffled. "I'm naked, in the middle of nowhere, and you're discussing marriage and kids!"

He remains motionless, blanketed in shadows, but I feel him glaring.

"I assume women have proposed to you? Cozied up beside you in bed, drunk on sex and musing about having your babies? I bet you thought they were crazy."

"Now I know how they feel."

"When did you have this epiphany? Before or after I jerked you off?"

"Don't do that." Blackness bleeds from his expression, his anger palpable, shuddering the air around him. "I fucking know you feel this, too."

Where are my clothes? I spin around, searching the stillness, covered head to toe in grass and mud and rain and confusion.

"You belong to me." He prowls closer. "I'll piss a circle around you if I have to. I'll move mountains and rearrange my entire existence. I'm not giving you up."

"You don't even know me." I spot the fence behind

him. My dress won't be far from there.

"Bullshit!" He advances, forcing me backward. "I know how your mind works. You're brilliant and genuine. You're passionate about what you believe in, and you're not afraid to fight. I know your expressions, your smiles, the octaves of your laughter, the loneliness behind your frown. You store your soul in your eyes. You fidget with your hair when you're nervous, let the ice melt in your soda before you drink it, and you hate to be alone. You've never had a one-night-stand."

"How do you—?"

"I *know*, Maybe. I listen when you speak, and I hear everything you don't say." He closes in, his strides long and determined. "I know you wear high-heels to feel professional, but you're not a news reporter."

"What?" My face chills, and my stomach bottoms out.

"I know you're not here for a job."

I stagger back, my boots squelching with each wobbly footfall. I'm naked and exposed, bereft and lost in the consuming glow of Jarret's eyes. "If you believe I lied—"

"I don't care about that."

He moves with me, shifting direction when I try to dart past him, blocking me from sprinting toward my clothes. But nudity isn't my biggest vulnerability.

He knows.

I'm not sure exactly what he's figured out, but he knows I'm not here to write a news story.

Why is he circling me like it doesn't matter? Why hasn't he kicked me out? Why is he staring at me like he wants to...? I grip my hair at the roots. Marriage? Children? I can't even.

"I'm a fashion journalist." I stumble away from him, maintaining several feet between us. "I write about clothing and makeup."

"I want you, Maybelline."

My breath stutters at the sound of my name on his lips. This is too much, too big. I have to push him away. "I don't want kids. Not now. Maybe not ever."

"I still want you." His boots squish in the mud as he chases, his arms stiff at his sides, his chest glistening with residual rain.

"I can't marry you." I hug my ribs, shivering in a curtain of cold, drippy hair.

"I'll change your mind."

My mind isn't the problem. Marrying him is a tangled, complicated impossibility. "I've only known you for nine days."

"I fell for you the first night."

There goes my heart. He might as well reach into my chest and yank out the miserable thing. It's his now, and I don't know how to proceed. I can't breathe, can't string together words, can't make my legs work.

He's inside me, stretching out and rearranging and taking over. I taste him in my throat, feel him burning in my chest, and hear him whispering in my head. He's talking, real adult conversation, and his declaration rips me apart.

I replay every word, aching for the truth in his gaze. A truth that has nothing to do with the one that led me here.

"This changes everything." My chest heaves beneath the tight fold of my arms.

"In the best way."

"It won't end well."

"That's where you're wrong." He takes another step toward me, pausing a few feet away. "It won't end. Period."

"Think about what you're saying."

"I don't need to think." He pounds a fist against his chest. "I feel it."

I marvel at his conviction. I've heard the words throughout my life, the *I love yous* muttered after sex, written in birthday cards, and tossed over shoulders on the way out the door. But I've never *felt* them broadcasted from someone with such soul-deep confidence.

He hasn't even uttered the trite sentiment. Instead, he communicates it with a look, lets it spill from his eyes, his pores, his breaths so profoundly and candidly it decimates me.

Tears rise, unbidden. Fearful tears. Grateful tears. Greedy, hopeful, naive tears.

I turn away and run like a coward, fully aware he'll catch me. He knows the land. He has longer legs, and he's determined. So fucking persistent. I don't stand a chance.

But I run anyway, stealing time to gather my wits. I can fight him, but I won't win.

Because I don't want to.

The tread of boots sounds behind me, gaining speed. My blood pressure explodes. Adrenaline floods my system, and my scalp crawls with dread and anticipation. He's going to capture me, restrain me, force me to bend, and blow my fucking mind.

I pick up my pace, but it's too late. His arms hook around my waist and lift me from the ground.

"Put me down!" Heart pounding, I kick my legs and gnash my teeth. "You don't understand—"

"Forget the past." His chest flexes against my back, his lips brushing my ear. "Move forward."

"I am moving forward."

"With me. I'm right here." He turns me in his arms to face him and coils the fall of my hair around his fist, holding on. "We'll do this together. Nothing's stopping us."

Eventually, my past will catch up, and it *will* stop us.

But if I leave now, it'll hurt. Deeply. Permanently. It'll hurt if I leave a year from now. It'll hurt no matter what. There's no avoiding the inevitable devastation.

My heart already decided. It moved in with him, slept in his arms, and surrendered itself in the middle of a thunderstorm.

My damn heart forgot that love sucks, that it scars the soul, tramples trust, and hollows out the body.

Anger flares in my chest. If I'm going to fight him, shaking and naked while considering my demise, it's only fair that he does the same.

"Remove your clothes." I take advantage of his shock and wriggle out of his embrace.

He's hidden in darkness as I step back. But with my next step, his face becomes clearer, lighter. By the time I edge a few feet away, a silver glow illuminates his gorgeous features—thick fringes of lashes, straight nose, sharp jawline, and strong lips that neither smile nor scowl.

I tilt my head back and lock onto the bright white moon. It's now in full view beside a waning mass of charcoal clouds.

Returning to Jarret, I find him watching me. He hasn't moved.

Hands at his sides, fly hanging open, bare chest rising and falling in the moonlight, he doesn't hurry toward our fated moment. He draws it out, as if waiting to see who will break first.

The moon shines a spotlight on his vigilant gaze, exposing the flare of his nostrils, the rigid tension in his stance, and the flex of hands at his sides.

I'm thrilled I can see him now, but it means he can also see *me*. Every naked flaw, spindly limb, and unattractive blemish.

I bar an arm across my small breasts and lower a hand between my legs.

"Don't hide from me." He prowls closer.

"Your clothes." I circle him, staying out of his reach.

"I prefer to do this in a bed."

"Like you did with McKenna?" My insides clench. "I thought you'd be more adventurous than that."

His jaw goes hard.

"I've never had sex outside of a bedroom." I stand taller, wrapped up in my arms. "I've never had sex without love."

Something menacing shifts across his face. "How many lovers?"

"One in high school. One in college." I swallow. "One after."

I've fallen in love three times. Had sex with three men. Failed three relationships. I swore there wouldn't be a fourth, and here I am, sucking at life.

With a nod, he wrestles off a boot. Then the other, followed by his socks.

His hands fall to his fly as he straightens and meets my eyes. "Be sure, Maybe."

I shake my head. "I'm not saying yes."

He searches my expression, inspecting and evaluating. When his eyes land on mine, the corner of his mouth crooks up.

He knows what I want. The illusion. The belief that he's taking and forcing, that I have no choice or power.

In reality, the word *stop* is my power. It's also the only power that matters, and we both know it.

In a fluid slide of motion, he strips the last of his clothes and stands at his full height, feet braced apart, chin lowered, and eyes tilted upward and fastened on mine.

Sculpted and chiseled from his hair to his feet, he unabashedly grips the base of his impressive erection and strokes. "Lie on your back."

"No." I won't make this easy. "If you want boring—"

He launches, and I swerve. His hand catches a fistful of curls, and my heart rate skyrockets. I can't untangle his grip without losing strands, so I do the only thing I can. I spin toward him and grab *his* hair.

It's thick and wet and so damn silky, but I manage to clutch a good hunk and pull with all my might.

"Fuck!" He releases a pained laugh, and the hand in my hair lets go.

With a squeal, I take off. Blood pumping, boots sloshing, I race through the night with a veracious wolf on my trail.

He sprints after me, groaning loudly. "You should see the way your ass moves."

My buttocks flexes instinctively, and I cringe. And stumble.

He grabs my arm and swings me around. Midnight lashes mantle the golden flames in his eyes as they blaze down upon me. The predatory beauty and ruthlessness in that gaze seizes my breath and gallops my pulse.

I press a hand against his chest, his skin rippling beneath my palm. I suck in air, panting and filling my lungs with his scent. He smells like rain and electricity, earth and grass, and something else, a quintessential toughness that's unique only to him—sweat and lust and vibrating life. It's all there, emanating from his skin.

He's the strongest, most potent creature I've ever encountered, a powerhouse of force and drive who lures as much as he terrifies.

And he wants me.

I shove at his massive chest. He doesn't budge. I yank on my arm in his grasp, both of us still slippery from the rain. I slide free, staggering with surprise.

Then I'm running again, veering left and right while staying in the vicinity of our clothes.

He swipes at me and growls, lunges and grunts, playing with me, letting me slip away long enough to resume the chase.

Surrounded by a dark field of nothingness, with his muscular body backlit by the moon and his cock standing proud, he's wild and ferocious. A gorgeous, majestic beast on the hunt.

His hair hangs over his brow, sticking to wet lashes. Whiskers darken his jaw. Tension stiffens the razored edges of his face as he stalks me like an animal would its mate.

Possessive and hungry, he grabs at me, missing and losing patience. "When I catch you—"

"I know."

Saliva rushes over my tongue, and my pussy throbs for the hard, thick rock of flesh between his legs.

Any panic left in my body is vanquished by the burn of his eyes. I've worked him into a frantic, heaving, ravenous monster who's no longer interested in playing.

Muscles flicker in his rigid jaw. Veins bulge along his flexing forearms. His fists squeeze and release at his sides. Yet somehow, he still holds tight to his control.

I've never seen anything as beautiful or frightening as this man on the brink of losing it. He robs the air from my chest and replaces it with red-hot heat that spreads south, pulsing and raging between my legs.

A heartbeat later, his restraint breaks. He moves so fast I feel him before I see his arms cage my waist. My feet leave the ground. My legs hook around his hips, and my hands fall through the soft strands of his dark hair.

He hoists me higher, and his lips sweep across my chest, feasting with open-mouth kisses, brutal nips, and scorching licks.

I arch against him, moaning. "You're a breast man."

"I'm a Maybe man." His hand stabs into my hair, cupping the back of my head and wrenching it down to plunder my mouth in a commanding kiss.

Smashed together, we can't seem to squeeze close enough, hips grinding, fingers scratching, lips sealed and sucking.

I loop my arms around the sturdy column of his neck, tilting my head left and right to deepen the angle, rubbing my tongue against the whip of his, biting and groaning and coming undone.

Desire erupts from everywhere as our connection sizzles and sparks, growing hotter, wetter. Every cell in my body buzzes and burns for his.

I slide down his solid chest, running my hands all over him, his skin like silk over steel. With a whimper against his lips, I squirm along his body, trying to meld us together, rubbing and grinding.

His erection prods against my aching center, his fingers digging into my backside. I could slam myself onto him and bounce on his cock while he's standing. I've never done it like that, but he's strong enough to support us.

With my legs encircling his waist and an arm locked around his neck, I reach between us and grip him.

"Greedy." He groans and knocks my hand away. "Impatient."

"Hungry." I rock against him, clinging to his strength. "Just body slam me."

"You want me to just shove it in, huh?" He grins.

"Whatever you have to do." I kiss him, starving and frantic. "Put me out of my misery."

"I want to hear you scream."

"Make me." I bite his lips.

"It's going to hurt."

"Now you're just being cocky."

"I'm not gentle."

"Stop talking and put it in me."

He drops to his knees in the grass and holds my legs around him so that I straddle his lap.

Framing my face in his hands, he rests his brow against mine. "Maybe."

The illusion crashes away, and reality seeps in. This is real. Him, me, and the final chance to say stop.

He's giving me that, waiting on my reaction with labored breaths.

"No maybes." I clutch his face, mirroring his hands. "I want you."

He pulls me tight to his chest and kisses me until I see stars. Then he leans back and grips my hips. "Hold on."

My fingers tremble as I grasp the broad shoulders of his heavily built body. Muscle sits upon muscle, forming stacks down his torso. I clench my legs around his narrow waist, my gaze imprisoned by the golden glow of his.

He wraps a hand around his cock, and that's when I feel it. The tremors skating along his arm. The shaking in his thighs beneath mine. The quiver in the breaths against my neck.

"Let go," I whisper.

His mouth parts. The fingers on my hip constrict. Then he thrusts, impaling me in one long, hard, brutal stroke.

We cry out together, losing eye contact for a stunned moment as we adjust and *feel.* The tip of him presses against the deepest part of me, his girth stretching neglected muscle and tissue.

When our gazes reconnect, he gathers me closer, making tight rocking stabs inside me, grinding without pulling out.

"You're fucking tight, Maybe." He presses a hand against my tailbone, the other twisting in my hair. "Am I hurting you?"

"A good hurt." The overwhelming fullness and pressure urges me to push down on him, seeking freedom from this undeniable need.

"How long has it been?"

"Since I had sex? Almost a year." I touch my lips to his. "Since it felt this right? Never."

That's all it takes. He lifts me and slams me back down on his cock. Over and over, he drives my body onto his, using my pussy like a fist to stroke himself off.

All I can do is hold on, shredding my vocal chords as I scream. I scream his name. I scream for a god. Maybe they're one and the same.

He looks like a warrior god. He fucks like a sex god. I'll happily worship him, and I do—with my mouth on his, my hands on his body, and my pussy squeezing him toward release.

He pounds into me, spreading my legs wider and tormenting my clit with talented fingers. His lips only leave mine to ravish my breasts, scattering brilliant sparks of need across my skin.

Then he lowers me to my back and fucks me into the ground. With my knee bent around his hip, he hammers relentlessly, grinding and plunging. His throaty groans infuse his kisses, his body a piston of flexing muscle and endless power as he thrusts into a frantic rhythm, hands on my ass, bruising and scratching.

He's a vicious storm—beautiful, violent, and uncontrollable. Crashing into me, he grunts and digs as if forcing all of him into all of me. This isn't sex. It's something more. Something I've never experienced or even fantasized about.

It's cruelty in its most primitive form, love in its deepest, most passionate state. It's animalistic mating, unbound and stripped bare, a connection that defies civility.

The bite of his teeth no longer hurts. The merciless press of his fingers isn't painful. His thrusts only scratch the surface of what he's unleashed in me. I want every brutal desire in his body. More pain. More pleasure. More *him.*

He fucks me into the night, thrusting so roughly and savagely the slam of his hips edges us through the grass. Pebbles scrape my back. Mud smears my skin. My lips throb from kissing. The heat from his body cooks me from the inside out, and still, we fight to prolong this.

I don't chase my release, but it creeps in, gathering and pressing against the inside of my skin in sparkling waves. I won't be able to hold it back much longer. He's right there with me, staring into my eyes, jaw tight, hands dropping to the ground and wringing the grass to death.

"I can't get enough." He wedges into me, breathing so hard it garbles his voice.

"We have tomorrow night." I arch against him. "And all the tomorrows after."

"Hearing you say that..." His eyes hood, and his hand rests against the side of my face. "You sealed your fate."

"What's my fate?" I burn with desire. Tremble with hope.

"This." He strokes in and out, slowing his pace. "*Us.* For an eternity."

I let myself believe that, just for the moment as he slides his hand to my throat and squeezes with ungodly pressure.

I choke, breathe, and everything inside me submits. His gaze dances over mine, never looking away as fear fuels arousal, worry gives way to pleasure, and resistance morphs into acceptance.

Pinned beneath this dangerous man, with his fist against my windpipe and his eyes blazing with frightening ferocity, I let go and give him my trust.

His lips part as he searches my face and registers my surrender. His breaths come faster, harder, competing with the rhythm of his hips.

"Together." He restrains my gaze as tightly as he holds my throat.

Bowing over me, he widens his muscled legs between the spread of mine and bears down. Then he rides us into the abyss.

I've always wanted to come on a man's cock, and as I fall apart around him, *with him*, I realize it's not his cock that's blowing my world into shards of ecstasy. It's the collar of his hand on my throat. It's his eyes, peering into the deepest reaches of my being. It's his bellow as he empties himself into my body. It's his total domination over my pleasure and his surrender to his own.

It's him.

Masturbation has always gotten the job done, but a Jarret-induced orgasm rocks the foundation of my existence.

We collapse together in a field of wet grass, heaving breaths, liquid limbs, and humming satisfaction.

Rolling to his back, he pulls me onto his chest and kisses me languidly. His tongue swirls around mine, his hands caressing with a tenderness that burns the backs of my eyes.

"Your body's talking to me." He wanders gentle fingertips down my spine.

"What's it saying?" I nuzzle the pocket of warmth at the base of his throat.

"You're content. Relieved. And anxious." He grips my hand, where it twists in the wet ends of my hair, and guides my palm to his chest. "Whatever you're worried about, let it go. I'll deal with anything that threatens us. You're not alone, Maybe."

I ache to believe him.

Tangled together under the moonlight, embraced by the velvet night, skin on skin, legs intertwined, and breathing as one, I let myself fall quiet and kiss him.

I let myself believe him. Just for a little while.

A little while stretches into a long while. Before I know it, summer cools into autumn, and three months gallop by.

Conor went back to school in August. She makes the long commute to campus every day, puts in a hellacious number of hours in the lab, and returns to the ranch every night to tuck in with her text books.

Jake is broody while she's gone, but the moment her motorcycle rolls onto the property, he's out the door to smother her in affection.

The morning her classes resumed, he followed her outside to the bike, knelt on the driveway, and held up a ring. He didn't just propose with any ring. The diamond belonged to his and Jarret's mother. Julep's ring. The one she was wearing when she died.

As Conor burst into tears and nodded her consent, I watched from the porch, with my throat constricting and panic in my gut. Standing beside me, Jarret reached for my hand and wove our fingers together.

He wants what they have, but he hasn't mentioned marriage since that night in the field.

In Conor's absence, I've thrown myself into picking up her chores on the ranch. I've learned so much about repairing fences, herding cattle from one pasture to the next, maintaining seasonal grasses, and cleaning corrals.

Jake pays me a regular salary. I was reluctant at first, but he manages the bookkeeping and argued it saves them on taxes if I'm on the payroll.

It feels good to be independent again, earning a living and doing a job I enjoy. My skin glows brighter. My hair loves braids, and my feet prefer sturdy boots over impractical heels. I find working outdoors makes me smile more and breathe easier. I feel healthier, livelier, *happier.*

Of course, a certain cowboy with an insatiable sex drive has a lot to do with that.

Standing in the shower in his bathroom, I let the water wash away the dirt from my body and the noise from my head. It's become my nightly ritual, my time away from the ever-present shadow at my side, to reevaluate and refocus.

I think about the envelope under the floor mat in my car. About the secrets we're hiding from each other. About the trust we've built on lies.

I know what we're doing isn't healthy. I know it's only a matter of time before everything unravels.

I also know that I've fallen deeply, madly, insanely in love with him.

With my track record, it would be easy to accuse myself of falling for every man who shows me attention. I've tried to compare this love to what I felt for the others, but I can't. This is too different. Too fresh. Too forbidden. What I feel for Jarret is twisted so intricately in wrong and right I can't make logical sense of it.

Since when is love logical anyway?

It doesn't matter. Neither of us have uttered the words. We don't talk about the future or the past. We cling to the present as tightly and desperately as possible, because we know what awaits outside our happy bubble.

As close as we've grown and as strong as we stand together, it's not enough. The truth is going to rip us apart.

So I ignore that envelope in my car for another night. I exit the shower and close the door on our secrets for just a little while longer.

Wrapped in a towel, I step into the bedroom and forget how to breathe.

Jarret sits on the edge of the bed, wearing black briefs and nothing else. In the background, *Hurricane* by Luke Combs thrums through hidden speakers.

He loves to play this song for me. He says it reminds him of the night we came together in a storm of electricity and blinding light.

His dark brown hair slicks away from his stern brow. His hands rest on his spread thighs. Back straight, chin tilted down, he fixes those striking eyes on mine.

Over the past three months, I've explored and memorized every inch of his gorgeous body. The hardness of his chest, the thickness of his biceps, the tight buds of his nipples when I run my tongue over them. I've never craved a man the way I crave him. Never been so obsessed with the carnal pleasures of flesh and sin.

But as much as I love his body, that isn't what holds me captive. It's the thunderous energy that vibrates from within him.

Like now.

"Remove the towel." The command in his voice is my weakness and my lifeline.

A shivery clench of unadulterated desire hits my core.

I slam my hands on my hips and give him the response that makes him harder than a rock. "No."

His eyes heat as he slowly rises from the bed.

He gets off on the illusion, just like I do. The feel of me struggling beneath him, the rapid pulse in my throat against his hand, the sense of forcing me against my will, all the while knowing he turns me on in a way no one else ever has.

I put up a good fight as he chases me through the room, bumping into walls, knocking over lamps, kicking, biting, and scratching skin. It ends with me bent over his lap, my face pressed against the mattress, and the towel long gone.

"Every night," he says, caressing a hand over my soon-to-be red bottom, "you come out of the bathroom with renewed tension. You try to shed it before you emerge, but it's still there."

How the hell does he pick up on that? His intuition is freaky, and it really scares me sometimes.

"I'm spanking you tonight as a reminder." He continues to stroke my bare butt, twisting me up with anticipation.

I writhe against his hand, earning a deliciously hard smack.

"Nothing matters," he says slowly, calmly, making me hang on every rumbling syllable, forcing me to focus only on him as I float in suspense for the pleasure he'll deliver, "except you, me, and the sound of my voice."

He lets his hand fly, and each time his palm meets my flesh, the burn erases anxieties about secrets and lies, missing persons and unfinished business. He reduces me to a physical creature existing only in the here and now, feeling the pain and pleasure, until all that exists is him and me and this sacred thing between us.

When my bottom becomes numb to the strikes and my body drifts on a cloud of endorphins, he rolls me onto the bed and stands, removing his briefs.

His erection juts from defined thighs, his gaze smoldering under the *V* of dark brows. The cords in his neck strain against his skin, his jaw locked down tight.

He doesn't always fuck me like he's fighting a war, but he needs that tonight. It's been a long day of herding, and he has his own tension to work out.

I flip to my stomach and scramble across the bed, yelping as his hand captures my ankle. He climbs over me, and my heart races.

His fingers slip between my legs, and he groans. "Fuck, you're wet."

I try to claw my way out from beneath him, panting from exertion and growing wetter by the second. He stays with me, crawling and grunting with a fist around his cock.

Every movement is an effort to bury himself inside me. He wrestles me, grabs at me, and I fight back, feeding off his urgency and squirming away.

He grips my legs and tries to climb onto my back, and I twist, gasping and panting. The thrust and miss of his hips makes him hotter and harder, and his groans darken into primal growls.

I love when he reaches this level of need, when he completely loses himself in the drive to plunder, claim, and fuck.

He finally pins me on my stomach, with his chest against my back, trapping me in the inescapable cage of his body. His knees roughly force my legs apart, and he rams into me with so much force it knocks the wind from my lungs.

"Christ, Maybe. Fuck!" With a grunt of relief, he gathers me close, imprisoning me with a hand against my throat and an arm around my stomach. "Always so wet and tight. So fucking perfect."

Then he goes wild, plunging and hammering with the strength and endurance of a stallion.

The headboard slams against the wall. The bed frame screeches. The sheets twist and unravel in my clawing hands. He groans at my ear, and I scream into the mattress.

He has the stamina to fuck for hours, and tonight, he does. Possessive and untamed, he impales me. Enslaved and owned, I welcome him. When his teeth sink into my shoulder, when the pleasure strangles his breaths, when the need in his body overrides his will to keep going, he tenses, presses his face against my neck, and groans long and deep.

We erupt together, explosive, shaking, and spent.

He crashes against my side, breathless and clinging with arms and legs. I fold into his chest and rest my lips against the warm, wet seam of his. We kiss leisurely, licking and tasting, until our heartbeats return to normal.

I need another shower. And twelve hours of sleep.

"I'm going to rinse off." I untangle our sweaty, languid limbs and leave him half-asleep on the bed.

"Hurry back," he mumbles into the pillow. "And bring the cream."

The cream takes the burn out of the marks on my body, but I love the tingling pain. I also love the cuddling aftercare.

I rush through the shower, pull on one of his t-shirts, and grab the tube of ointment. When I open the door to the bedroom, the distinctive scent of weed hits my nose.

Stretched out on the bed beside the open window, he lies on his back, hands folded behind his head, with a joint between his lips.

He only smokes when his aches are more than he can bear. I'm not fond of the smell, but my God, he's sexy when he's all sprawled out and mellow, like a lazy lion. The sheet twists around his hips, the rest of him bare and utterly at ease.

I set the cream on the nightstand and pick up his phone. Scrolling through his playlist, I select *Might As*

Well Get Stoned by Chris Stapleton and gently sway as the song floats through the room.

"You overdid it today." I join him on the bed, slotting my legs beneath his head so he can use my lap as a pillow. "Then you overdid it again tonight. You should've told me you were hurting."

The smoldering joint protrudes from the corner of his sexy mouth. He cracks open an eye, squinting up at me through the smoke.

"Why are you so beautiful?" he mumbles, jostling the joint.

"I don't know how to answer that." I laugh, running my fingers through his hair. "Why are you so large?"

He glances down at his groin.

"Oh, for the love." I pluck the spliff from his lips and replace it with a kiss, savoring the taste of smoke and rebellion on his mouth. "I was talking about your personality."

"You think my personality is…*large*?"

"Uh, yeah." I return the weed to his lips, holding it as he takes a drag. "You know what else I think?"

He exhales a thick cloud toward the window and stares up at me expectantly.

"I think three months with you isn't enough." The truth tumbles out, and I curse myself for speaking without thinking.

He looks at me, really looks, with golden eyes that see more than they should. His hand floats to my face, caressing a trail of wonder and warmth.

"Cache that." He directs his gaze at the joint in my hand.

I twist to the side and put it out in the ashtray on the windowsill.

When I turn back, his arms close around me and pull me tight, chest to chest, legs entangled.

"I think a lifetime with you isn't enough." He rests his forehead against mine, breathing me in.

He's right. No amount of time is enough, yet I feel us ticking closer and closer toward expiration. One false move, a slipped word, a knock from the past, and this ends.

The thought makes me cold and hollow inside.

I've spent the best three months of my life with him. He takes me dancing at the Big Sugar. Drives me to Tulsa to dine at vegetarian restaurants. Brings me with him every week to visit Lorne. Works beside me all day every day. Sleeps with his arms around me every night. Restrains me, flogs me, chokes me, spanks me, and gives me more pleasure and joy than I ever hoped for.

And he never asks me about my secrets. Never volunteers his own. That's our limit. The line we silently drew and never cross.

He grabs the tube from the nightstand and lifts my shirt to rub the cool cream into my heated bottom. He kisses my lips while he cares for me, murmurs how beautiful I am as sleep pulls me under.

He shackled my heart with his, and I wish he would lose the key to that lock. The steady beat of his love against mine empowers me, strengthens me, makes me believe that as long as we're together, it's enough.

We're enough.

THREE MONTHS LATER...

I trudge through the snow toward the stable, dragging my boots to create a manageable path for the dawdlers behind me. The icy wind blasts my face, and I laugh back at it, adjusting the Stetson lower on my forehead.

"I hate that you're enjoying this." Maybe stomps and groans and releases a frustrated sigh.

Grinning, I turn around to check on her. "All you have to do is ask for help."

"No way. You always get to be the alpha." She tugs on the braided lead connected to Chicken's halter. "I'm determined to be the alpha in *this* relationship."

She digs her boots in, yanks on the rope with all her might, and falls on her ass.

I bite down on my lip, but my grin pulls free.

She insisted we take her three-foot-tall, four-hundred-pound weanling for a walk, despite the foot of snow that dumped on us overnight. Chicken decided midway through the hike she wants no part of it and planted her hooves.

Frost clings to her black nose. Her black ears twitch restlessly, the rest of her so white I can't see where she ends and the snow begins.

"You've spoiled her by keeping her in the stable." I rest my gloved hands on my hips.

"I'd rather she sleep with us." She climbs to her feet, dusting off her jeans.

"That's a hard no."

"Aww, but look how cute she is." She bends down and presses a kiss between Chicken's stubborn brown eyes.

I don't know about the calf, but there's a fuckton of cuteness happening with Maybe bent over like that. Snowflakes stick to her blond braids beneath the Stetson. White clouds plume from her pink lips, and her puffer coat lifts up her lower back, revealing a round, firm, gorgeous ass in tight jeans.

A groan sounds in my throat, and she straightens, arching a brow at me.

"Here." I remove a wadded napkin from my coat pocket, unravel a treat, and toss it to her.

"An apple fritter?" She inspects the fried bread in her gloved hand. "Can she eat this?"

"Ask her." I've been sneaking fritters to the damn calf for the past week.

She turns and holds out the treat. "Look what I have, Chicken. Can you eat—?"

Chicken launches for it, and Maybe jumps back with a shriek, hugging the fritter to her chest.

"Oh my God." She lets out a musical sound of surprise as she stumbles backward to evade the charging calf. "Slow down, you greedy girl."

She spins on her heel and takes off toward the stable, laughing and tromping through the snow, with Chicken bounding after her.

I catch up with them inside and find Chicken in

her stall, gobbling up torn pieces of the fritter in Maybe's open palms.

"She loves it." She blinks up at me, her blue eyes as luminous as her smile.

I smile back, overwhelmed by the ripples of warmth swirling through my blood.

Sinking into her body the first time completely redefined my existence. But nothing compares to moments like this, when her happiness is so blinding it crackles the molecules in the air.

When the fritter is gone, she hugs the calf, fusses over the bedding, and checks the automated feeder.

It's not an all-inclusive chicken resort, but it allows her to pamper and coddle her very own rescued critter. It makes her smile, and that means more to me than anything else in the world.

She's lived here for six months. She works for the ranch and spent the holidays with my family—Thanksgiving, Christmas, New Year's. She's become one of us, wedging right into the fold without even trying. They adore her.

I adore her. Cherish her. Worship the ground she walks on. I fucking love her with everything inside me, and I'm sick of holding back the words, the promise I want to make to her, and the secrets I ache to tell her.

I trust her to keep my skeletons buried. My family trusts her. Whatever she's hiding from me, whatever drove her here six months ago, no longer matters.

I've waited long enough.

She says her goodbyes to Chicken and follows me to the door. When I step outside and head toward the house, I don't hear the crunch of her boots behind me. I stop and look back.

Standing in the doorway of the stable, she burrows down into her puffer coat, arms wrapped around her, and legs squeezed together. Her breaths huff out like white smoke from beneath the hat, and her entire body trembles.

It's frigidly cold today, but she's been working in wintry temperatures for over a month. I toss her an impatient scowl.

"What?" She glares at the snow. "Chicken doesn't like it, either."

"This is her first winter, so she has an excuse. But you..."

"Yes. I'm cold. I know it's not nearly as cold here as it is in Chicago, but I'm still cold. Don't judge me."

"I'm definitely judging." I pivot back toward the house and start walking.

Two strides later, a snowball slams into the back of my neck and crumbles beneath the collar of my jacket.

I turn, and she races past me, hurling more snowballs from a pre-made pile in her arms.

The sneaky, little—

A ball of white flies past my face, so close it grazes my cheek.

She squeals with laughter and speeds off toward the parking lot, grabbing a stash of already-formed snowballs along her path.

I don't know when she set this up, but my insides alight with adrenaline at the prospect of playing with her.

Dropping to my knees, I pack and mold as pelting snow rains down on my head. I haven't done this since I was kid, and dammit, I can't stop the snowballs from falling apart. "How do you know how to do this so well?"

"I grew up in Chicago, baby." She stands ten feet away, ammo clutched in each hand, and winks. "I know how to play in the snow."

I finally figure out how to pack small lumpy balls and spend the next twenty minutes chasing her around the cars in the lot, ducking and weaving and volleying ice grenades back and forth.

I haven't laughed this hard in years. She's so damn

invigorating and addictive, a flurry of energy and rosy cheeks, youthfulness and angelic beauty. Her love for life is magnetic, her spirit inspiring. I want to spend the rest of my days chasing her fire and basking in her heat.

When the pelting hail of snow falls quiet, I scan the lot, searching for her mischievous grin. She either used up her arsenal or she's planning an attack.

"Maybe?" My boots crunch the snow as I circle the cars, heart pounding in anticipation.

Something stirs behind me. I pivot, and her chest collides with mine. Her arms encircle my back, and I hoist her up. She wraps her legs around my hips, and we sink into a kiss that scatters birds and melts snow.

Her lips are cold, her mouth wet and warm as I plunge my tongue in languorous strokes. There's no biting. No bruising or urgency. No games or wars. It's just us, feeling, tasting, and savoring the realism in our togetherness.

"I love you." I snap my eyes closed, startled by the sound of the words I've said to her so many times in my head.

She lowers her feet to the ground and rests a gloved hand on my cheek, prompting me to look at her.

"I love you, too." Her gaze slips over my face and returns to my eyes. "So much it hurts."

Needle pricks stampede across my skin, and my heart pummels my ribcage. Chills and heat and the vibration of her declaration—it's the best feeling.

It's the right time.

The rock in my pocket burns to be removed. I've been carrying it around for so long, waiting, dreading, hoping.

I know that what I do next will upset the balance we've so carefully and diligently maintained. But I've only been delaying the inevitable. We share the same destiny, and I want the world to know it.

My mouth dries as I slide off my gloves and lower to one knee.

"Jarret?" Confusion creaks her voice.

My hand shakes as I shove it into my pocket and slip out the ring. I had it custom made months ago. A two-caret diamond set in a gold band with a delicate leaf pattern along the sides. It reminds me of an enchanted meadow, straight out of Alice in Wonderland.

I'll be making payments on it for the rest of my life, but I don't care. I just want her happy.

I lift my eyes to hers and hold up the ring. "Marry me."

She stares at the diamond, and her mouth drops open. She closes it, opens it, and her eyes flood with horrified tears.

"Jarret..." She staggers back, shaking her head. "I can't."

My heart falls out of my chest and bleeds in the snow. My lungs slam together, and I bite down so hard on my tongue I taste iron.

But I knew this wouldn't be easy. Maybe Quinn doesn't do anything without a fight. So I push away the rejection and pull my insides back together. My muscles tense. My blood heats, and determination surges beneath my skin.

"You *can.*" I rise to my feet and clench the ring in my fist.

"You don't understand." Her chin quivers, and tears streak down her pale cheeks.

"You love me. I love you." My voice rises to a guttural shout. "There's nothing else to understand!"

"Oh, God." Her shoulders hunch, and her gloved hands fly to her mouth as she turns away, wobbling in the opposite direction of the house.

"What are you doing?" I trail her through the lot with a painful knot in my stomach. "Talk to me."

"I will." She picks up her pace and lurches toward

her car. "I have to…" A sob rips from her chest. "I need to show you."

She stops at the driver's side door, clutches the handle, and pauses. Agony and conflict shake through her tiny frame, and it's all I can do to keep from roaring. I can't stand to see her upset.

"Whatever it is…" I return the ring to my pocket and pull her tight against my chest. "We'll get through it. I'm not letting go. Understand?"

She stares up at me, her eyes vivid, radiant, watery blue against the backdrop of snow. She blinks, and a lone tear clings to the lower fringe of her lashes.

"I never wanted to see your lashes wet." I catch the droplet with my finger and squeeze it in the ball of my hand. "I'm so sorry I made you cry."

"It's not you." Her eyes close, and her expression crumples.

"You're stunning, even when you're crying." Cupping the back of her head, I guide her face to my lips and kiss each eyelid. Damp lashes flutter against my skin, and I kiss those, too. "What can I do?"

"You're doing everything right." She turns back to the car door and opens it. "We should've had this conversation months ago."

She bends down toward the floorboard and reappears with a large envelope clutched to her chest.

That's where she kept her secrets? All this time, I could've looked in her car, but I never considered it. I told her I would wait until she was ready to give me the truth, and she left the envelope in the car, trusting me not to take it.

"I love you, Maybelline Quinn." I hold out a hand to her.

With a jerky nod, she grips my fingers. Then she follows me into the house, down the hall, and into our bedroom.

We remove our outerwear in silence, watching each other without looking away. She sits on the bed to tug off the boots. The boots from my childhood. She could've replaced them with the money she's earning. Instead, she wears them every day and even now, she sets them on the floor with affectionate care.

Lifting the envelope from the pile of coats and hats, she finds my eyes across the room. "I would've said yes."

"But..." My throat closes, and a swarm of bees invade my stomach.

She clutches her neck, her expression washed in misery. "I'm already married."

A knife twists inside one simple word.

Married.

How is that possible? Maybe is mine. She's been mine. My fists clench as denial clamps down on my lungs.

Married.

I repeat it in my head, weighing the declaration against her actions over the past six months.

She was resistant from day one, physically and emotionally averse to having a relationship with me. But there are so many explanations for that—her fear of sexual intimacy, her suspicions about my past, and her connection to the list of dead men.

My chest squeezes around my heart as my thoughts take me farther and farther down a horrifying path.

In the back of my mind, I suspected she had some kind of family tie to my dad's business partners. Her mother died of cancer. Her father, however, she never mentions.

But a husband?

Had I considered that possibility? Perhaps deep down I always knew and refused to let myself acknowledge it.

"Did he send you here?" I ask with more calm than I feel. "Is he using you in some kind of ploy against me?"

"What?" She shakes her head rapidly. "No!"

"Who is he?"

"I don't know anymore." She hovers near the closed door of the bedroom, watching me warily.

"What does that mean?" I shake uncontrollably as a flood of questions rise in my throat.

Do I know him? Is she looking for him? Does she love him?

Why didn't she tell me?

His identity is chief of my concerns. Levi Tibbs was the youngest of my victims and the first person she mentioned when I met her in the bar. But I can't fathom her marrying a rapist and hired hit man.

Except she fell in love with *me*.

A serial murderer.

She loves me.

That's the only reason I haven't completely lost my shit.

She fell in love with me while she was still married. He might be looking for her. She might be looking for him. But she's with *me*.

If she's married to a dead man, she's a widow. If he's still alive, she can divorce him. We'll work through this. I refuse to consider any other option.

"I met him on a dating site two years ago." She lowers the envelope, staring at it through a glaze of tears. "It was a whirlwind romance. He swept into my life, swept me off my feet, and swept out of it within a year."

"Is he one of the names on your list?"

"I...I need to tell you some things first. Things that will anger you, and I don't want you to hurt him." She shudders with a stifled cry, knocking more tears loose. "I loved him."

The torment in her voice is a thousand knives stabbing my chest.

"I thought he loved me." She shuffles to the bed and perches on the edge. "Until he left for work one morning and never returned."

So he's missing.

She's had three lovers. Three relationships. One in high school, one in college, and *one after.* Not once did she fucking imply she was married.

It can't be Levi Tibbs, because he didn't disappear until after I met her. Whomever it is, I want to kill him for hurting her.

How morbidly ironic that he may have already died at my hands.

But how can that be? My mind sifts through the names and faces of the dead bodies in the ravine. They all lived alone in different parts of the country. None were from Chicago. None were married. None shared her last name. Although, Jake and I didn't dig very deep into their personal lives. We had neither the time nor the money to investigate. We just wanted them dead, removed as a threat, and we were prepared for parents, siblings, lovers, anyone who cared about their miserable existences to come looking for them.

Except no one came.

Until six months ago.

Her husband left her, and she did what? Sold her belongings and drove to Sandbank to find him? How did she know to come here? What does she think happened to him?

A blizzard of impatience rages inside me, but I force myself to remain still and composed. "I need his name."

She closes her eyes and makes a distraught sound

in her throat. "I'm..." She clutches the envelope on her lap, creasing the edges. "I'm afraid."

Afraid of my reaction? Afraid I'll confirm what she already suspects?

"Tell me, Maybe." I step toward her.

She flinches and covers her mouth with a hand, holding in a sob.

Fuck, this isn't good. What the hell is she scared to tell me?

"Let's start with the day he left." I lower onto the bed beside her, rest an arm around her back, and kiss her shoulder.

She softens beneath my touch and pulls in a deep breath.

"He said he was going out of town. Just a day trip to Oklahoma to meet with an investor. He never came home." She stares at the envelope on her lap, unblinking. "He never called. Never answered his phone or messages. He was just... *Gone."*

The haunted hush in her voice constricts my throat.

How many phones did I destroy and throw into the ravine with the bodies? Most of them were burner phones, all of them locked with passwords. I didn't even try to hack into them. I didn't care.

Her husband is dead. I'd bet my life on it. And I'm going to have to tell her.

"Did you call the cops?" I rub a hand along her spine.

"No. First, I checked our credit card and bank accounts, hoping to find activity that would pinpoint his location." She stiffens beneath my fingers. "That's when life as I knew it fell apart."

She doubles over and presses her hands to her face. I bend with her, hugging her with a lead weight in my stomach.

"I was so naive." She releases a hicupping cry. "I

married him within weeks of meeting him and turned over all the finances to him. I signed documents and transferred accounts so he could access everything. Every dollar I earned and invested since college. He said he knew how to grow my money, *our* money. He owned a small investment firm." She straightens, bristling with anger. "He lied."

The killer inside me sharpens its claws and distorts my voice. "What do you mean?"

She winces at my tone. "He cleaned me out. Took every penny I had. Since he was handling the bills, I turned over all my advances and royalties to him. I didn't know he stopped making the mortgage payments on our condo. I lost that, too. He left me with *nothing*. No car. No savings. All I had was the few clothes to my name and the diamond on my finger, which turned out to be a twenty-dollar piece of glass. On top of all that, my mom had *just* died. When I met with the attorney, I learned that my husband worked with my mom behind my back to manage her finances and..."

"He cleaned her out, too."

She nods stiffly and swipes at the river of tears on her cheeks. "She was sitting on a wealth of old money, an inheritance passed down through generations in my family. She trusted him because I trusted him. It's all gone."

The son of a bitch left her homeless and broke and stole from her dying mother. Who the fuck would do that?

Any one of the selfish, ruthless men buried in the ravine.

The pound of my heart thrashes in my ears.

Did her money end up in my father's hands? Did it pay off his debts and fund the drilling on Julep Ranch? My mind spins to connect the dots, but the answers can wait.

"I'm so sorry, Maybe." I gather her in my arms and rest my forehead against hers. "I would do anything to take away your pain."

"You've been..." She clings to my shoulders, her breaths shredding between tears. "You've been so good to me, Jarret."

She glances down at her lap, and I follow her gaze to the envelope. Whatever it contains seems to be her greatest torment. I don't know if it's evidence against her husband or my family or something else entirely. My fingers twitch to yank it away, but I won't push her. She's so fucking brave and strong I refuse to take that from her.

"When I discovered the state of our finances, I was scared *for him.*" She releases me and faces forward, her voice flattening. "I assumed he was in trouble and needed the money. He left behind his clothes, his personal belongings, and his computer. I was going to call the cops, but then..." She grits her teeth. "I figured out his computer passwords and pried into his life. Emails with your dad. Documents on his hard drive. There was so much I didn't know about my husband."

My thoughts drift back to one of the first conversations I had with her, when I asked her how we got on her radar. "You said you were following a lead on a different project, and it led you to my father."

"The project was my missing husband. The lead was Dalton Cassidy."

"Conor and Lorne's father?" My head jerks back. "He's been dead for..."

"Four years. I heard about him but never met him."

I swallow around a hot ember. "How did your husband know Dalton?"

She lifts the envelope and holds it out to me as a fresh wave of tears soaks her cheeks. "Please, don't hate me."

I accept the envelope and touch my lips to her grooved forehead. "I could never hate you."

"Open it." She grips the ends of her braids, twisting the strands around her fingers.

I guide her hands to her lap and turn my attention to the documents. As I lift them from the unsealed envelope, my eyes lock on the header, honing in on three words.

Petition for Divorce

As I read the names, my heart stops, and the papers crinkle in my clenched hands.

Petitioner: Maybelline Cassidy
Respondent: Rogan Cassidy

The room tilts, and the air evaporates from my lungs. "Cassidy?"

"Quinn is my maiden name. When Rogan left me, I changed my name back." She hugs her torso and stares at the floor. "I need to find him, Jarret. If I can serve the papers and talk to him—"

"Slow the fuck down!" My voice comes out louder than I intended, making her flinch. "I'm still trying to wrap my head around the names."

She closes her eyes and sucks in a serrated breath. Then she drags her gaze to mine. "Rogan Schroeder. That's the name he used in his email correspondence with your dad."

"But his last name is Cassidy?"

"Yes." She inches away.

I drag her back by her arm. "How—? Look at me, Maybe." I wait for the connection of her eyes and ask in a softer tone, "How is he a Cassidy?"

"He's Dalton's son."

Ice hits my stomach, and my head spins with dizziness.

Is it possible? A surface investigation on Rogan Schroeder showed he lived alone in Texas. The ID in his wallet confirmed his Texas address. But given his line of work, it makes sense he used a false identity and fake driver's license.

"Rogan's older," she says in a shaky voice. "Almost forty. Dalton knocked up Rogan's mom after high school and stuck around long enough to give Rogan his last name. Then he bailed and married Ava O'Conor. During the year I was with Rogan, he made some snide comments about how his dad started a new family and owned all this rich land while he and his mom struggled to make ends meet."

"I didn't know." I set the papers aside and brace my elbows on my knees, rubbing my face. "Conor and Lorne..."

"Rogan knows about them, but they don't know he exists. Dalton wanted it that way. He paid the required child support and kept in touch with Rogan, but he wasn't around."

Rogan Schroeder was a Cassidy.

I close my eyes, recalling his dark hair, dark eyes, overly confident and charismatic demeanor. He was a good-looking man, and despite the fourteen-year age difference, I can see the similarities between him and Lorne.

I killed Lorne's and Conor's brother. Maybe's husband.

Bile rises, but I swallow it down with the reminder that Rogan was a sleazy piece of shit and a threat to Conor's life.

"Was he motivated by revenge?" I ask. "A scorned son with daddy issues?"

"I don't know. Other than a few comments, he didn't talk about his family. I know it bothers him, but not enough to..."

"To do what?"

"I haven't pieced everything together. The first thing I found on his computer was a rent agreement. He paid the lease on the apartment Dalton and Conor stayed at in Chicago, and I thought it was odd. Rogan isn't a charitable guy, especially not with the man who abandoned him. The only reason he would help Dalton was if he was getting something in return. He either moved Dalton and Conor there to keep them close or to keep them away from the ranch. I believe Dalton offered a piece of the land in exchange for help."

My hands flex and release.

"I dug deeper and..." She stands and paces through the room. "I found copies of Ava O'Conor's trust and learned about the stipulations on the Power of Attorney and the rightful owners of the land. I knew she was Lorne's and Conor's mom, but I didn't understand why he would have those documents. When I went online and researched the Cassidys, things started to click."

"You found out what happened here. With Conor and Levi Tibbs..."

She nods, her expression darkening. "I spent days going through Rogan's email. That's how I found your father."

I rake a hand through my hair. "What did the emails say?"

"They were vague. Nothing about the attack on Conor or a ploy to keep her away from the ranch, but there was an undercurrent between the words that made me uneasy. Discussions about meeting times. The drilling on the land. Updates on Lorne's and Conor's whereabouts. Conversations about missing business partners. That's how I got the list of names. I surmised enough to know Rogan and your dad worked out an agreement. Dalton was dead, but Rogan was already tied in. He was helping your dad with his debts in exchange for a cut of the land. And it was *my* money funding the partnership."

My stomach hardens, and my voice comes out as a growl. "What did you do, Maybe?"

"I emailed your dad from Rogan's account and demanded to meet with him."

I surge from the bed. "You could've gotten yourself killed!"

She stumbles back, eyes wide. "Of everything I've told you, that's..." She shakes her head in disbelief. "That's what you're upset about? Don't you get it? My husband played a part in keeping Conor and Lorne off their land so he could profit from it." She narrows her eyes. "Or maybe you were in on it?"

"I had nothing to do with that or the money that was taken from you."

She pulls in a deep breath, her eyes huge and searching. "I believe you."

My pulse crashes through my veins. Not once has she mentioned murder—Rogan's intent to kill or my blood-soaked history. She doesn't know.

Her innocence is so fucking beautiful and devastating it takes my breath away.

"Why didn't you tell me you were married?" I step toward her.

"The first couple of weeks I was here, I had a lot of reasons. You owned a business that was pulled out of debt with stolen money. You lived in an extravagant estate while I lived in my car. You were thriving while I was barely surviving. Your father isn't in the picture, and my husband is missing. All evidence points to your involvement. I didn't trust you."

All of that is true, and it fucking wrecks me that her trust was used against her. No wonder she fought me as hard as she did.

"And now?" I step closer, leaving a few feet

between us. "You said you were afraid."

"I trust you not to hurt me, but over the past six months, it became harder and harder to tell you. I fell in love with you while married to Conor's brother. We've been so happy and content I fell into a dream I didn't want to wake up from. Ignorance is bliss, right? But dreams end, and now we stand in the moment of truth." She swallows hard and gives me steady eye contact. "I know you had something to do with Rogan's disappearance. Did you threaten him? Force him to go into hiding? Your dad said you know where he is."

"I'll tell you." Dread eats away my insides as I pace a circle around her. "I need to know about your meeting with my dad. You emailed him and..."

"I told him I was a news reporter and threatened to sell an incriminating story if he didn't meet with me. He gave me his address, and I packed up what little I had left, bought a cheap car, and drove to Texas."

"Did you tell him you were Rogan's wife?"

"No, but he knew. When I arrived, he knew my name and everything about me. Rogan must've told him."

An overwhelming surge of protectiveness ripples through me, and I can't stop myself from cupping her face and lifting her forehead to mine. "You're a beautiful, *naive* woman. You drove across the country by yourself, met with a dangerous man you didn't know, and not once did you call the cops. I should spank you for that."

Her cheeks warm beneath my hands. "Let me ask you this. If I stole money from you and disappeared, would you call the cops?"

"No." I'm so certain I don't even think about it. "I would hunt you down and punish you."

"That's what I did, although the punishment I had in mind isn't the same as yours." She sighs. "I was determined to find him, get answers, and drag him through a miserable legal battle. That is, until I met you."

"Your priorities shifted." I stroke a thumb across her cheekbone.

"You must think I'm horribly flaky and incompetent."

"Because you chose to stay with me rather than pursue your deceitful, manipulative thief of a husband?"

She smiles sadly. "I need you to know I didn't come here to create family drama for Conor. I'm married to her brother, a brother she doesn't know she has, and I didn't want her to find out about him from a scorned wife. I guess I wanted her to think the best of him, to know him the way I knew him in the beginning. A tiny part of me still holds onto hope that he got himself into financial trouble and wasn't involved in the attack on her."

While her optimism never ceases to amaze me, it's also tragic. Rogan had it out for Conor and Lorne the moment he discovered the oil on their land. He stole from his wife and hired contract killers with the intent to murder.

"What did my father tell you?" I lean back, watching her expression.

"He said his sons turned on him, and he's out of the loop. Said he doesn't know what's going on with the ranch or my money, but you and Jake know. You know where to find Rogan. He sent me to you with a warning. He said what you're doing is illegal and I should watch my back."

"A warning you ignored."

"You warned me, too." She lifts a shoulder.

I remember it well. The night I told her I could be a coldblooded psychopath, I said she should run. She didn't.

If I tell her I killed her husband, she *will* run.

"Have you met your dad's girlfriend?" She watches me with suspicion.

"Raina? Yeah, she lived here a few weeks. Why?"

"She's stunning. And *young.* I don't know your dad well enough to make assumptions, but I don't understand why she's with him. It's not just an age thing. He's an asshole. I mean, he talks down to her and not in an attractive way."

"What are you saying?"

"I don't know. Call it woman's intuition, but I sensed something malignant between them. Like she didn't want to be there."

"I felt the same and asked her if she was in trouble. She snapped at me."

"Okay." She sighs. "Well, she has my phone number and hasn't tried to contact me."

"What? How?"

"On my way out, I told your dad to call me if he had anything else to share. I did it for *her* benefit. I insisted he write it down, and as he did, I met her eyes and said the numbers. She got the message."

"She won't call."

"I know." She straightens her spine and meets my gaze with refocused strength. "Where's Rogan, Jarret?"

Buried at the bottom of the ravine with his truck and phone.

At my silence, she grips my arm. "If my money is soaked up in the ranch, I'll let it go. And I'm not on a mission to win Rogan back. I just want the divorce, and I… I need a moment with him, to look him in the eyes and tell him I know what he did. I need that closure." She lowers her hand and steps back. "If you still want me after that, if you can forgive me for deceiving you, I want to stay." A tear skates down her cheek. "I want to say yes to your proposal."

Her words annihilate me, and the self-disparaging look in her eyes guts me. She's asking for forgiveness when none is needed. I'm the one stained in sins. I can't give her the divorce she wants or the closure she needs. I robbed that from her.

I hover on the precipice between right and wrong, good and bad, and everything inside me tilts toward doing the dishonorable thing. The thing that wipes all this away and leaves me standing on a pedestal of integrity.

It's on the tip of my tongue to put all the blame on my father. He paved the trails of sin through Julep Ranch. He involved her husband and spent her money. I want to tell her Rogan died at his hands and convince her to let it go. I could do that so goddamn easily. She loves me. She'll let me heal her and protect her, and with time, she'll move on. With me.

The truth is impossible. It's ugly, unforgiving, and it shakes me down the center of my soul.

She fell out of love with Rogan because she believes he stole from her and left her. But did he?

He left his belongings behind. He told her he would invest her money. Deep down, I know there's a possibility he intended to return to her with a profit on his investments. I mean, how could he leave her? She's beauty, innocence, compassion, and everything perfect in the world. No man would part with that.

If I tell her the truth, she'll know I'm the reason her husband never returned.

If I don't tell her, I'll have to live with that lie for the rest of my life.

What do I do?

What kind of man am I?

I think I'm the wrong man. I'm John Holsten's son. The selfish liar. Coldblooded murderer. Ruthless lover.

But she makes me want to be the right man. Selfless. Vulnerable. Buckled on my knees beneath the trust in her huge blue eyes. She makes me want to be the man deserving of that precious trust.

My hand shakes as I reach for her and grip her

fingers. With a forceful tug, I lead her to the bed and motion for her to sit.

She lowers, her gaze alert and flicking over mine.

I kneel at her feet and rest my hand on her lap, palm up. "We made a blood oath the night Conor was raped. The four of us passed around a blade as Levi Tibbs lay unconscious at our feet."

Her expression softens as she runs her fingers along my scar.

"We swore to one another..." The wood flooring grinds against my knees, balancing the flood of pain from my memory of that night. "We vowed to kill him when he was released from prison."

A soft gasp slips past her lips. "He was released." Her fingers twitch against my palm. "Is he—?"

"Dead? Yes. We killed him a few hours before you showed up at the ranch."

She yanks her hand away, bowing backward. "No, Jarret—"

"I'm not finished." I grip her hips and wedge my chest between her legs, holding her against me. "Your husband was a loan shark who extorted money, lent it to desperate people, and charged outrageous interest rates. He paid off my father's debts and expected a share of the oil in return. He wasn't involved in the initial attack on Conor and Lorne, but he spent the next five years ensuring they wouldn't return to the ranch."

She clutches at my shoulders, her chest rising and falling with the rush of her breaths.

"He hired contract killers." I loosen my fingers on her hips, stroking her through the shirt in an attempt to comfort her. "He ordered them to kill Conor if she stepped foot on the ranch."

"She's his sister. He wouldn't do that. How could he?"

"I have evidence, Maybe. Video recordings of my

dad's conversations with him."

"Oh God." Her eyes fill with tears. "Where is he, Jarret?"

"He's dead." My fingers dig into her waist.

She scrambles back, kicking in her desperation for space. I loosen my grip, giving her what she needs.

"How do you know?" She climbs off the far side of the bed, shaking violently. "Did you see it...happen?"

"I was there." I remain on my knees with my heart in my hands and force out the words. "I killed him."

My hands shake. My lungs heave for air, and the room narrows to the tick, tick, ticking time bomb in my chest.

Rogan is dead.

Murdered.

Gone.

The horror in my gut wages a war against the love in my heart.

Jarret killed my husband, and I still love him. *Jarret.* I love Jarret.

I'm a cheater.

Not just any cheater. I cheated on my husband with his murderer.

I wrap my arms around the hollow, frigid cavity of my ribs and chase my thoughts deeper into hell.

What if Rogan didn't leave me? What if he always planned to come home?

He's dead, and I never reported him missing. What kind of worthless, fucked-up person am I?

And can I even accuse him of stealing? I gave him full authority to invest my money. Technically, *our* money, since we were married. Did he let our finances slip into the red because he was gambling the money with the hope of making us rich? Was he really willing to kill Conor and Lorne to ensure that his investment turned a profit?

I don't condone Rogan's investment methods or his behavior. It makes me violently sick to my stomach. But I never bothered to ask or investigate what he was doing with my money. I was swamped with magazine deadlines. He said he would handle the bills and our retirement, and I trusted him to do that.

Still, that doesn't give me a pass. I was negligent. Unsuspicious. Blinded by love. That's on me.

But if he wasn't purposefully stealing from me, if he had no intention of leaving me, that changes my entire perspective. He could've been on his way home that very night to tell me what he was doing.

Or he could've truly taken my money and left.

I'll never be able to ask him.

I'll never know.

Jarret rises to his full height, his expression predatory as he prowls around the bed. A feral glow flares in his eyes, yet his movements are cautious, restrained, *uncertain.*

I raise a hand, gulping down breaths and holding back a cry. "Don't come any closer."

He stops at the foot of the mattress, and a shadow of hurt crosses his face before he closes it off.

"How?" I back up, keeping the corner of the bed between us, my voice shrill. "How did he die?"

"Don't, Maybe." His head angles away, his rigid jaw a dark slash of warning. "Ask me anything but that."

My mind runs rampant. Was Rogan stabbed? Shot? Strangled? Starved? Dismembered? Beheaded? Drowned? Set on fire? Run over by a truck? Trampled by a horse? Skinned alive?

The more I think about it, the harder the tears fall.

"I can't do this." I grip my head and tack my eyes shut as a terrible keening noise escapes my chest. "I'm imagining horrible things, and the images are getting worse and worse. This will eat at me, Jarret. It'll haunt me into madness." I find his eyes a few feet away. "Please. I have to know."

He steps toward me, and I stumble back.

His features harden. "I pushed him into the ravine before we filled it in."

A cry hides behind the knot in my throat. "He died on impact?"

"No," he says quietly. "I think his back broke. He was conscious and unable to move."

Alive. Paralyzed. Defenseless. What were his final thoughts? Did he think about me while he lay in the dirt and confront his death?

Pain and misery drips from my eyes and nose, racking my body with uncontrollable tremors. "What did you do?"

"I had dump trucks on standby, already loaded with dirt."

I clap a hand over my mouth as saliva rushes in, followed by bile, nausea, the sudden urge to puke.

He closes his eyes, opens them. "I buried him alive."

I take off at a run, shoving past him and stumbling into the bathroom. I barely make it to the toilet as the contents of my stomach erupt. I heave repeatedly, brutally, sobbing in a convulsion of snot and spit.

He kneels beside me and caresses my back, his eyes burning into the side of my face.

Minutes pass. My stomach settles. My mind dissolves into numb shock. He hands me a towel and a glass of water.

His tenderness fills me with difficult feelings. He's too close, too overwhelming. Physically and emotionally.

I need distance.

I need answers.

I clean my face with the towel, drink the water, and clear my voice. "When did he die?"

"Six months before I met you."

The time line matches his disappearance.

He's been dead for a year, the same amount of time I was married to him. And I've been sleeping with his killer six of those months.

"Where?" I ask.

"He was in Sandbank, on his way to a meeting with my dad."

"Did he say anything? Obviously, he didn't mention me. But did he defend himself or say he needed to get home?"

"We didn't give him the opportunity."

"What do you mean?"

"We gagged him immediately to keep him quiet. I'm sorry, Maybe. If I'd known he was married..."

"You would've killed him anyway."

"Yes."

"If you'd known he was Conor's brother?"

"She'll ask the same question, and I'll give her the same answer. Yes, I would've killed him. I've hurt her deeply over the past six years. I hate myself for it, but she's alive. I will never regret that."

I admire his honor and devotion, even if his methods are vicious and illegal.

"And the other missing people?" I sit back on my heels, clutching the braid of my hair.

"Hit men. Loan sharks. Levi Tibbs. They all threatened Conor's life, and they're all in the ravine."

Another wave of nausea hits my stomach, but I'm empty. Drained. Hollowed out. I have a lot of soul-searching to do, and it's not going to happen on this bathroom floor.

I move to stand, and he helps me, crowding in,

breathing against my neck.

"Jarret."

"Maybe."

We watch each other, motionless, drawn together, even now, in a way I've never felt with another person.

I hold still, constricted on all sides by reality. Secrets and betrayal. Covered in blood. Smothered by love. Amid it escapes an agonized sob, followed by his soothing shush. Then his arms, his warmth, his lips in my hair.

He's ruined me. There will be no more attempts at forever. Not for me. He might not be the first man I loved, but he's the only one who left a mark. If I walk away from this, I walk away from love indefinitely. That's my penance.

"I can't begin to imagine how hard this is for you." He surrounds me with his scent, his heat, his brain-scrambling presence. "Tell me what you need."

"Space." I wriggle away and push past him, heading out of the bathroom and toward the pile of coats on the bedroom floor.

"How much space?" He trails after me.

"Acres. Miles. Months. Years. Forever. I don't know." I shove my feet into the boots.

"I know you're upset. Talk to me." He touches my chin, lifting it. "Which part of this is the hardest?"

"Everything. All of it." I shrug on the coat and set the Stetson on my head. "I don't even know where to start, Jarret."

"Try."

I stare at the door, itching to escape as I contemplate his question out loud.

"Looking back at my marriage, I feel so removed from it that it confuses my private memories with the ones I placed outside myself when he disappeared. I put on a brave front and let myself become that callous mask." I slide on the gloves, cold and wet from melted snow. "I despised him for leaving me. But now I don't know if he actually did. What I do know is that when we were together, life was good. I was happy with him. We didn't have the passion and fire that you and I have, but I felt something for him. I can't just sweep that under the rug and brush off my hands. I need to sort these feelings."

"Sort it here." He steps into my space. "With me."

"No." I back toward the door. "I'm so wrapped up in you I let six months blur by before I told you I was married. Nothing else exists when you're all up in my space. Give me some breathing room."

His jaw clenches. Then he grips his brow and nods.

I hurry through the house, out the front door, and make a beeline for the stable. Inside the building, it's warm and quiet and filled with warm, welcoming nuzzles from Chicken.

I sit beside her in her stall, stroking the white cowlicks on her head.

And I cry.

Trembling, sobbing, blubbering nonsense pollutes the stable and unsettles the horses.

I beat myself up for being so weak and emotional and dry my eyes.

Then I cry some more.

Why is this so hard? Either I stay or leave. Simple as that.

If I look deep inside, the answer is written all over my trampled heart. I've loved a lot in twenty-six years, and it's never been enough.

I loved my dad when I was little, and he left me without offering a reason.

I loved Chris in high school, and he left me to pursue a job in New York.

I loved Scott in college and he left me for another woman.

I loved Rogan, and he... He probably left me, too.

None of them wanted to keep me. None fought for me in any way. Perhaps they never loved me. Perhaps what I felt for them wasn't love at all. Perhaps *I* am not enough.

Was Rogan even with me for *me?* He knew I had money, and his sights were set on Julep Ranch before he met me. He hired hit men, for Christ's sake. If he was willing to murder his own family to satisfy his goal, he could've married me for money.

Jarret's the first and only man who's ever given me a sense of mutual attachment. He loves me with the same depth and intensity that I love him. At least, I think he does. What if I'm wrong? Would he fight for me? Do I want him to?

He's murdered people. Bad men for good reasons. But he's still a killer. And I love him regardless. I'm not okay with that.

This isn't about who's a better man, who I love more, or who loves me in return.

It's about acceptance.

Can I accept the path I'm on, the choices I've made, and the woman I've become? Can I stand at Jarret's side twenty years from now and accept the crimes, deceit, and deaths that led me there?

I can forgive him, but I don't know how to forgive myself.

If I stay, it must be with a guilt-free conscience. No deep-seeded resentment, confusion, or distrust. If I walk back into his arms with any doubts at all, they'll fester and multiply and poison everything good in us.

I lost myself in him for six months without telling him about Rogan. Because I was scared. What's stopping me from falling into that trap again? I don't want to wake up fifty years from now and realize I've been living in a toxic relationship built on great sex and...

Fear.

That's the single, biggest reason I didn't run the moment he told me he killed Rogan.

I'm afraid I'm not strong enough to leave. I'm afraid of his reaction if I try. I'm afraid he'll hunt me down, and he *will*. He'll snarl and rage and throw his weight around.

More than that, I'm afraid I'll hurt him. If he truly loves me, the level of the anguish of what might have been but can never be will damage him.

I'm so afraid, but fear isn't the reason to stay.

Hours pass. Sunlight fades outside the stable door. The dirt floor digs against my butt. Chicken slips in and out of sleep.

I have answers to some of the questions that drove me to Sandbank, but I don't have closure. If anything, I'm more lost now than I was when Rogan disappeared.

I'm lost.

All the illusions in the world cannot remove that reality.

My relationship with Jarret is too entangled in my unfinished business with Rogan. I need to dig myself out of this mess before I'm so far gone I don't know who I am.

I've never walked away from anything, and maybe that's the problem.

I need to walk away.

Now.

Get up.

My gaze drifts to the door. He'll come looking for me any moment. He'll rest those gorgeous, commanding eyes on me and persuade me to stay.

Go now.

It takes a sea of courage and a mountain of resolve to make my legs move. Hugging Chicken goodbye reduces me to a tear-soaked blob of wobbly limbs and strangled breaths.

With harrowing steps, I make it to the door, across the field of snow, and stop at the front porch, where Jarret waits.

Jake and Conor sit beside him on the stairs, and the first thing I notice is her puffy, red-rimmed eyes.

Jarret told them.

She knows she had a brother. A brother who wanted her dead. She knows I was married to him and didn't tell her.

Her pain and my guilt sit between us, and it's eternal.

"I'm sorry," I whisper into the cold night air. "I'm leaving."

"You're not going anywhere!" Jarret surges to his feet, eyes wild and breaths steaming.

Agony rips through my chest and quivers my voice. "I'll take your secrets to the grave." I pat at my pockets. Looking for... *Shit.* "I need my keys."

And my purse, phone, money. My wages are deposited in my bank account, but I need my wallet. I didn't think through this.

There's no way I'm going back into that house. If I do, I won't leave.

"I'll grab them." Conor stands and disappears inside.

Jarret charges toward me, and I turn, hurrying to the car without looking at him. I'm defenseless against his gaze, fracturing and bleeding beneath the sound of his chasing footfalls.

I speed up my gait, following the tracks in the snow from our snowball fight. Every step plagues me with the relentless wishing for his arms around me, the press of his warm body, and the authority in his voice.

The pain is too great, cleaving my insides and causing my strides to falter. Walking away from Jarret Holsten is the hardest thing I've ever done.

"Do you still love him?" He grabs my arm and swings me around. "If he were alive, would you take him back?"

"No and no." I yank free of his grip.

"Then what is it? Why are you running?"

"You know why." I spin back to the car and reach for the door handle.

"Because I killed him?"

"You killed. I cheated. We built our relationship on a bed of secrets and distrust. I can't make peace with that, and you shouldn't be able to, either."

"He was gone. You didn't cheat. As for our relationship, it was built on love, Maybe."

"Love." I grimace. "How many times has love found me and dumped me? In the end, I'm lost."

"I won't leave you. I would sell my soul if it meant never losing you."

I reel in a world of emotion and feeling, drowning in the torment of *if only.* It's a tragedy to feel this much for another person. A burden and a curse.

"I don't know what to do or where I'm supposed to be or how to process what I'm feeling. I'm lost, Jarret." I suck in a shuddering breath. "You have to let me go."

"For how long?"

"Forever."

"No." His jaw turns to stone. "Never."

It's the reaction I feared. The one I have no armor against. I'm cracking apart inside so painfully I have to separate from myself to deal with it.

I have to convince us both of the ugly truth. "We've been playing a twisted game. The only winning move is to walk away. You had to know this would end eventually."

"You're wrong." He grips my nape, his fingers ice cold against my skin. "We both won the second you showed up at the ranch."

"But I came here searching for answers. I've been

searching for so long and feel like I'm everywhere and nowhere at all."

"You're where you're supposed to be, where you belong."

"I own nothing."

"You own *me.*"

My lungs lose air, and tears careen down my face. The impulse to fall at his feet steals the strength from my legs. I pivot and open the car door, leaning on it for support.

"We're in different seasons of our lives." I scan the glistening snowdrifts, blanketing the night with ice-white dust. "Your heart is in spring, floating in the enchantment of first love. You're still hopeful, still planting seeds and eager to watch them grow. But I'm in the autumn of my life. I've loved. I've lost, and now it's late. I'm tired, Jarret. I can't give you what you deserve."

"You're giving up."

"I'm giving *you* up. Freeing you to move on. You think you love me, but when you find the next one, you'll thank me."

"Is that what I am to you? Just another man to love and lose?"

No. That's why this hurts so goddamn much. I've been through breakups, walkouts, and abandonments. I cried. I moved on.

Jarret Holsten isn't a man I can move on from. He's the man I will never know as deeply as I want even as he forever owns my heart. This isn't a break-up. It's a separation of souls.

So strong is the barbed wire that stitches us together that the process of separating myself from him leaves behind bleeding, shredded hunks.

But I don't tell him this. He'll cling to it with a determination that will crush my own.

Instead, I gather the remains of my resolve and

say, "I'm sorry."

I'm always sorry. Always regretting. Apologies mean nothing if I keep doing things I'm sorry for. But it's different this time. I'm the one walking away, not the other way around. Does that mean I'm finally doing the right thing? Or did I finally meet the right man?

I'm crumbling. Talking myself out of this. Losing my willpower. I slide in behind the steering wheel and reach for the door handle.

"I'll change your mind." He grips the door, preventing me from closing it.

"Not this time. Let go."

"I'll heal the damage I've done. I'll carry you through this."

"Do you have such little confidence in me? You think I can't heal on my own? That I need to be *carried*?"

"No." A pained whisper. "You're right." A sheen of wetness dilutes his golden eyes, and he steps back, hunching into the warmth of his coat. "You don't need me."

Everything inside me collapses and shatters, as if he swung a mallet at my chest. "Jarret, that's not—"

"I'll wait." He stands taller, shoulders back, and adopts the confident stance so intrinsic to who he is. "Take your space, your time, whatever you need. But I won't let you take forever. That belongs to me. Your forever is *mine*."

He doesn't give me a chance to argue. Strong and swift, his strides carry him across the lot and into the shadows on the front porch.

He's letting me go with a stipulation. It's temporary.

If I can't give in, and he can't let go, we'll come to an impasse. He'll grow bored. Lose interest. He has so many better options.

Options I can't think about. Women I refuse to imagine warming his bed.

I can't do this. It's not too late to change my mind.

I grip the steering wheel, forcing myself to stay in the car as a sob breaks free, followed by tears, choking breaths, trembling bones. I'm falling apart.

Conor emerges from the porch with a bag and my purse and sprints across the snowy lot in a whipping tangle of red hair.

I wipe my face as she approaches the car, my gaze drifting to the stable.

She leans in and glances out through the windshield. "Chicken will always have a home here."

"Thank you." I take a breath and let it out.

"I called my phone from yours, so you have my number. Here." She plops my purse on my lap. "Don't say I never gave you anything."

"Conor…"

"I packed as much of your things as I could." She tosses the bag into the passenger seat. "When you land, wherever that may be, text me your address. If you don't, he'll hire a private investigator with money he doesn't have, and he *will* find you. If you tell me where you are, I'll be able to give him updates and keep him away as long as I can. Okay?"

I look back at the silhouette standing beside Jake in the shadows of the porch.

She follows my gaze and returns to me. "He'll be okay. He has us. You're the one I'm worried about. I know how badly this hurts. I've been there."

She's a helluva lot stronger than I am.

I remove the keys from the purse with a shaky hand. "I'm doing the right thing."

"You're doing the brave thing. He'll wait. For as long as it takes."

"I don't want him to wait."

"That's not up to you." She steps back and shoves her hands in her coat pockets. "Text me. You won't want to, but you'll do it. No matter what happens with Jarret, Lorne and I are your family."

Her soft smile hits hard, but her words center me. I don't know if I'll ever reach out to her. I'm not that brave. But it's nice to know she wants me to.

She closes the door and returns to the porch. I don't watch her retreat or let my eyes drift to the dark shadow under the overhang.

I put the car in gear and maneuver through the snow and onto the dirt road. My chest is so tight I can't breathe, but I hold it together until the ranch fades in the rearview mirror.

When the misery floods in, it's an avalanche. Uncertainty claws from my chest. Determination holds my foot to the gas pedal. Heartbreak fills the car with godawful noise.

I turn on the radio and cry harder as *Just A Fool* by Christina Aguilera & Blake Shelton tortures me with cruel lyrics.

It's okay. I'll be okay. I might be falling apart, but it's an opportunity to rebuild myself. I'm lost, but I'm going to find myself. I'm doing this for me.

Except I know that's a lie. I'm doing it for him.

He deserves a woman who doesn't resent him, who isn't afraid of him, who wouldn't even consider walking away from him.

I'm not good enough.

When I reach the edge of town, I leave the *could've been's, should've been's,* and *never will be's,* and head south.

Destination unknown.

"You need to be patient." Conor glares at me, her eyes as green as her sweater.

Two auburn braids fall past her shoulders in the same style Maybe wore, and it pisses me off.

I slam the refrigerator door, wobbling the contents. "It's been two months."

Two fucking months and Maybe hasn't called. No messages. No updates. Nothing. I'm confined in a persistent fog of rage and helplessness. My patience flew the coop the moment she drove away.

Jake leans against the back counter, his face a tapestry of blue and yellow bruises. Mine looks worse. We talk with our fists, and we've been talking a lot lately.

"I'm calling the private investigator." I pop the cap on a beer and move to push past Conor.

She blocks my path, anchors her fists on her hips, and raises an eyebrow.

I know that look. It judges and scolds with a terrible reminder. Not too long ago, we shut her out of our lives. We let her believe we abandoned her for six years, and here I am, raging about being ignored for two months.

"Fine." I grit my teeth. "I'll give her more time."

"Thank you." She gentles her expression. "And try to be a little more tolerable."

I can't promise that. Anger's my trusted companion. It feeds me and keeps me breathing.

With a long draw from the beer, I storm out of the kitchen and into my bedroom.

Maybe's hair tie sits on the nightstand next to the cream I used on her welts. There's a bottle of mint shampoo in the shower, little cotton shorts under my pillow, and random girly things in the closet. Her sweet, feminine scent lingers in every corner, and I'm terrified it'll fade before I see her again.

I'm crawling inside my skin, missing her, cursing her, hating her, and aching for her. If she saw me in this state, she would be horrified.

I writhe in my bed at night, fucking my fist like a sex-addicted fiend. I snap at everyone who looks at me. My best friend has become a white calf named Chicken, and I can't eat meat without feeling ill. I'm twisted-up, banged-up, so fucking desperate for her I can't stand myself.

Does she think she's the only one hurting? I want to bloody her ass for leaving me. I want to punish myself for letting her leave.

Is she safe? Does she think about me? Is she coming to terms with what happened? Or has she moved on with someone else?

My vision turns red, and I pace the room, vibrating with fury and needing an outlet. The walls close in around me, huge sections demolished from repeated collisions with my hands.

My fists flex.

From my pocket, I remove my phone and pull up *Fuck You Bitch* by Wheeler Walker Jr.

Buckled

As the sneering song croons through the speakers, I move to a pristine wall and lay into it.

Swinging my fists, I break through sheetrock and send up a cloud of dust.

Fuck her. I let my arms fly, savoring the pain.

I hate her. I punch harder. Right hand. Left hand. My knuckles throb.

I fucking love her. I grip my head and roar.

FOUR MONTHS LATER…

I wake. The room is empty. The walls are bare, the air stale.

Jarret isn't here. He isn't near.

"I don't care." I push out of bed and move toward the window, opening it wide.

The summer morning breeze brushes its emptiness against my face and stirs the frizzy ends of my hair. It's not the same breeze that kisses Julep Ranch. It doesn't caress my skin or cleanse my lungs. It doesn't carry the warmth of his breaths.

It's insubstantial. Meaningless. I can't relate to it.

I'm truly lost.

Closing the window, I let my fingers linger on the sill. Traffic motors by on the narrow street three stories below. People stroll along, walking dogs and carrying coffee cups. Purpose propels their steps. They have places to go. Loved ones to see.

Since living here, I've kept to myself and evaded all forms of relationships. I can't risk anyone discovering

I was married. Rogan was never reported missing, and if someone starts prying and retracing my steps, they might uncover the crimes at Julep Ranch.

I left Jarret because I want him to be free of my misery. I want him to be happy, unshackled by his past, and never ever confined to prison walls.

Where are you?

Are you alone?

Do you miss me?

Are you happy?

Dangerous thoughts. They possess my mind like demons, stifled by willpower but always fighting for dominance, hissing temptations under heated breath, and easily summoned in moments of weakness.

It's been six months since I fled the ranch. That night, I drove south and ended up in a small town in middle Texas that reminds me of Sandbank.

I checked in at a motel and ate at a diner across the street. The server was exhausted and didn't hold back her complaints about the waitress who just quit.

I asked for the job. I don't know why. I guess it felt like an omen. Within a week, I was earning tips and moving into an apartment down the road.

Conor started texting me a month later. She checks in regularly, always asking about me, giving me updates on Chicken, and never mentioning Jarret. My responses are vague.

I'm fine.

I'm safe.

I'm not ready to tell you where I'm at.

Until last night.

She didn't ask for my address. She demanded it. I knew my time of avoidance was over, so I sent it to her.

It's a four-hour drive from the ranch. I expected him to be here this morning, but I'm glad he's not. I'm not strong enough to battle him. I'm too selfish and fragile right now to send him back to his life without me.

Buckled

I think about him constantly. When I'm hurrying out the door for work, I imagine his tongue on my neck, and my skin shivers. When I'm running in the park behind my apartment, I hear his voice in my head, and my body heats. When I'm waiting tables during the lunch rush, I feel the tickle of his fingers between my legs, and my thighs clench.

I miss him more during the day when I'm busy than at night when I'm lonely.

I miss him with excruciating agony, and those pangs are permanent.

Stepping back from the window, I grab my phone and set *Furnace Room Lullaby* by Neko Case on repeat.

The haunting country song serenades me as I shower and get ready for work. I finish piling my hair into a bun and tilt my head at the sound of honking on the street.

Not just one horn. Multiple cars blare repeatedly, which is odd for this quiet little town.

I wander to the window and freeze.

Jarret's truck sits out front with a trailer hitched to the back. The rig takes up more than half of the narrow street, preventing traffic from moving in either direction.

Standing on the front lawn three stories below, he stares up at me from beneath his hat, a braided lead in his hand, and Chicken beside him.

My heart rate explodes with fear and elation, and the hairs on my nape stand on end.

He's here.

He brought Chicken.

I can't breathe.

God, he's gorgeous. Tight jeans, fitted t-shirt, tanned skin, muscles flexing from here to there. His face hides in the shade of his hat, but I feel the burn of his predatory eyes along my skin.

He came for me.

That means he hasn't moved on.

But he has to. He can't be here. How do I make him understand that without hurting him? How far will I twist and break him so he can be free of me?

I don't have it in me to be cruel, but we can't fall back together. I'm too mixed-up in guilt and distrust. He murdered my husband, and I didn't tell him I was married. He's a killer, and I'm deceitful. The blood has seeped too deep, the wounds too infected. We're a toxic combination.

I have to stay away, even if it means wrapping myself in the hell of my own undoing.

We stare at each other through the glass, across the distance. He doesn't move. Doesn't try to speak or gesture at me to come out. He just watches, ignoring the honking around him, disregarding the entire world, as if I'm the only thing that exists.

We're in our own universe, and I can almost hear his heartbeat in the magic of the moment.

He's waiting for me. Waiting for me to go to him. Waiting for me to take him back. Doesn't he realize how much happier he'll be if he just lets me go?

With a steeling breath, I close my eyes. Then I step out of view from the window. Sliding down the wall, I land on my heels and hug my knees to my chest.

The song cycles three more times. Tears sting my face, hot and relentless, pouring from splintered cracks.

Then the honking stops. I peek out the window.

He's gone.

A week passes before I see him again. He brings Chicken and stands under my window. Nothing more. Just his unyielding stance, his silence, his direct eye contact. He's sending an unmistakable message.

I'll wait.

As summer withers into autumn, his visits continue. Once a week. Twice a week. The days are irregular. Sometimes he comes alone and watches me run in the park. Often, he arrives at night and sits beneath my window.

How do I deal with this? Indirect resistance to his presence, avoidance of conversation, procrastination—these are the only tactics I have. Of course, they're not effective.

Meanwhile, I'm tormented by the fact that he spends eight hours in his truck on the days he visits me. He's missing work, which he can't afford to do. He's stalking, which is the complete opposite of moving on. And he's making me crazy.

I find myself looking for him, searching the streets, trembling on pins and needles for his next visit.

Then winter plunges the temperatures below freezing, and his routine changes.

He shows up at the diner where I work.

On my lunch break, I sit at the bar, watching the ice melt in my soda. He lowers onto the stool beside me and orders coffee from the server.

We sit together in silence as flurries of snow whistle past the windows. If anyone's watching us, they don't know we have history. They don't realize how out of place and lost we are. A widow and a murderer, stuck in a broken love story.

Then he looks at me, and an electric spark tingles from my scalp to my toes and deep inside my bones. In that moment, I've never felt so alone.

I wish I'd never met him. I resent the unwavering love I feel for him. I silently will him to leave.

He finishes his coffee and walks out the door without a word or a glance.

And that's how we spend the winter. Sitting at the bar during my lunch break. Sharing a moment of longing, regret, and uncertainty. Those are my feelings. He broadcasts something entirely different.

There's no verbal conversation, but he

communicates. With his eyes resting on the side of my face. With his breath pacing the erratic rush of mine. With his company intruding on my life and invading my every thought.

He still loves me. He wants me back, and he won't give up.

I'm fully aware I've fallen into a passive-aggressive pattern with him, and as the months wear on, Jarret remains silently aggressive, waiting for me all up in my personal space.

Then one night, a year after I left him, his aggressiveness reaches new levels.

I've been pursuing the local paper since I arrived in this town, damn-near begging for an opportunity to write for them. Fashion, entertainment, community news… I've offered to cover any column, full-time or part-time.

The owner, Keegan Mitchell, finally agrees to meet with me at a fancy steakhouse in town. It's a strange venue for an interview, and not because I'm a vegetarian. I prefer to talk in his office, but he insists on dinner.

Over a course of wine and salad, Keegan asks about my education and experience. He has my resume, so the questions feel a little redundant. Maybe he didn't have time to look over it?

I answer enthusiastically, and he smiles and bobs his head.

He's a nice-looking man. Black hair, energetic eyes, shorter than average, a tad too skinny, and a few years my elder—he reminds me of Tom Cruise with that overstretched smile.

"I noticed there's no ring." He cocks his chin at my hand. "Not married?"

"Not married."

"No boyfriend?"

I fight the impulse to squirm. I'm not sure how this line of questioning applies to the job, but I push back my shoulders and keep my professional face in place. "I assure you my personal life won't interfere with work."

"Very good." He nods, and his gaze dips to my chest before he catches himself. "Why do you want this job?"

My brow furrows.

I went to college to be a journalist. Writing about fashion was the only job I could land after school. Given my mom's love for makeup and glitter, I had a solid background on the subject. But after working on the ranch and soaking in the outdoors, I lost my passion for office work.

I want this job because I want to move on with my life. Waiting tables isn't moving on. It feels more like I'm just... Waiting.

Since I can't say any of this, I open my mouth to deliver a canned response.

"Stand up." The low, deep voice reverberates against my back, shooting a shiver down my spine.

I twist in the chair, my heart in my stomach, and meet the blazing, feral eyes of the one man who scares me more than any other. "What are you doing here?"

He steps to my side and turns that menacing gaze on Keegan. "Who the fuck are you?"

"Jarret," I whisper harshly.

"I'm Keegan Mitchell, and you're making the lady uncomfortable. I'm going to have to ask you to leave."

It's the absolute wrong thing to say. The cords go taut in Jarret's neck, and his hands clench and release at his sides.

"The lady," he spits past grinding teeth, "belongs to me. And if you look at her chest one more time, I'll tear you limb from limb, starting with your dick."

My face heats. My vision clouds, and every inch of me stiffens.

Any chance I had at this job is gone.

I turn my attention to Keegan and try to keep the fury out of my voice. "I'm so sorry. If you'll excuse us for just a minute—"

"Don't worry, sweetheart. I can deal with this." He rises from the chair and stands in a face-off with Jarret.

Six inches shorter and a fraction of the muscle mass, Keegan must be suffering from Napoleon syndrome. Or stupidity.

"Time for you to leave." He scowls at Jarret and reaches for me.

His fingers curl around my wrist, and he tries to pull me over some imaginary line, as if he has a claim on me.

I yank my arm free as Jarret grips Keegan's collar and neck with both hands, lifts him, and tosses him across an open table.

Place settings and flower arrangements crash to the floor. Gasps shudder from surrounding patrons, and two suit-clad servers rush toward us and stop.

My eyes burn. My throat constricts, my heartbeat sluggish and loud in my ears.

Keegan pulls himself to his feet and stumbles back, dazed and unsure.

"Stay away from her." Jarret puts his huge body in front of me, facing Keegan with his hands folded behind him.

The back of the Stetson tips upward with the dip of his chin. Muscles twitch across his shoulder blades and biceps, his neck a column of golden skin and strength. Whatever look he gives Keegan causes the man to take another step back.

"I don't want to fight you." Keegan tosses up his hands and bumps into a table. Then he fumbles for his coat and casts me a worried look.

"You better go." I slide on my own coat and snatch my purse, humiliated and seething. "I'll settle things with the restaurant."

I just want to get the fuck out of here. I've spent the last year avoiding attention and trying not to become the target of small town gossip.

Keegan pushes out the door without a backward look, and I lift my wallet from my purse. I don't have much money, barely enough to pay the rent on my studio apartment. But there are broken dishes and flower vases and a dinner tab. Do I have the cash to cover that?

Jarret tosses a few large bills on the table, more than enough to pay for the expenses.

His fingers rest possessively on my lower back, his mouth at my ear. "Let's go."

A voracious shiver weakens my knees, and I mentally slap myself. "I'm not going anywhere with you."

"Fine." He sets his hands on his hips. "We'll do this here."

A fever spreads up my neck. "We're not doing anything, anywhere."

I breeze past him and make a beeline for the door. He chases me out and through the parking lot. The chilly night air bites my skin, but my blood, my muscles, everything inside me cooks with anger.

A few feet from my car, he catches me around the waist and twists me to face him. "Were you going to fuck that weaselly motherfucker?"

"What?" My eyes bulge. "I was on a job interview!"

His expression blanches for a fleeting second before his gaze narrows ruthlessly. "He intended to be deep inside your cunt before the night was over."

"You're so fucking sick and twisted." I shove at his chest, causing his arms to constrict tighter. "Not everything is about sex."

"A man doesn't take you to dinner without making it about sex. He couldn't keep his eyes off you. Every second he sat at that table, he imagined your tight pussy squeezing around his dick." His voice rises to a shout.

"The napkin on his lap couldn't hide his fucking hard-on!"

My stomach sinks. My teeth slam together, and I push harder against him, breaking free from his grip. "Fuck you!"

"You know I'm right, Maybe."

Hard to argue when I picked up on those unsettling vibes during dinner.

I spin toward my car, sliding on the icy pavement in my heels. He sticks to my side, ready to catch my fall but doesn't touch me as I hurry to the driver's side door.

"Even if that's true..." I dig out my keys and unlock the car. "You had no right to step in."

"You're mine." He crowds me against the door, the force of his breaths forming stony clouds between us. "I protect what's mine."

My heart skips. Oh, how I ache to be his.

But I'm not.

Regardless, I won't let him or any other man make me feel like I can't take care of myself.

"By storming in there and ruining my meeting, you basically told me you think I'm weak and incapable of surviving without your manly interference. You think so little of me you have to save me from a job interview, because my judgment's so poor and my willpower's so pathetic I don't know how to walk away from a bad situation."

"I don't think any of that." His face turns to granite. "You walked away from me."

A sharp twinge cuts through my chest. "You don't love me, Jarret. If you did, you would let me struggle, let me work through my trials, and step in only to guide me toward independence instead of insecurity."

"I'm not built that way. I can't bear to see you struggle, and you're already so powerfully independent I could never take that away from you." His eyes harden in the glow of the streetlight. "I love you so goddamn much

I can't function without you. I can't sleep. I can't work. I can't fucking breathe when you're four fucking hours away."

I love him, too. More than he can possibly know.

I have to let him go.

If I had any doubts before tonight, I don't now. We're a combustible vortex of acid and corrosion, gunpowder and sparks. One lit match and we'll go up in flames.

"Go home." I open the car door.

He shoves it closed. "You're going home with me."

"No." I advance on him and stab a finger against his chest. "We're over. No more standing under my window, stalking me in the park, or lurking around my diner. Go home and do *not* come back." I suck down the pain in my throat and turn back to the car. "If I see you again, I'll slap you with a restraining order."

"Threaten me all you want." He clasps a yank of my hair and drags my face to his. "I will *never* let you go."

"Stop." The word falls from my lips and hangs between us.

His eyes widen, and his hand loosens but doesn't release.

"Stop," I say louder, firmer.

In the year and a half I've known him, I've never used that word.

The grip in my hair vanishes, and he lowers his arms, his chin, his voice. "You've always held all the power. You don't even realize how much control you have."

He cups the back of my head and touches his lips to my brow.

As he turns away, the barbed wire around us unravels and snaps. As he crosses the parking lot and steps onto the street, my throat burns, and my hands shake to reach for him.

I stand there long after he fades into the darkness.

I wait for him to return.

I wait for months.

This time, he's gone for good.

Love hurts.

It's an emotional abuser, insidious and manipulative, charming its way into unsuspecting hearts before beating the ever-loving shit out of the defenseless insides.

Love is as invisible as the wounds it inflicts and as lethal as a knife. When it's taken away, all that remains is pain.

Unlearning that pain is impossible. It's a road with no exit ramps or turnoffs. Once it carves its way through the soul, there's no choice but to hold on and ride it to the dark, bitter, lonely end.

Love heals.

It's a universal balm that repairs fractures, soothes pain, and stitches the heart into wholeness again.

Love is meant to buckle the strongest and fiercest person. It's the very thing the soul cries for. To recoil from that is to reject the most powerful medicine, the greatest cure for loneliness.

With love, even the darkest season of guilt and betrayal can be defeated.

SIX MONTHS LATER…

Today is the same as every other day. I wake. I wait tables. I run in the park. I go home.

At night, I write boring fashion articles for a small print magazine in Dallas. It doesn't pay much, but it utilizes my degree.

It keeps my mind occupied.

While my mundane routine hasn't changed, today is a six-month milestone in a string of milestones marking Jarret-related changes in my life.

I met him six months after Rogan disappeared.

I lived with him for six months.

I didn't see him for six months, until he appeared beneath my window.

He stalked me for six months, until I told him to stop.

Today marks six months since the last time I saw him.

Something should've happened. I searched my surroundings from dawn to dusk, trying to pick him out in a crowd, scanning streets for his truck, fully expecting him to show, as if he knows the significance of the date.

But he's not here. It's eleven at night, and I'm just as alone as I was yesterday.

I've known Jarret for two years now, exceeding the longest relationship I've ever had with anyone besides my mom. Not that I'm in a relationship with him. But my heart is. I left the battered, bleeding thing at Julep Ranch a year and a half ago, knowing I would never get it back.

Conor and I stopped texting shortly after Jarret walked away. It was too painful to respond to her questions with assurances I didn't feel.

The good news is I finally figured myself out. The bad news?

I'm a miserable fucking wreck.

I've given a lot of thought to the guilt I've been carrying. I shouldn't have married Rogan without getting to know him first. I should've reported him missing. I shouldn't have fallen in love with one man while married to another. Clinging to all these *should have's* and *shouldn't have's* was just a way for me to feel sorry for myself.

Rather than continuing down that self-destructive path, I've decided to treat it as a gift. It's taken me eighteen months to come to one crucial conclusion.

I can't and won't regret what happened.

If I hadn't made all those mistakes, I wouldn't have met Jarret. I wouldn't have experienced what it is to truly love someone and feel that love reciprocated. The best six months of my life were on that ranch, working side by side with a man who refused to walk away from me.

That's the detrimental part. In the end, I forced him to leave. I used my safe word like a brandished weapon, cut him at his knees, and removed his power. He left because I gave him no choice.

He loved me, and he risked that love to tell me he killed Rogan. He could've easily lied and prevented me from running. But he didn't. He did the honorable thing and told me the truth. In return, I hurt him.

After eighteen months of searching, self-analyzing, and introspection, I now realize what I experienced in my relationships before Jarret wasn't love. I replaced each lover with a new lover, but true love can't be replaced.

True love is finding my soulmate when I wasn't searching for him. It was the depth of my smile when I worked beside him. It was putting his happiness over mine.

True love isn't about being inseparable. It's being separated for over a year, and feeling even stronger, deeper in love.

I love him.

Distance didn't erase it. Time didn't expunge it. Losing him didn't make it go away.

I love him. I miss him, and I'm a wretched, disgusting mess without him. I make myself sick wondering how he's doing, what he's thinking, and if he's happy. But I can't go back. Not after the way I ended things.

He's strong enough to have healed himself by now. It's been six months since I've seen him. Six months is plenty of time for him to move on and find someone else. I won't sabotage his happiness in any way.

But what if he's not happy?

If he's still alone, if he's suffering even a fraction of the misery I am, I want to know.

I *need* to know.

Anyone can say, *I love you.* But if he didn't move on, if he waited all this time, that's more proof than words can ever express.

Lying on the mattress in a studio apartment I've never furnished, I roll to my side and reach for my phone on the floor.

Radio silence with Conor means I'm in the dark with regard to the entire family. She should be finished with school now, and Lorne is coming up on eight years served in prison. He could be up for parole any time.

I clutch the phone tightly and stare at the screen. I miss them so much and want to know everything that's going on with them.

I'll just send a short text to Conor, a friendly greeting, and go from there.

As I pull up the messaging screen, the phone buzzes with an incoming call, making me jump.

Private Number

Who would be ringing this late? Probably a misdial or drunken attempt to call someone else.

I accept the call. "Hello?"

"Maybe Quinn?" A woman whispers.

"Who's calling?"

"It's Raina Benally. I'm..." Her voice rasps through the phone. "We met at John Holsten's house."

"Yes, I remember." My pulse speeds up. "I gave you my number. Is everything okay?"

Silence.

It lasts so long I check the screen. We're still connected.

"Raina? Are you there?"

"I need help." Her words are strained, as if she's forcing them out.

"What happened?"

"I... I have to go." A rustling sound scratches through the line. "I'll call you back."

"Wait. I'm about three hours away. Are you still at John's house?"

"You can't come here. Promise me."

A chill crawls over my scalp. "If you're in trouble, I'm calling the cops."

"No!" A cry chokes her voice. "No cops. Please. I'll call you back."

The line disconnects.

Fucking shit, what the hell was that?

Is she hurt? In danger? Why did she have to call me back? She was whispering and sounded really fucking scared.

My breathing accelerates. I don't know what to do.

I throw on jeans, a t-shirt, and shove my feet into Jarret's boots. Then I wait.

Thirty minutes later, she hasn't called back.

I try redialing the private number. It's blocked.

Grabbing my keys and purse, I race to my car and start the drive toward northern Texas. I still have John's address, and I still carry the small knife under the driver's seat. Not that I intend on using the latter, but she said, *No cops.*

Does that mean she's involved in something criminal? The whole fucking family is covered in blood. I should turn around and stay the fuck out of it.

Except I gave her my number with the unspoken offer to help. God, that was over two years ago. What if he's been hurting her or holding her against her will all this time?

I hit the gas and drive through the night. Eyes gritty and head heavy, I arrive on his rural road after three in the morning.

He lives on a small plot of land, surrounded by fields and woods. No neighbors. Nowhere to hide my car.

I park on the shoulder about a quarter of a mile from the house. Setting my phone on vibrate, I slip it and the knife into my pocket. Then I walk the rest of the way.

The June heat has cooled off beneath the shade of nightfall, leaving a sticky, mosquito-loving mugginess. I swat at the bloodsuckers on my arms and quiet my footfalls on the poorly paved road.

At the gravel driveway, I remain hidden in the shadows of overgrown shrubs. Darkness envelops his house. Outside, inside, nothing stirs.

Raina told me not to come, so I don't plan on rolling right up to the front door. *Yet.*

I check my phone to make sure I didn't miss a call and linger for another ten minutes, certain they're asleep. There's nothing I can do tonight.

Exhaustion pulls on my eyelids as I make the trek back to the car. The motel in town appeared vacant when I passed through earlier. I'll stay there tonight so that when she calls, I'll be close.

Twenty minutes later, I pay the clerk, shuffle into a musty room, and fall into an uneasy sleep.

Early the next morning, I wake on a lumpy bed and immediately check my phone. No missed calls.

The knot in my stomach tightens. Something's wrong.

How long should I wait? What if she never contacts me?

I call in sick to the diner, shower, and grab breakfast from the bakery next door. Then I return to the room and pace.

I need Jarret. If I asked him for help, he would come. He's only two hours away. But what if he rejects my call? What if a woman answers his phone?

My chest clenches. I can't deal with that right now. Besides, the last words I hurled at him were along the lines of *let me work through my own problems.*

Another hour of pacing and waiting works me into a frazzled panic. It's almost noon before I decide on a plan. Or the beginnings of one. It's enough to spur me into the car, armed with questions for John Holsten.

I park in his driveway, shaking and sweating. I chewed the shit out of my cheek on the way here, leaving a shredded gouge against my tongue. I can't do this.

Yes, I can. It's not like he's going to kill me.

Would he?

With the knife and phone in my pocket, I head to the door and knock.

Footsteps approach from within, seizing my lungs. The door opens, and John Holsten stands on the threshold, wearing an oily smirk.

An undershirt hangs untucked from black trousers. His black and silver hair greases around his ears, long overdue for a trim. He's also in desperate need of a shave. And a shower.

"Maybe Quinn." His brown eyes sweep over me and pause on the boots. "Didn't think I'd see you again. Still looking for your husband?"

"Not exactly."

He gives my boots another narrowed glance. "My boy had a pair of those. Looked just like 'em."

"Jarret gave them to me." My toes flex against the soles. "May I come in?"

"Please." He steps aside, his gaze crawling over my skin as I slide by him. "Something to drink?"

"No, thank you." I quickly inspect the sitting room filled with heavy wooden furniture.

Nothing seems out of place. The kitchen sits in the back. Empty. The doorway beside it leads to a small bathroom. The hallway to the left gives way to two more doors. One opens to a bedroom. The other is closed.

"Where's Raina today?" I lower onto the armchair with a direct view of that closed door.

"She's not feeling well. Too much whiskey last night, I'm afraid." He winks and pours himself a glass of the stuff from the liquor cabinet in the sitting room.

"I'm sorry to hear that." Dread builds in my throat. "I hope she feels better."

"So you found Rogan Cassidy?" He sits in the chair across from me, heaving his round gut over his belt.

I assume he knows Rogan's dead, but I won't

admit to anything that incriminates Jarret and Jake. "Yes, but he's not speaking to me."

He chuckles. "I s'pose he's not."

"I thought you could help me fill in some gaps."

He lifts the tumbler to his lips, studying me over the rim. "Ask your questions."

I start with the easy ones. How long did he know Rogan? When did they meet? How often did they talk? I know the answers, but I'm here to keep him talking with the hope that Raina will emerge from that room.

I speak loud enough for her to hear my voice. If she opens the door, she'll see me.

After ten minutes of stalling, there hasn't been a peep from the hallway, and I've run out of easy questions.

"Did Rogan…?" I pull in a deep breath and release it. "Did he deliberately steal from me with no intention of returning?"

John leans back in the chair and balances the whiskey glass on his knee. "He took you to the cleaners, sugar. You were one of many. Just another con in a long list of cons."

"What?" My voice strangles as ice prickles my cheeks.

"He married you for your inheritance. Same with the others before you." He cocks his head. "You didn't know he was married six times?"

"No." My fingers bite into the armrests, and my stomach sours with disgust.

"The man was a con-artist. Mighty good at it, too. Till he got greedy. My boys would've never given up that land. Too much attachment to it."

The room wobbles around me, distorting his voice.

I was just the target of a con. All that guilt and self-loathing over a man who didn't love me was a joke. I really am naive.

"How are my boys?" His eyes drop to my boots

again.

"I don't know."

"What happened?"

"I worked on the ranch for a while. They didn't trust me. I didn't trust them. It was a waste of time."

It was the best time of my life. When I'm finished here, I'm going to call Conor and beg for an update on their lives.

"I miss it." He kicks out a boot, sprawling in the chair. "Nothing beats herding cattle on a hot day like this."

As he drones on about his life on the ranch, I steal peeks at the door down the hall. Is she actually in the room? Is she hurt? I need to see her.

My plan got me into the house. Whatever comes after is on a wing and a prayer.

"May I use your bathroom?" I need time to think, without his wandering eyes and nonstop jabber.

"Behind you." He gestures at the door.

"Thank you." I shut myself inside the small room and pinch the bridge of my nose.

I need an excuse to go into that bedroom, but I don't have one. I could demand to see her. My threats worked on him before, and I have enough evidence against him to make him sweat.

Problem is I would never follow through. If I reported John Holsten to the authorities, he would take Jarret and Jake down with him.

I have nothing.

Flushing the toilet, I step out and into an empty room. A shadow passes across the window, and I spot John outside. Standing on the porch, he holds a phone to his ear, head down and back to me.

I lurch into motion.

Shutting the bathroom door, I slip into the hall. If he glances inside, he'll think I'm still on the toilet.

Adrenaline spikes my veins at a full pelt as I sprint toward the closed-off bedroom. I grip the handle, push, and it doesn't give.

What the—?

There! On the top edge of the door, a barrel bolt holds it in place. I slide it open and shove, stumbling in and...

"Oh my God." The sharp scent of blood hits my nose, and I gag.

The room is unfurnished, the wood floors smeared with dark crimson stains. A heavy blanket hangs over a single window, letting in a crack of light. I follow that dim glow to the corner, where the bruised and bloody form of a woman's body curls in on itself.

Steel shackles encircle her wrists, connected to chains that fasten to the wall. Her face is unrecognizable, swollen and lacerated, black and blue, and caked in dried gore.

Full-body tremors hold me frozen as I glance at the empty hall. The moment he ends his phone call, he'll be inside the house, waiting for me to emerge from the bathroom.

If he knows I found Raina, he'll kill me. After seeing the damage he's done to her, I have no doubt. I need to be quick.

My stomach solidifies into a block of ice as I run toward her and drop to my knees.

Padlocks secure the shackles, the chains unyielding when I yank on them.

"Raina?" I shake her bruised shoulder, rousing a moan from her throat. "Where's the key?"

She blinks up at me with one good eye, the other sealed shut.

"The key." I grip the cuffs on her wrists, my pulse careening into dizzying levels. "Where?"

"Kitchen." Her tongue darts out, wetting busted lips. "Hook."

"Hook where?" I strain my hearing, listening for the creak of the front door.

If he comes in, I need an exit plan.

The window.

I hurry toward it and sweep aside the blanket. No bars. It faces the woods out back and a shed that sits at the tree line.

Two window locks give way after a little force, but it doesn't open. I put all my strength into it, grunting and losing precious seconds.

"Painted shut," she whispers from the floor.

"Can you walk?" I remove the blade from my pocket and cut around the seams.

"Don't know."

The window lifts, and the bottled breath in my chest bursts free.

"The hook?" I close the window, leave it unlocked, and run to the door.

"Wall. Next to fridge."

"Try to stand. I'll be back."

"No cops." Her hoarse plea follows me out the door.

I close it behind me, return the lock, and listen.

His voice muffles through the thin walls, indiscernible but definitely outside. I take off toward the kitchen, locate the hook, the key. *Oh, thank fuck.*

As I come around the corner of the sitting room, he stands outside the window and lowers the phone from his ear.

I have two seconds before he turns around, and I use those to swing open the bathroom door and position my body to appear as if I'm just coming out.

He meets my gaze through the glass, and I hold my breath. After a suffocating moment of eye contact, he turns toward the front door.

I exhale loudly, wheezing, trembling, and burning

up with chills. The key goes in my pocket. A soft smile settles onto my face, and I calmly lower onto the armchair.

If I bolt, it'll make him suspicious. So I prepare myself for a horrifying chitchat with a monster while pretending a woman isn't broken and chained in a room down the hall.

"Sorry about that." He steps inside and closes the door. "Had a little emergency recently. Couldn't ignore that call."

"Everything okay?"

"Much better." He scrutinizes me for the span of a hundred thundering heartbeats. Then a grin curls his lips. "Now where were we?"

"The stallion you tried to break..."

"Ah, yes. That there was some fine breeding."

He returns to his chair and proceeds to tell me all about his horses, John Deere tractors, and the winter that wouldn't quit.

My mind flails through the agonizing discussion, tormenting me with scenarios that end with me shackled in that blood-stained room beside Raina. I need to get out of here. Every second I delay is a second he could look into my eyes and register my fear.

I wait for a pause in his storytelling, and when it finally comes, I leap on it.

"I should get going." I reach for my keys. "I have a long drive back."

"Where to?"

"I'd rather not say." I stand and offer my hand. "Thank you for answering my questions."

"It's been a pleasure." He grips my fingers, and his thumb slides over my wrist, spreading a revolted shudder through my body.

He walks me out and stands on the porch as I move in a petrified fog to the car. He continues to watch me as I pull out of the driveway.

I turn in the direction I came, and the moment he's out of view, I lose it.

My lungs burst, shoving air past my parched throat. My hands shake violently against the steering wheel, and tears pour from my eyes.

I'm terrified to go back, but I have no choice. He'll notice that key missing, and when he does, Raina's chance for survival disintegrates.

Pulling off onto a dirt path nestled in trees, I park the car out of view of the road. Then I type a message to Jarret. I outline the situation and provide the address of his dad's house.

But I don't send the text. It's my emergency plan.

My parking spot is a five-minute hike from the house, through a field. I hope to hell Raina can make that trek. She's around my weight, and I won't be able to carry her.

From my overnight bag, I remove a casual sundress. I don't have extra shoes, but at least she'll have something to wear.

The walk back is a harrowing test of bravery. I'm not a courageous person, but I am stubborn. That stubbornness keeps me moving. The phone in my pocket gives me strength.

If something happens, I'll press send on that message, and Jarret will come.

When I reach the house, I approach from the back, keeping to the trees. My heart pounds so viciously I feel like my ribs are breaking.

I sprint toward the room where she's held and arrive at the window. It groans with the hoist of my hands, and I freeze. Every organ in my body turns to stone, waiting for a blade or bullet to run through me.

Nothing happens.

I poke my head under the glass pane and find Raina swaying on her feet in the middle of the room, the chains stretched as far as they can go.

She holds out her hands, rattling the metal links. I toss the key, and she catches it.

Lowering to the floor, she works the locks. It takes forever. Minutes. Hours. The space between my shoulders contracts and itches, and saliva thickens into a dry paste in my mouth.

Hurry. Faster. Come on.

I should climb in and help her, but that's where my bravery ends. I entered the house of horrors once. I won't do it again.

Finally, she rises, arms free, and focuses her good eye on me.

I stretch an arm through the window, while keeping my attention on the open space behind me.

She staggers toward me and falls against the sill. We go slow and quiet. She climbs. I pull. Her body is so damaged and malnourished her bruises have bruises, her bones press beneath her skin, and some of the lacerations rip open as she falls through the window with a silent cry.

I release a held breath and loop her arm over my shoulders. "Now we run."

The forty-foot dash to the tree line is the part I dread most. Can she run? Will he see us? Will bullets plow down our heart-pounding escape?

My blood catches fire, my limbs functioning on their own. I'm disconnected from everything but the ever-present drum of my pulse.

Her feet move in pace with mine, her naked body eking out the last of its strength. When we make it to the cover of foliage and thistles, she tries to collapse.

I hold her up and wrangle the dress over her head. "This isn't over until we reach the car. Five minutes. You can do this."

"Yeah." She grimaces as she works the dress over the gouges and cuts on her torso and hips. "Ready."

By the time we reach the car, I'm dragging her. My muscles burn. Hot flashes blot my vision, and my jaw aches from clenching.

As I fold her abused body into the backseat, she mumbles, "No cops."

A frightening thought runs through me. "Does he know where I live?"

"No." She releases a pained groan and passes out.

I grip the roof of the car to prevent myself from following her under. Hours of extreme stress has taken its toll. But I won't be able to relax until we're in my apartment.

My legs protest the walk to the driver's seat. My back aches as I lower behind the steering wheel.

I have a three-hour drive left. Three hours to figure out what to do with Raina Benally.

Three hours to decide if I should call Jarret.

Raina sleeps the entire duration of the drive. With a vise around my chest, I maintain the speed limit and watch the rearview mirror for signs of John Holsten.

It's a mentally agonizing, physically exhausting race to my apartment. Even harder is walking her up three flights of stairs without suspicious glances from my neighbors.

My Stetson and sunglasses hide her face, but her pain is palpable, shaking her tiny frame with every step.

Inside, I bathe her, feed her broth, treat her wounds, and tuck her into bed, during which I press her for answers. How long has he been hurting her? Why can't I call the cops or take her to a hospital? What is she not telling me?

She refuses to talk. It could be the pain, a mental breakdown, or something else, but she hasn't spoken since we left John's house.

I let her sleep and shuffle to the window. A storm just blew in, and I'm drawn by the rain pelting against the glass.

The clap of thunder electrifies my skin and fills me with a nostalgia that hugs my soul. The electric flickering of lightning illuminates my mind with images and sensations of a wild night with a perfect man. White bolts streak toward the earth, stirring treacherous longings for the one I let go.

I've starved myself for so long I don't know how to escape the cage I trapped myself in. I live in the confines of my own destruction, running a self-torturing marathon on bloody knees. But lightning storms release me from that hell, if only for a little while.

I feel him in the charged air, see his eyes burning in the violent limbs of light, and hear his roar in the rumble of thunder. Storms connect me to him, but whenever they pass, I go cold inside, my soul incomplete, my feelings numb.

Rain whips against the window inches from my face. It calls to me, my eyes fixed on the raging sky, my body gravitating toward the steel clouds that dissolve into the black landscape.

A jolting flash flickers and dies, and in that explosion of light, I see him beneath the window.

My heart stops, and I fall against the glass, pressing closer and begging my eyes to adjust to the darkness.

He can't be real. I'm losing my mind.

Another flare of light burns the sky, winking in and out through a series of jagged bolts. In the span of that illumination, he stares up at me in the rain, finding and holding my gaze.

My breaths rush out, heaving my chest.

He's here.

He's really fucking here.

His eyes widen, blinking against the downpour. He looks surprised, like he didn't expect me to be here, either.

Rain sluices off the brim of his hat and crashes against the solid silhouette of his wide stance. He doesn't move, doesn't look away.

He waits.

I slip away from the window and press my back against the wall, fighting to catch my breath.

He still loves me.

In the bed across the room, Raina doesn't stir, deep in sleep, escaping the torment of her pain.

No more waiting.

I run to the door on silent feet, down the stairs, and smash into the falling sheets of rain.

His shoulders jerk back when he sees me, his hands slipping into his front pockets, his entire body soaked and dripping.

I pause a foot away, my voice stuck in my throat, my gaze glued to his.

"Where did you go?" Muscles twitch along his jaw, his eyes flinty. "I thought you left, and I fucking lost it."

My mind spins, and I shake my head in confusion. "How did you—?"

"I live at the motel." He stabs a finger toward the center of town. "Your car's been gone since yesterday."

"What?" I swallow. Blink. Swallow again. "You live here? For how long?"

"Six months." He squints at me, challenging me to go off on him. "I drive home a couple of times a week to catch up on work. Otherwise, I'm here."

I clutch my neck, trembling, drenched, but somehow still standing as eighteen months of pain release from my body.

He never left. Never walked away.

He never abandoned me.

"I bought a truck you wouldn't recognize, so I could follow you. Watch you. I couldn't..." His hands lift to his face, and his shoulders roll forward, his huge frame shuddering beneath the deluge of rain. "I can't let you go."

"Jarret..." I cup a hand over my mouth, muffling a cry.

"Living without you is a form of death. A death I refuse to accept." He lowers his arms. Then he drops to his knees, head bowed, buckled at my feet. "You can't hide your pain from me. Your isolation, the bruises under your eyes, the permanent sadness on your lips..." His gaze lifts, stark against the strobe of lightning. "I see you. I see your misery, heartbreak, longing. It's lived in your eyes since you left, trapped in turmoil. But I see love, too. It's still there, Maybe, and I swear to God, if you would just accept it, if you would give me a chance, I'll set you free. Let me take part in your pain, walk with you, sit with you, watch over you, something, anything... Just...let me join you in the hurt." His throat bobs. "Come home."

The downpour ebbs into a gentle drizzle, beading droplets on the hard planes of his upturned face. I stand over him, drowning in rain, affection, love, and *acceptance.*

I reach toward his jaw, slide trembling fingers along his whiskers, and apply upward pressure beneath his chin. "Stand up."

His brows gather, and he slowly rises. I keep my hand on his face, cradling the sharp edges and shivering with a flood of emotion.

"Yes." I put all the answers into that one word.

"Yes?" His breath hitches, eyes searching.

"You're right, about all of it." I step closer, slipping my boots in the space between his. "I fucked up, and I've come to terms with that. I accept the mistakes, the secrets, the guilt, the wrong turns, and the dark back roads. I accept everything that's happened that led us here, and ninety years from now, I'll remember you standing in the rain, begging me to come home. And I'll never regret that I did."

Raindrops cling to his lashes, and amid the

wetness, wells something deeper, stronger.

Happiness.

"*Ninety* years?" He touches my cheek.

"Give or take. No regrets."

"Then I can finally give this back to you." He shoves a hand in his pocket and pulls out the engagement ring. "Maybe, will you—?"

"Yes." I hold out my hand, fingers extended and shaking. "You've been carrying it all this time?"

"Every day." He slides the diamond band onto my hand, fitting it snugly in place.

I pull back to take a closer look, but his fingers clamp down, holding tight to mine. He stares at me, and I stare at him, doused in a milestone of acceptance.

We move at the same time, crashing together in a stumbling, uncoordinated leap and kiss. Our foreheads bump. He staggers backward, and our lips touch and glance off, clumsy and awkward, without the connection we crave.

I right my footing and rub my brow, squirming with nervousness. "Should I have swooped in differently? I feel like I came in too hard."

"Hard is good." He grips the back of my neck and drags me against him, chest to chest.

"I was too eager, though." I clutch his wide shoulders, and wings flap in my stomach. "We angled the same way, and our teeth hit. Maybe I should've dipped when you dove? And there's also the rain. We're all slippery and—"

"Let's not overthink it." His gaze dips to my mouth.

"Okay. Yeah, kind of loses the magic." I inhale deeply, savoring the warmth of his breaths. "Can we try again?"

"Which part?"

"All of it."

His eyes spark. "I fucking love you."

"I love—"

He devours my words, kissing me like there's no choice. His tongue swirls past my lips, tasting and plunging as the light shower runs down our faces to where our mouths meet.

Cold drops, sultry air, and the distant rumble of thunder—there's something celestial about kissing this man in the rain. It's a frenzied moment that refuses to wait. An outpour of love desperate for connection, uncaring about soaked clothes or chilled skin. It's a rebellion against threatening winds and depressing conditions. Nature brings the rain, but we stand against it, united in mutual need.

He presses his lips firmly against mine, controlling the depth and asserting the rhythm. The heat of his mouth is my home, the clench of his fingers my sanctuary. He's my greatest torment and constant salvation, my beginning, my end, and all the roads between. The whole damn world should stop on its axis and take note, because no man alive knows how to love a woman like he does.

He lifts me up his chest, and I cup his face, knocking off his hat and sinking into the hungry eyes that drive me crazy.

"God, I missed you." My legs encircle his waist, and my hair falls around him, becoming one with his dark soaked strands.

He kisses droplets from my lips, and I smile against his.

"There it is." He sweeps my hair aside and nibbles a path to my ear.

"What?" I sink into his arms.

"Your smile." He palms my butt through the jeans and yanks me closer. "I haven't seen it in eighteen months."

"I'm sorry I hurt you." I bury my face in the curve

of his shoulder.

"Hey." He grips the back of my hair and captures my eyes. "I hurt you, too. No regrets, remember?"

"And no secrets."

"No lies."

"No more deals." I bite my lip.

"No more waiting." His expression tightens, his cheekbones like blades beneath the aggression in his gaze.

Does he know how hot he is when he looks at me like that? How it makes me want to smother his face in ravenous kisses?

"I can't believe you're here." My head swims, my blood pumping with ecstasy as I take in his gorgeous features.

"I can't believe you're real." He plants his mouth against mine, binding us in a kiss so unquenchable we claw at each other to dig deeper, closer, and it's not enough.

He bends to grab his hat. His feet move beneath us, splashing through puddles and carrying us toward the entrance to my apartment. Rain falls down around us, washing away pain and intensifying the heat of our bodies.

The past ceases to exist, blurred and forgotten as I grab hold of the future with arms and legs. By the time he stumbles into the dimly lit stairwell, our need for each other has exploded into a raging fire.

My back hits the wall, and he grinds against me, torturing the throb between my legs. The chill that soaks through our jeans doesn't matter. We're a furnace of desire and urgency, ripping at clothes, biting lips, and scoring skin.

Our groans echo off concrete walls. Our bodies writhe, and his boots squeak across wet floors as he swings me toward the stairs.

We make it halfway up the first flight before he lowers me on the steps to deepen the kiss and rock between my legs.

"Need inside you." He licks my tongue, panting against my lips.

I don't know who needs who more as the roll and kick of my hips battles the grind and thrust of his.

"Three flights." He cranes his neck and groans at the staircase high above us. "We'll never make it."

Good, because Raina's in my bed, and I'm not going to kill the moment with that conversation.

"My neighbors go to work early." I grip his hair, bringing his mouth back to mine. "They're already asleep."

He pulls back to look at me, his eyes like every fantasy I've ever had of him, every moment I longed for over the past eighteen months.

Then he kisses me with hail and lightning. Crashing in with a persuasive tongue. Lighting me up with dominant strokes. Owning me with the thunder of his heart.

I wrap my entire being around it—the kiss, the look, the stolen moment that could've so easily slipped through my fingers. But our path is set, fated and indelible.

He gathers me close and shifts us up two more stairs. "We should—"

"Here." I reach for my fly and release the button. "Right now."

He's on board, already tearing at his belt and zipper and breathing as hard as I am. His mouth doesn't leave mine as he drags off my boots and everything beneath my waist. His jeans are next, shoved down to his thighs.

Then we're on each other, panting with need, burning with desire, and trembling with hunger. He bites my nipples through the wet t-shirt, and I yank on his hair, writhing beneath him, aching, pulsing, grinding to get closer.

His fingers find my hot, wet center, and he sinks two inside, groaning against my lips. I buck against him and reach for his cock. I'm too worked up for foreplay. It's been too fucking long to draw this out.

"Please, Jarret." I squeeze the steely length of him. "Hurry."

He glances down between us, lips parted as he glides the head of his cock along my slit. "I haven't been with anyone."

"Me, neither. And I still have the IUD." I release a breath and meet his eyes. "Someday… Not now, but someday, I want kids with you."

His cheeks lift with a smile he can't contain, and he grabs the side of my head, his other hand clenched around his dick.

"Fucking love you." He thrusts hard and deep. "Ahhhh, Christ, Maybe."

His forehead drops to mine. His hands fall to my hips, and he doesn't give me time to adjust. He fucks me with a speed and urgency that bounces my breasts and stretches my inner muscles.

Arms sliding beneath me, he leverages me off the steps and prevents my back from grinding into concrete. His hunger, his power, his love—all of it slams into me, rough and fast, like a hammering piston as he unleashes a year and a half of celibacy.

I palm his ass, delighting in the flex and clench of hard muscles as he wedges himself deeper, harder between my legs, bowing over me, forcing me to open wider, demanding I accept every long vicious inch of him.

His eyes stay with me, absorbing my expressions and cementing the connection. Our hips move in tandem at the quickest pace we've ever fucked, but our heads hold together, foreheads touching, breaths joined, gazes locked in a trance.

"You're going to make me come." I lean in and lick his lips.

"I'm with you." He presses a hand against my lower back and grinds against my clit, deepening the strokes. "Come on my cock."

My entire body erupts, pulsing and clenching. I open my mouth to scream, but there's no sound. No air. Only him and the overwhelming pleasure he ripples through us.

He comes with me, jerking his hips, his face slack, and his low long groan reverberating through the stairwell.

"Fuck, Maybe." He braces his hands on the step on either side of my head, staring down at me, breathless. "That felt so damn good."

I clench around his softening cock, exquisitely replete and struggling to focus.

"Don't bother getting dressed." He rocks his hips, stroking in and out. "As soon as we get upstairs, I'm spreading you out on the bed and worshiping you properly."

The bed that's currently occupied.

I close my eyes. "There's something I need to tell you."

It's after one in the morning when I pull the truck under the archway of Julep Ranch. Maybe's head lolls on my shoulder, her minty scent teasing my inhales and warming my blood.

I still can't believe she took me back. I hoped. Fuck, I hoped with every goddamn breath I took, and I would've never given up. But when she ran out of her apartment in the rain, the sight of her suspended me in a dream.

I've yet to wake from that dream.

We have a lot to discuss, eighteen months to catch up on. Not to mention the reckless stunt she pulled with my father.

My hand clenches around the steering wheel as anger reignites.

When she told me Rogan conned her, I wanted to kill him all over again. Then she described her rescue mission with Raina. I had to lock my rage down tight. Punching walls and roaring at the top of my lungs wouldn't have been the best way to welcome her back into my life.

She's alive and unharmed, and I'm focusing all my energy on that. Her punishment will come later.

Beside her, Raina curls up against the door, frozen in the kind of stiff sleep that doesn't bring rest.

She hasn't spoken since I found her in Maybe's apartment five hours ago. She's barely been conscious. I looked over her wounds. A lot of bruises, welts, and knife cuts. But nothing appears infected or broken. *On the outside.*

What lies behind her haunted eyes is something else entirely. She doesn't need an ER doctor. She needs a psychiatrist.

As I park the truck in front of the house, the front door opens, and Jake steps out.

I called him before I left the apartment, and we decided this was the best place for Raina until we know what happened.

She's lived with my father for over two years. I'm certain she knows every secret we've buried, every crime we've committed. Hell, she probably knows more about my family than I do. She's a huge fucking liability.

The fact that she doesn't want the cops involved is a blessing. But it also puts me on high alert. She's either done something or she intends to do something. Something outside of the law. While it's a way of thinking I can relate to, I don't want my family caught in the crossfire.

Jake opens the passenger door and lifts her into his arms. He takes in the swollen damage to her face, his eyes hardening with murderous fury before lifting to mine.

"Jesus." He shifts her against his chest, making her groan. "Dad did this?"

"Yeah." I cradle Maybe against me and carry her out of the truck.

"I can walk." She loops her arms around my neck

and nuzzles her face against my throat.

With a chuckle, I kiss her brow and follow Jake inside.

She didn't have much in her apartment. The clothes and few things she collected in Texas sit in the bed of my truck. Her car stayed behind. If she wants it, I'll have it towed home.

In the house, Jake pauses in the foyer, glancing between the living room and the hall to my wing.

"Lorne's room." I don't want Raina sleeping on the couch.

Maybe pops her head up and clutches my shoulders. "But Lorne comes home in two days."

My chest rises at the glorious sound of those words. "We'll figure it out."

On the way home, I updated her on the highlights of my life, outside of stalking her every move.

Conor graduated and is now officially a Doctor of Veterinary Medicine. Jake finished building her clinic over the filled-in ravine. Chicken is spoiled rotten, hand-fed and pampered like a family pet by everyone who lives here. And Lorne earned an early release from prison. He'll be home in two days.

Raina's arrival settles a cloud over our excitement. But I'm holding my entire world in my arms. Nothing can put a damper on the lofty, buzzing feeling in my chest.

Jake carries Raina down the hall, and I trail behind him. In Lorne's room, Maybe squirms against me until I set her down.

"Where's Conor?" She hurries through the room, gathering sheets and blankets.

I help her make the bed, anxious to get her into my own.

"She's asleep." Jake lowers Raina onto the mattress, taking care with her injuries. "She'll be pissed I didn't wake her."

Maybe spends the next few minutes fussing over our new house guest, while Jake and I hover, sharing an unspoken feeling of distrust for the abused woman.

I don't know what to do with her. Perhaps a good night's sleep will loosen her tongue tomorrow. Until then, I just want to wrangle up my girl and bury my nose against her skin.

"Maybe." I crook a finger at her. "Let's go."

She pretends to ignore me, focusing her attention on Raina. "Are you sure I can't get you anything?"

Raina lies on her side with her back to Maybe. No response. Not a twitch.

"I'll be in the room at the end of the hall if you need me." Maybe rises from the bed, looking uncertain.

"She lived here for a month." I grip her hand and guide her into the hall. "She knows her way around."

"But you've remodeled this wing since then, right?"

"Yeah."

Probably a good thing. Reminders of my father are exactly what she doesn't need right now.

I should've killed him when I had the chance. But if I had, Maybe might not have shown up on my doorstep two years ago.

When we reach our bedroom, I lead her to the bathroom. After our reunion in the rain and on the filthy stairs, we could both use a shower.

I undress her slowly, kissing every inch of her skin as I unveil it. Then I remove my clothes and follow her under the warm spray.

I wash her, touch her, and reacquaint myself with her breathy noises and ticklish curves. I didn't intend to fuck her in here, but when she backs against the tiles and opens her legs, I'm a goner.

Holding her up against the wall, I sink inside her with unhurried strokes. I love her gently, tenderly, relishing the connection, the feel of her clamping around me, the taste of her lips, and the devotion in her eyes.

When we come, it's a powerful tide of fulfillment and wonder, slow kissing and spent bodies. Limbs intertwined and reluctant to separate, we sink deep into each other, gazes locked, lost in the best way possible.

Later, she falls asleep with her head on my pillow, her breath against my lips, and her leg hooked around my hip.

I watch her sleep, unwilling to close my eyes, refusing to erase the sight of her.

During my darkest moments, my love for her kept my mind from sinking into the mire. As deep as I fell, she was my solid ground, steadying me, lifting me back on my feet.

The feelings I harbor for her will never end. Not when my body ceases to function. Not when my soul releases for whatever comes next. Even in death, I won't let her go.

She's my serenity and my fire, my first and last breath.

Lying beside her is my favorite place, and for the rest of my life and into the next, she's all mine.

The next night, Maybe stands naked in the stable with her forehead against the wooden support beam. I prowl a circuit around her, fingers clenching the crop, heart thumping, and adrenaline coursing through my veins. This must be what a cat feels like while waiting to pounce on a mouse.

My belt binds her wrists in front of her, preventing her from pushing me away. My rope binds her ankles, restraining her from running. Not that she would. She wants this badly, evidenced by the wetness glistening on her inner thighs.

"Tell me why we're here." I pause behind her.

"Because it pleases you."

Goddamn, I love this woman. "Not a lie, but it's the wrong answer."

"Because you're cruel." She shifts her weight, wagging that gorgeous ass at me.

I burn to welt all that pristine skin. It's been so fucking long since I played with her.

Leaning over her back, I put my mouth at her ear.

"Try again."

She shivers and rolls her brow against the post. "Because I risked my life when I went to your dad's house."

"And..."

"I didn't call you for help."

I kiss her shoulder, igniting more shivers. "You're independent and remarkably brave. I will never try to suppress that. But we're a team, Maybe. You and me. We'll face every battle together from now on."

"As equals." She shoots a narrowed glare over her shoulder.

"Yeah." A grin pulls my lips, loaded with affection. "As equals."

She straightens away from the pole, squaring her shoulders. Nothing restrains her to it except my will. She'll stand there and submit to my mouth and teeth, my hands and words, and my pleasure and punishment.

"Tell me your safe word." I step back, flicking the crop against my leg as blood rushes to my groin.

"Stop."

"What happens when you use it?"

"You untie me." She twists her neck and gives me a foxy smirk. "Then you'll take me to bed and love me forever."

Excitement glows on her face and in her voice, and my cock jerks against my zipper.

No more waiting.

She gulps when the first strike lands. By the sixth swing, her ass blooms with pink welts.

I check on her expression between hits, and it doesn't take long for her eyes to drift. With each added whack, she stiffens slightly, then falls into a deeper calm, a softer peace, waiting to obey me.

Ten minutes in, her body sags with a peaceful energy. Some people need pain to be free. Others need to deliver it to harness a sense of control. We're not those people. We simply enjoy walking along the edge of our comfort zones, challenging each other, and flirting with endorphin-induced pleasure.

When we're playing, it isn't about sex. It's about expression, discovery, and catharsis. But after?

We have the best fucking sex in the wake of a good beating.

I drop the crop and tackle my fly. Then I take her, slamming into her tight, hot cunt from behind and losing my ever-loving mind. I thrust and bite and squeeze her tits, rutting against her like an animal.

She loves it, and I love her, any way and any chance I can have her.

A hard fuck, a vanilla tumble, a red welt, a tender kiss—I love her in all the colors and levels of intensity, and she lets me.

I'm a lucky son of a bitch.

The anticipation is a nervous kind of energy. It tingles through the four of us like an electric current, jolting my heart and lifting the tiny hairs on my arms.

We stand shoulder to shoulder outside Oklahoma State Penitentiary, awaiting Lorne's release. I'm so fucking giddy I want to run, shout, and tell the world how momentous this day is. I can't even fathom how Jarret, Jake, and Conor must feel.

They stare at the gate, as if their brains are on fast-forward without an off switch. Lorne will walk out of that hell any second. He'll climb into Jake's truck and go home for the first time in eight years.

Eight goddamn years.

Conor talked to him yesterday, updating him on everything that transpired in the past couple of days. Raina is still holed up in his room, refusing to speak, eat, or leave the bed. Lorne said to leave her alone and he'd deal with it when he got home.

With regard to me, he learned about Rogan Cassidy and my relationship to him months ago, but I haven't seen him since I left.

Jarret assures me Lorne holds no ill feelings toward me, but I'll be the judge of that. He has every right to resent me, and I'll do everything in my power to prove my rightful place in his family.

I love Jarret, his best friend and brother, and I'm not going anywhere.

"You okay?" Jarret gives me a sidelong glance and tightens his hand around my fingers.

"Me? How are *you* doing?"

"Never been happier, Maybe." He leans down and brushes his lips against mine.

A mechanical noise sounds at the gate, and he straightens. Activity stirs beyond the glass door of the building.

It's happening. Lorne's finally coming home.

My heart takes flight. My knees bounce, and...

My phone buzzes in my pocket. I grit my teeth.

Jarret glances at me. "You need to answer that. If it's your landlord..."

"I know." I'm trying to close up everything I left behind in Texas, including my lease on the apartment. "Terrible timing."

I remove the phone and glance at the screen.

Private number.

He reads it with me and arches a brow. I shrug and connect the call.

"Hello?"

"You took something of mine." John Holsten's voice growls through the line. "I want it back."

My pulse whooshes in my ears, and my eyes dart to Jarret's, widening.

He yanks the phone from my hand. "Hello? Hello?"

His jaw sets, and he glances at the screen.

Disconnected.

"Who was that?" He searches my face, registering my alarm.

Conor and Jake lean around Jarret, giving me the same inspection.

"John Holsten." I clear the lump in my throat and tell them what he said.

"He knows we're here." Jarret hooks an arm around my shoulders and wedges me against him.

"I agree." Jake turns back to the gate as it slides open. "He's trying to ruin this moment."

"We won't let him." Conor stands between the guys, chin raised and eyes straight ahead.

Just like that, all worry and fear lifts and sweeps away with the warm breeze.

Together, we stand in a unified line as Lorne emerges through the gate. His eyes lock onto his sister, and she breaks into a run, arms outstretched and a shriek pealing from her lungs.

When she leaps into his embrace, I feel it.

It bubbles out of me in a burst of laughter. It circulates through the unbreakable bond of the four people around me. It glimmers in the golden eyes of the man at my side.

Love.

The most powerful healing force in the universe.

TRAILS OF SIN series concludes with:

BOOTED, Book 3
Lorne's story

Other books by

Pam Godwin

LOVE TRIANGLE ROMANCE
TANGLED LIES TRILOGY
One is a Promise
Two is a Lie
Three is a War

DARK ROMANCE
DELIVER SERIES
Deliver #1
Vanquish #2
Disclaim #3
Devastate #4
Take #5
Manipulate #6
Unshackle #7
Dominate #8
Complicate #9

DARK PARANORMAL ROMANCE
TRILOGY OF EVE
Heart of Eve
Dead of Eve #1
Blood of Eve #2
Dawn of Eve #3

DARK ALASKAN ROMANCE
FROZEN FATE
Hills of Shivers and Shadows #1
Cage of Ice and Echoes #2
Heart of Frost and Scars #3

STUDENT-TEACHER / PRIEST
Lessons In Sin

STUDENT-TEACHER ROMANCE
Dark Notes

ROCK-STAR DARK ROMANCE
Beneath the Burn

BILLIONAIRE REVENGE
Dirty Ties

OLDER WOMAN / YOUNGER MAN
Incentive

DARK HISTORICAL PIRATE ROMANCE
King of Libertines
Sea of Ruin

Legends by Kelsea Ballerini
Hell On Heels by Pistol Annies
Wine & Vinegar by The Wild Feathers
Whips and Things by David Allan Coe
Get Along by Kenny Chesney
The Cowboy in Me by Tim McGraw
From The Ground Up by Dan + Shay
Hurricane by Luke Combs
Might As Well Get Stoned by Chris Stapleton
Just A Fool by Christina Aguilera & Blake Shelton
Fuck You Bitch by Wheeler Walker Jr.
Furnace Room Lullaby by Neko Case
Love Hurts by Melinda Schneider & Beccy Cole
Love Heals by Levi Hummon & Alison Krauss

About Pam Godwin

New York Times, Wall Street Journal, and USA Today bestselling author, Pam Godwin, lives in the Midwest with her husband, cats, retired greyhounds, and an old, foul-mouthed parrot. She traveled the world for seven years, attended three universities, married the vocalist of her favorite rock band, and retired from her quantitative analyst career in 2014 to write full-time.
Her interests veer toward the unconventional: bourbon, full-body tattoos, and tragic villains. Equally peculiar are her aversions to sleeping, eating meat, and dolls with blinking eyes.

EMAIL: pamgodwinauthor@gmail.com

www.ingramcontent.com/pod-product-compliance
Lightning Source LLC
Chambersburg PA
CBHW020459310726
48979CB00016B/2716/J
* 9 7 8 1 9 6 6 5 3 7 0 6 9 *